She Remembered the Summer She Had Shared with Rink.

Caroline stared at the moon through the branches of the trees outside her window. How glorious those days had been! He shared his dreams with her and she confided her secrets.

Every stolen hour they had spent together had been golden, and only partially because of the summer sun. Because one day it had rained.

That day had been the most golden of all.

Caroline let her tears stream unchecked. She prayed for forgiveness, but she didn't think she was absolved. Because she tried to weep for Roscoe, her husband, but her tears were all for Rink, her love.

Dear Reader:

There is an electricity between two people in love that makes everything they do magic, larger than life. This is what we bring you in SILHOUETTE INTIMATE MOMENTS.

SILHOUETTE INTIMATE MOMENTS are longer, more sensuous romance novels filled with adventure, suspense, glamor or melodrama. These books have an element no one else has tapped: excitement.

We are proud to present the very best romance has to offer from the very best romance writers. In the coming months look for some of your favorite authors such as Elizabeth Lowell, Nora Roberts, Erin St. Claire and Brooke Hastings.

SILHOUETTE INTIMATE MOMENTS are for the woman who wants more than she has ever had before. These books are for you.

Karen Solem
Editor-in-Chief
Silhouette Books

Bittersweet Rain

Erin St. Claire

Silhouette Intimate Moments
Published by Silhouette Books New York
America's Publisher of Contemporary Romance

SILHOUETTE BOOKS, a Division of Simon & Schuster, Inc.
1230 Avenue of the Americas, New York, N.Y. 10020

Distributed by Pocket Books

ISBN: 0-671-47608-4

First Silhouette Books printing November, 1984

10 9 8 7 6 5 4 3 2 1

America's Publisher of Contemporary Romance

Printed in the U.S.A.

Books by Erin St. Claire

Silhouette Desire

Silhouette Intimate Moments

Chapter 1

"YOU'RE CERTAIN?"

The doctor nodded bleakly. His operating room greens were still fresh. He hadn't been in surgery long enough to sweat them. "I'm sorry, Mrs. Lancaster. It's extensive and rampant."

"There's nothing you can do?"

"Beyond keeping him comfortable and as free of pain as possible, no." He touched her arm and glanced meaningfully at the man standing by her side. "He doesn't have too long. A few weeks at the most."

"I see." She blotted her eyes with a crumpled, damp tissue.

The doctor's heart went out to her. When family members reacted to bad news with hysteria, he felt competent to handle them. This valorous acceptance from a woman so feminine and frail-looking left him feeling callow and awkward. "If he had come in for a checkup sooner, maybe . . ."

She smiled a sad, wistful smile. "But he wouldn't. I

begged him to see you when his stomach kept bothering him. He insisted it was nothing more than indigestion.''

"We all know how stubborn Roscoe can be," the man with her said. Gently Granger Hopkins folded Caroline Lancaster's fingers around his arm. "Can she see him?"

"In a few hours," the doctor replied. "He'll be under anesthetic until this afternoon. Why don't you go home for a while and get some rest?"

Caroline nodded and let Granger, an attorney and friend, lead her toward the elevator. They waited for it in glum silence. She was dazed but not surprised. Never had her life been rosy and without complication. Why had she idealistically clung to the hope that Roscoe's exploratory surgery would prove that he had nothing more than a treatable ulcer?

"Are you all right?" Granger asked softly when the elevator doors closed behind them and they were free from prying eyes.

She drew in a deep, shuddering breath. "As all right as a woman can be when she finds out her husband is going to die. Soon."

"I'm sorry."

She looked up at him and smiled. Granger's heart melted. Her smiles, which were often sweetly apologetic for some invisible deficiency, had a way of touching both men and women. "I know you are, Granger. I can't tell you how glad I am to have you as a friend."

They crossed the lobby of the newly refurbished hospital. Personnel and visitors glanced at Caroline and then quickly away. The averted faces were curious but deferential. Everyone already knew. When a leading citizen in a town the size of Winstonville was dying, the news spread like wildfire.

Granger escorted Caroline to her car and opened the door for her. She got inside but didn't turn on the ignition. She sat, staring dejectedly ahead, lost in thought, in worry, in grief. So many things to see to. Where would she start?

"Rink will have to be notified."

The name went through her like an ice pick, cold, needle-sharp and piercing. It punctured all her vital organs. His name thundered through her head. The pain of hearing it paralyzed her.

"Caroline, did you hear me? I said—"

"Yes, I heard you."

"Before he went into surgery, Roscoe made me promise to contact Rink if the prognosis was bad."

Eyes the elusive color of woodsmoke sought the lawyer's. "He asked you to contact Rink?"

"Yes. He was most emphatic about it."

"I'm surprised. I thought the quarrel between them was irreconcilable."

"Roscoe is dying, Caroline. I think he knew when he went into the hospital that he'd never leave it. He wants to see his son before he dies."

"They haven't seen or spoken to each other in twelve years, Granger. I don't know if Rink will come back."

"He will when he knows the circumstances."

Would he? Oh, God, would he? Would she see him again? How would she feel when she did? What would he look like? It had happened so long ago. Twelve years ago. Her hands gripped the padded steering wheel of her Lincoln. Her palms were damp. She went damp all over.

"Don't worry about it," Granger said, sensing her distress. "Since you don't know Rink, I'll call and tell him."

Caroline didn't correct his assumption that she didn't know Rink. That they had known each other had been a well-kept secret for twelve years. She didn't intend now to start revealing it. Instead she laid her hand over Granger's where it rested on the windowsill of the car door. "Thank you for everything."

His face was plain and lumpy and as long and drooping as a basset hound's. His cheeks hung like empty leather pouches on either side of his jaw. Incongruously, when she touched him, he blushed like a schoolboy. He was rumpled and stooped, slow-moving, soft-spoken and kind, but his demeanor had fooled many. Behind that caricature of a face operated a shrewd, though scrupulously honest, mind. "I'm glad to be of any help I can. Is there anything else?"

She shook her head. It was a relief that he had volunteered to call Rink. How would she ever have brought herself to do that? "I have to tell Laura Jane." The gray eyes filled with tears. "That won't be easy."

"You'll handle it better than anyone else could." He patted her hand and backed away. "I'll call you this afternoon and if you like, I'll drive you back to the hospital whenever you want to return."

She nodded, started the car and engaged the gears. The town was bustling as she drove through it. Roscoe's surgery had been scheduled early that morning. By now the workday's business was in full swing. People were going about their daily routines, unaware that Caroline Dawson Lancaster's world had once again been turned upside down.

The man she had looked to, first as an employer, then as a husband, was going to die. Her future, which for a short while had seemed secure, was once more precarious. Not only would Roscoe's death mean the loss of someone important to her, it would mean the loss of her new station in life as well.

She drove past the Lancaster Gin. They were gearing up for a heavy cotton crop this year. The foremen would have to be told about Roscoe's condition soon. That would be left up to her, since she had been tending to the gin's business for several months, ever since Roscoe's health had prevented him from handling it himself. The foremen would pass on the word to the workers. Before long everyone in town would know that Roscoe Lancaster was dying.

It had been a hot gossip item when Caroline Dawson married Roscoe Lancaster, who was more than thirty years her senior. Folks had said that that trashy Dawson girl had bettered herself all right, living at The Retreat and driving a shiny new Lincoln, always dressed fit to kill no matter what the occasion. Shoot! Who did she think she was? Everybody could remember when she wore patched clothes and worked at Woolworth's after school. Now that she was Mrs. Roscoe Lancaster, married to the richest man in the county, she put on airs.

Actually, Caroline avoided the townsfolk because she couldn't stand their speculative glances, glances that told her they were wondering just what kind of witchcraft she had practiced on ol' Roscoe to get him to marry her after being a widower for so many years.

Soon those same people would be coming to her to pay their respects. She closed her eyes briefly and shuddered at the thought. Only the sight of The Retreat could lift her despondency. Until the day she died, a mere glimpse of the house would thrill her. From the first time she had seen it as a little girl, creeping through the woods and peering through the trees at the mansion, it had enchanted her.

It was encircled by stately live oaks. Their massive branches, dripping curly gray moss, spread over it protectively like embracing arms. The house sat like a Southern coquette with her wide hooped skirts ballooned around her. The brick was kept painted a pristine white. A file of Corinthian columns adorned the front, three on each side of the front door. They supported the second-story balcony over the wide veranda that surrounded the house. White wicker furniture dotted the porch. It was brought in only during the cold, wet winter months.

White wrought iron, as lacy as a petticoat, bordered the balcony. Forest-green shutters flanked tall windows that gleamed like mirrors in the sunlight.

Summer insects buzzed crazily, ecstatically, around the profusion of blooming flowers, their colors so brilliant and rich they hurt the eyes. No place on earth had greener grass than that which spread like a carpet around The Retreat.

An aura of serenity hovered over the house like the magic mist that surrounded the castle in a fairy tale. For almost as long as she could remember, the house had represented all that was desirable in the world. Now she lived in it. After today, she knew her residence would be temporary.

She brought the car to a stop on the gravel drive that arced in front of the house. For a moment, she collected her thoughts and built up the resources from which she would have to draw strength for the next few hours. It wouldn't be a pleasant afternoon.

The entrance hall was dim after the blinding sunshine outside. The Retreat was a typically designed plantation house of the antebellum period. A wide central foyer ran from the front door to the back. Opening off one side of it were the formal dining room and the library, the room Roscoe used as his office. On the other side were the formal and informal parlors, divided from the foyer and from each other by enormous sliding doors which disappeared into the walls. To Caroline's recollection the doors had never been used. A sweeping curved staircase rose majestically to the second floor and its four bedroom suites.

The house was cool, a haven against the summer humidity. Caroline peeled off her suit jacket, hung it on the coatrack and plucked at the silk blouse that was damply sticking to her back.

"Well? What's the news?"

The housekeeper, Mrs. Haney, who had been at The

Retreat since Marlena Winston had married Roscoe Lancaster, stood in the arched doorway that led into the dining room. Having come from the kitchen beyond, she was drying her large, rough, capable hands, which matched the rest of her, on a muslin cup towel.

Caroline went to her slowly and embraced her. The housekeeper's stout arms closed around the slender woman. "Bad, then?" she asked softly, stroking Caroline's back.

"The worst. Cancer. He won't be coming home."

Haney's enormous bosom heaved on a sob that she didn't let go of. Together the two women leaned into each other, offering and accepting solace. Haney wasn't all that fond of Roscoe, though she had tolerated him for over thirty-five years. Her grief was mostly for the ones he would leave behind, including his young widow.

Haney had at first been suspicious and resentful of the new mistress of The Retreat. But when she saw that Caroline wasn't going to change anything in the house, that she intended to leave it as Marlena had wanted it to be, she began to be won over. Of course, the girl couldn't help coming from trash. Haney wouldn't be so prejudiced as to judge her by her folks. Caroline treated Laura Jane affectionately and kindly. That was reason enough for sainthood in Haney's book.

"Haney? Caroline? What's the matter?" They turned to see Laura Jane standing on the bottom stair. At twenty-two, Roscoe's daughter looked little more than an adolescent. Her soft brown hair hung straight from a center part. It framed a face whose features were so delicate they looked ethereal. Her complexion was as translucent as porcelain. Her waiflike eyes were large and soulful and velvety brown, surrounded by long lashes. Her figure had matured only as far as her mind. She was like an exquisite bud not quite in full flower. All the curves of womanhood were there, but they would never ripen. Just as her mind had stopped developing, so had her body. She would forever remain untouched by time.

"Is Daddy's operation over? Is he coming home?"

"Good morning, Laura Jane," Caroline said, going to her stepdaughter, who was only five years younger than herself if one measured in years alone. She looped the girl's arm through hers. "Will you walk with me outside? It's a beautiful day."

"All right. But why is Haney crying?" Haney was dabbing her eyes on the cup towel.

"She's sad."

"Why?"

Caroline propelled the young woman through the front door and out onto the veranda. "Because of Roscoe. He's very sick, Laura Jane."

"I know. His stomach hurts all the time."

"The doctor said it's not going to get any better."

They strolled over the well-manicured lawn. A team of workmen came twice a week to keep the grounds at The Retreat in immaculate condition, no matter the season. Laura Jane plucked a daisy from a clump growing near the lichen-covered brick path. "Has Daddy got cancer?"

Sometimes her astuteness surprised them. "Yes, he does," Caroline replied. She wouldn't shelter Laura Jane from the severity of her father's illness. That would be cruel.

"I've heard a lot about cancer on television." She stopped and faced Caroline. The two women were about the same height and their eyes were on a level. "Daddy could die with cancer."

Caroline nodded. "He *is* going to die, Laura Jane. The doctor said he could die in a week or so."

The deep brown eyes remained tearless. Laura Jane raised the daisy to her nose as she pondered the news. Finally she looked up at Caroline again. "He'll go to Heaven, won't he?"

"I guess so. . . . Yes, yes, of course he will."

"Then Daddy'll be with Mama again. She's been there a long time. She'll be glad to see him. And I'll still have you and Haney and Steve." She glanced toward the stables. "And Rink. Rink writes to me every week. He says he'll always love me and take care of me. Do you think he will, Caroline?"

"Of course he will." Caroline clamped her lips together to keep from crying. Would Rink ever keep a promise? Even to his sister?

"Then why doesn't he live with us?" Laura Jane demanded logically.

"Maybe he'll come home soon." She wasn't going to tell the girl that Rink would be there until she knew for certain that he would be.

Laura Jane's mind was at peace. "Steve's waiting for me. The mare had her foal last night. Come see it."

Taking Caroline's hand, she dragged her toward the stable. Caroline envied Laura Jane's resilience and wished she could approach Roscoe's death with the simple faith in the future that his daughter had.

The air in the large stable was warm and thick and smelled pleasantly of horseflesh, leather and hay. "Steve," Laura Jane called out merrily.

"Here," the low voice responded.

Steve Bishop was manager of the Lancaster stables. Raising thoroughbreds was an avocation of Roscoe's, though he bothered little with the actual care of the horses. Bishop stepped out into the center aisle from one of the stalls. He wasn't very tall but was powerfully built. His features were heavy and coarse, but somehow their expression softened the bluntness of his face. He wore his hair long, usually with a bandana sweat band around his head or, as now, with a straw cowboy hat on it. His jeans were old and frayed, his boots dusty, his shirt sweat-stained. But his face was alight with a smile as Laura Jane skipped toward him. Only his eyes never lost their look of sadness and disillusionment, even when he smiled. They seemed much older than his thirty-seven years.

"Steve, we came to see the foal," Laura Jane said breathlessly.

"Right in there." He tilted his head toward the stall he had just left.

Laura Jane went inside it. Steve searched Caroline's eyes inquisitively. "Cancer," she said in answer to his silent question. "Only a matter of time."

Steve cursed under his breath and glanced toward the young woman kneeling in the hay, crooning to the foal. "Have you told her?"

"Yes. She accepted it better than any of us."

He nodded and smiled at Caroline ruefully. "Yes. She would."

"Oh, Steve, she's beautiful, isn't she?"

He touched Caroline's shoulder briefly, self-consciously, then went into the stall. Caroline followed and watched him as he awkwardly knelt down beside Laura Jane. The Vietnam War had left him without the lower half of his left leg. He wore a prosthesis that was virtually indiscernible unless he had to bend it, as now.

"She is pretty, isn't she? And her mama's so proud of her." He patted the mare's rump, but his eyes were on Laura Jane. Caroline watched as he reached up and pulled free a straw that had attached itself to Laura Jane's hair. His fingers lightly grazed her flawless cheek. Laura Jane raised her eyes to him and they smiled at each other.

Caroline was momentarily stunned by the intimate exchange. Were these two in love with each other? She didn't quite know what to make of the idea. Tactfully she withdrew, but Steve looked up at her. "Mrs. Lancaster, if there's anything I can do . . ." He left the offer open-ended.

"Thank you, Steve. For the time being just carry on as you have been."

"Yes, ma'am." He knew she had been instrumental in Roscoe's hiring him. She had been working for Roscoe when Steve Bishop had showed up to apply for the job of stable manager, carrying his bitterness in front of him like a shield. His ponytail had grown halfway down his back, his denim vest was covered with peace signs and patches with antiwar and anti-American slogans on them. He had been surly and belligerent, almost daring Roscoe to give him a job, a chance, when so many others had refused to.

Caroline had seen through his disguise and into the real man. He was desperate. She felt an automatic affinity with him. She knew the hurt that could come from being labeled, knew what it was like to be judged by an appearance and background one couldn't help. Because the veteran said he had worked on a horse ranch in California before the war, Caroline had talked Roscoe into hiring him.

Roscoe had never regretted it. Steve had cut his hair and modified his appearance immediately, as though the trappings of rebellion were no longer necessary. He worked diligently, conscientiously, and had a rapport with the thoroughbred horses that was uncanny. The man had only needed a vote of confidence to restore his self-esteem.

Caroline mused on all that as she went back toward the house. Steve and Laura Jane in love. She shook her head, smiling, as she entered the foyer. The telephone was ringing and she automatically picked it up before Haney had a chance. "Hello?"

"Caroline, Granger."

"Yes?"

"I've spoken with Rink. He'll arrive some time this evening."

There were a million things to be done in the afternoon, a million people to notify. Roscoe had no living relatives save his son and daughter, so there was no family to be concerned with. But everyone in the county, and many in the state of Mississippi, would want to know of Roscoe's illness. Caroline divided the list with Granger and spent a great deal of time on the telephone.

"Haney, you'd better get Rink's old room in order. He's coming home tonight."

At that the housekeeper burst into copious tears. "Praise God, praise God. I've been praying for the day my baby would come home. His mama is dancing in Heaven today. She surely is. All that room needs is fresh bed linens. I've been keeping it clean against the day he'd come back to it. Lordy, Lordy, I can't wait to clap eyes on him."

Caroline tried not to think of the moment when she would have to look at the prodigal son, speak to him. She busied herself with the myriad tasks at hand.

Nor did she think of Roscoe's imminent death. That would come later, in private. Not even when she visited the hospital late in the afternoon and sat by his bedside did she let herself dwell on the thought that he would never leave the place. He was still a captive of the anesthetic, but she thought a small pressure was applied to her hand when she took his and squeezed it in good-bye.

At dinner, she told Laura Jane about Rink's coming home. The girl jumped out of her chair, grabbed Haney and began to dance her around the room. "He promised he would come back someday, didn't he, Haney? Rink's coming *home!* I've got to tell Steve." She raced out the back door toward the stables, where Steve had an apartment.

"That girl's gonna make a nuisance out of herself if she doesn't leave that young man alone."

Caroline smiled secretly. "I don't think so." Haney cocked one inquiring eyebrow, but Caroline didn't elaborate. She picked up her glass of mint-sprigged iced tea and went out onto the front veranda. As she sat down in a wicker rocking chair, her head fell back onto the flowered cushion and her eyes closed.

This was the time she loved best at The Retreat, the early evening, when lights from inside the house shone through the windows and made them look like jewels. Shadows were long and darkly hued and melded into one another so that there were no sharp angles or distinct shapes. The sky overhead was a rare and lovely shade of violet, dense and impenetrable. The trees were looming black etchings against it. Bullfrogs down on the river channel croaked hoarsely and cicadas filled the breeze-less, humid air with their shrill soprano notes. The rich delta earth smelled of fecundity. Each flower gave off a unique and heady perfume.

After long moments of rest, Caroline opened her eyes. That was when she saw him.

He was standing motionless beneath the branches of a sprawling live oak. Her heart rocketed into her throat and her vision blurred. She didn't know if he were real or a mirage. Dizziness assailed her and she gripped the slippery iced-tea glass hard to keep it from sliding through her cold, stiff fingers.

He nudged himself away from the trunk of the tree and moved, pantherlike and silent, coming closer until he stood at the brick steps leading up to the porch.

He was only a shadow among many, but there was no mistaking the clean masculine lines of his shape as he stood with his feet widely separated. Physically the years had been kind to him. He was no less trim than the first time she had seen him. Darkness hid his face from her, but she caught the shine of straight white teeth as he smiled slowly.

It was an indolent smile if it matched his tone of voice. "Well as I live and breathe, if it isn't Caroline Dawson." He placed one booted foot on the bottom step and bent at the waist to prop his arms on his knee. He looked up at her and the light from the entrance hall fell on his features. Her heart constricted with pain . . . and love. "Only it's Lancaster now, isn't it?"

"Yes, it's Lancaster now. Hello, Rink."

That face! That face had haunted her dreams and filled her fantasies. It was still the most marvelous face she had ever seen. Good in his twenties, he was magnificent in his thirties. Black hair, the Devil's own, intimated the wildness of his spirit with swirling strands that defied control. His eyes, which had mystified her from the first time she had seen them, intrigued her anew. People with no imagination would call them light brown. But they were gold, like the purest dark honey, the finest liquor, like sparkling topazes.

The last time she'd seen him, those eyes were blazing with passion. *Tomorrow. . . . Tomorrow, baby. Here. In our place. Oh, God, Caroline, kiss me again.* Then: *Tomorrow, tomorrow.* Only he hadn't returned the next day or ever again.

"Funny," he commented in a tone that left her to believe it wasn't funny at all, "us sharing the same last name."

There was no answer for that. She wanted to shout that they could have shared the same last name years ago if he hadn't been a liar, if he hadn't betrayed her. Some things were better left unsaid. "I didn't hear your car."

"I flew in, landed on the airstrip and walked from there."

The landing strip was about a mile away. "Oh. Why?"

"Maybe I didn't know what kind of welcome I was going to get."

"This is your home, Rink."

His curse was vicious and rank. "Yeah, sure it is."

She wet her lips with her tongue and wished she had

the courage to try standing. She feared to, afraid her legs wouldn't support her. "You haven't asked about your father."

"Granger filled me in."

"You know he's dying, then."

"Yes. And he wants to see me. Wonders never cease."

His scathing remark brought her out of the chair without having to think about it. "He's a sick old man, Rink. Not at all the way you remember him."

"If he's got one breath of life in his body, he's exactly the way I remember him."

"I won't argue with you about this."

"I'm not arguing."

"And I won't have you upsetting him or Laura Jane or Haney. They're looking forward to seeing you."

"*You* won't have? My, my. You do consider yourself mistress of The Retreat, don't you?"

"Please, Rink. The next few weeks are going to be difficult enough without—"

"I know, I know." His long sigh reached her where she stood tensely on the porch, her hands clasped tightly together. She had set her glass of tea on the porch railing for fear of dropping it. "I can't wait to see them, either," he said and glanced toward the stables. "I saw Laura Jane come out of the house a while ago, but didn't want to suddenly appear out of the dark and scare her. I remember her as a little girl. I can't believe she's all grown-up."

An image of Laura Jane and Steve kneeling in the hay of the stall together, his rough fingers brushing her cheek, came to Caroline's mind. She wondered what Rink would think of his sister's romance. It made her uneasy to surmise. "She's a woman now, Rink."

She felt his eyes on her, touring, analyzing, assessing. Like warm brandy they poured over her and touched everywhere. "And you," he said softly. "You're all grown-up now, too, aren't you, Caroline? A woman."

She was remarkably unchanged. The beauty of the fifteen-year-old girl he had known had only mellowed. He had hoped to find her fat, disheveled, frumpy, with lackluster hair and heavy thighs. Instead she was still reed slender, with a waist that looked like a strong Gulf breeze would snap her in two. Her breasts had matured to a soft fullness, but they were still high, round and achingly touchable. *Damn her!* How often had his father touched her?

He took the steps up to the porch slowly, like a predator who wasn't hungry but only wanted to torment his prey. The golden eyes, gleaming through the darkness, held hers. The wide sensuous lips were fixed in a sly, knowing smile, as though he knew she was remembering things she wished she could forget, like how his lips felt on her mouth, on her throat, on her breasts.

She spun on her heel. "I'll call Haney. She'll be—"

His hand flashed out to manacle her wrist and she was jerked to a halt. He forced her around to face him. "Hold on a minute," he said silkily. "After twelve years, don't you think we can greet each other more cordially?"

His free hand wrapped around the back of her neck and brought her face up dangerously close to his. "Remember, we're kinfolks now," he whispered tauntingly. Then his lips swooped down on hers, hard and angry. He took them brutally with his mouth, punishing her for all the nights he had had to think about her, his unspoiled Caroline, sharing her bed, her body, with his father.

Her fists dug into his chest. There was a roaring in her ears. Her knees went to jelly. She fought him. She fought herself harder. Because she wanted to fling her arms around him and hold him close, to know again the thrill of being in his embrace.

But this wasn't an embrace, it was an insult. She struggled for all she was worth to tear her mouth free.

When she succeeded, he slid his hands into his jeans pockets and grinned with mocking triumph at her outraged expression and bruised lips. "Greetings, Mom," he drawled.

Chapter 2

CAROLINE GASPED, HER BREASTS HEAVING WITH ANGER and humiliation. "What a wretched thing to say! How can you be so horrible?"

"How could you marry that rotten old man who just happens to be my father?"

"He isn't rotten. He's been good to me."

His laugh was a short barking sound. "Oh, I can see how good to you he's been. Are those pearls in your ears? Diamonds on your hand? You've come up in the world, haven't you, Caroline of the river? You live in The Retreat now. And didn't you tell me one time you'd give anything to live in a house like this?" He leaned over her and spoke in a low growl. "Let me guess what you gave my father before he married you."

She slapped him hard. It happened before she could measure the wisdom of it. One instant he was grinding out his insults and the next her palm was cracking across his hard cheek. It made her hand burn and she hoped his cheek felt the same sting.

He backed away, grinning a sardonic smile that made her angrier than his deprecating words. "Whatever I gave him, it was more than you did these last twelve years. He was heartbroken, living alone in this house, pining for you."

He laughed again. "Pining? That's good, Caroline. Pining." One knee bent so that his weight was shifted to his other leg in an arrogant stance. His arms crossed over his chest and he tilted his head. "Why is it so difficult for me to envision my father pining over anything? Especially my absence."

"I'm sure he wanted you here."

"He was as glad to see the last of me as I was of him," he said harshly. "Spare me any more sentimentality. If you attribute it to Roscoe, I assure you, you imagined it."

"I don't know what your quarrel was, but he's sick now, Rink. Dying. Please don't make things harder than they already are."

"Whose idea was it to notify me, yours or Granger's?"

"Roscoe's."

"That's what Granger said, but I don't believe it."

"It's the truth."

"Then he sure as hell has an ulterior motive."

"Roscoe wants to see his son before he dies!" she exclaimed. "That's motive enough."

"Not for Roscoe it's not. He's a cunning, manipulative bastard and if he got me here to watch him die, believe me he has a reason."

"You shouldn't speak to me this way about him. He's my husband."

"That's your problem."

"Caroline? Who's— Oh, my Lord. *Rink!*" Haney barreled through the screen door and embraced Rink in a hug that would have squeezed the life out of a less brawny man. He hugged her back just as hard. Tears came to Caroline's eyes as she watched the bitterness and derision leave his face to be replaced by a wide grin of pure joy. His golden eyes were now lit with happiness, his teeth gleamed whitely behind a broad smile.

"Haney! God, how I've missed you."

"You could have written more often," she sniffed, drawing herself up and trying to look indignant.

"I apologize," he said humbly, though his eyes were as mischievous as they had been every time the housekeeper had caught him with his hand in the cookie jar. He'd always gotten away with it. He did now.

"I see that you've met Caroline," Haney said, beaming at the two of them.

"Oh, yes. I've met Caroline. We've been getting to know each other."

The housekeeper missed the glance he gave Caroline. "You haven't been eating right, I can see that. Making money hand over fist, picture showing up in the newspaper all the time, and still you look like you never get a decent meal. Well, get on inside. I've got supper warmed over for you."

"And pecan pie. I can smell it from here," he teased, pushing her through the door.

"I didn't bake it special for you."

"Now, come on, Haney. You and I both know better."

"And it's a coincidence that we had chicken gumbo for supper, too."

For weeks after Caroline had moved into The Retreat as its new mistress, she had felt like a visitor who didn't really belong. But months had passed. Laura Jane had accepted her as a friend. Haney had come to like her. But now, seeing Rink in his home, hearing the sound of his boots on the antique hardwood floors and hearing his voice echo through the high-ceilinged rooms, Caroline once again felt like an interloper. Rink belonged here. She didn't.

By the time she had followed them into the kitchen, Haney had Rink sitting at the large round oak table with a heaping plate of food in front of him. He was surveying the room. "Nothing's changed," he said warmly.

"I had the kitchen painted a couple of years ago," Haney told him. "But I told Mr. Lancaster that I wasn't going to change the color. I wanted everything to stay the same for the day when you came home."

Rink swallowed and moved a forkful of food around his plate. "I'm not home for good, Haney. Only until Daddy . . . gets settled down again."

Haney's busy hands paused in their endless tasks. She looked down at the man as though he were still a young boy in her charge. "I don't want you to go running off again, Rink. This is where you belong."

His eyes flicked toward Caroline then back down to his plate. "There's nothing for me here anymore," he said angrily before shoving another bite into his mouth.

"Yes there is . . . Laura Jane," Caroline reminded him softly. Rather than hovering inside the door, she forced herself to enter the kitchen. She didn't want Rink to know that his presence intimidated her in her own house. She wasn't Roscoe's widow yet, and as his wife she certainly had a right to be here. Going to the refrigerator, she poured herself another glass of iced tea which she really didn't want.

"Bless her heart, Rink," Haney contributed as she polished an already gleaming glass. "She beats me to the mailbox every day looking for a letter from you. On her account you shouldn't have stayed away, no matter the bad words between you and your daddy."

"I hated not being here for her. Is she all right?"

"Sure, sure. Pretty as a picture."

"That's not what I mean."

Haney thumped the glass onto the counter. "I know what you meant," she said tightly. "And yes, she's fine.

I know by the way you've asked about her in your letters that you have no idea what Laura Jane is really like, Rink. She may not have been much for book learning, but she's smart as a whip about some things. You didn't stay around to watch over her, but you're as possessive as a mama bear with her cub. Watch out. She's a grown-up lady now and might not take kindly to being treated like a breakable object. She's a beautiful young woman. If folks got a chance to meet her, few would even realize she was different.''

"But she is," he insisted.

"Not so different," Caroline said. "She knows exactly what's going on in the world, but her emotions are fragile. I worry more about her vulnerability than what mental deficiencies she has. If someone she loves should disappoint her, she might never recover.''

His eyes never left hers as he wiped his mouth with a linen napkin, tossed it down and pushed his chair away from the table. "Thanks for the sermon, Sister Caroline. I'll try to keep it in mind.''

"I didn't necessarily mean—"

"Of course you did," he snapped and reached for the coffeepot, sloshing a generous amount into his cup.

"Rink Lancaster, you've got no call to light into Caroline that way." Haney was shocked by the automatic antipathy between these two. They hadn't known each other for five minutes, yet each time they looked at each other sparks flew. Apparently Rink didn't cotton to the idea of his daddy taking a bride as young as Caroline. But he'd been gone for twelve years. What difference had Roscoe's marriage made to him? Unless it had something to do with The Retreat. "Where are the manners your mama and I drilled into you? You remember that Caroline is your daddy's wife and deserves your respect as such.''

Rink, his eyes still on Caroline, lifted one corner of

his mouth in a mocking smile. "My stepmother. I keep forgetting that."

"Here comes Laura Jane," Haney said, glancing worriedly at the two in the kitchen. "Don't upset her, Rink. She's already had one shock today and she took it well."

Laura Jane's soft voice trailed through the screen door before she pulled it open. She froze, her willowy body poised like a Grecian statue in the doorway as she spied her brother. For a moment her face remained blank, then it began to glow and the glow spread to her eyes, over her cheeks and became the most radiant of smiles. "Rink," she whispered.

She launched herself against him, folding her thin arms around his neck and burying her face in his shirt collar. His arms went around her and he rocked her back and forth while hugging her tight. His eyes were squeezed shut against the emotions that assailed him. Laura Jane was the first to pull back. With fingers that looked too fragile to have life in them, she explored her brother's face, his hair, his shoulders, as though to reassure herself that he was truly there.

"You're so tall," she remarked. "And strong." She laughed, gripping his biceps.

"You're beautiful and so grown-up." His eyes took in all of her, a beautifully delicate young woman. Then they both started laughing with the sheer joy of seeing each other. They hugged again.

"Daddy's going to die, Rink," Laura Jane said solemnly when they finally released each other. "Did Caroline tell you?"

"Yes," he said softly and ran his finger along her chin.

"But now you're here. And Haney and Caroline and Steve . . . Oh, my goodness! I forgot to introduce you." She turned to the stable manager, who had walked with her back to the house and who was now standing just inside the screened back door. Laura Jane took his hand and pulled him forward. "Steve Bishop, this is my brother, Rink."

Steve had to disengage his fingers from Laura Jane's in order to shake hands with Rink, who was staring at him with guarded eyes. "Mr. Lancaster, nice to meet you."

"Call me Rink," he said, shaking Steve's hand with a firm grip. "How long have you worked here?"

"A little more than a year."

Rink glanced at his sister and then back at the stable manager. "Laura Jane has mentioned you in her letters."

"One of the mares had a foal yesterday, Rink," Laura Jane informed him excitedly. "Steve helped her."

"And I need to get back to them," Steve said.

"Why don't you stay and have a piece of pie with us?" Haney offered.

He looked at Rink, then away. "No thank you. I need to check on that filly."

"I'll be over to see her in the morning, Steve. Is that all right?" Laura Jane inquired, taking his hand again.

"Sure," he said softly, smiling down into her guileless face. "She'd miss you if you didn't come to visit."

He pulled his hand free and went to the back door. "Good night, Steve," Laura Jane called.

"Good night, Laura Jane," he replied. Then he touched the brim of his straw cowboy hat in a salute to everyone else and disappeared into the darkness, limping slightly.

Rink stared after him, bracing himself in the doorjamb. Haney bustled around, slicing generous portions of pecan pie and scooping vanilla ice cream on top.

"None for me, thank you, Haney," Caroline said. From the corner of her eye, she saw Rink turn around to look in her direction. "It's been a long day. I think I'll go upstairs."

"Do you need anything?" Haney asked, concerned.

"A good night's sleep," Caroline said. She leaned over Laura Jane and brushed a kiss on her cheek. "Good night. Tomorrow we'll go to the hospital and you can see your father."

"Yes, I want to. Good night. Isn't it wonderful that Rink's home, Caroline?"

"Yes, it is." Caroline straightened and met Rink's eyes. "Haney has your room ready for you. Good night, Rink."

Before he could respond, she was out the door and making her way through the dining room and up the stairs. Being in the same room with him was proving too much for her. Besides, he and Laura Jane and Haney, who had been a mother to them after Marlena had died, deserved some time alone together.

Her tread down the upstairs hallway was muffled by the Oriental runner that extended its length. Her bedroom was softly lighted by two bedside lamps. She switched one of them off. Darkness seemed comforting tonight, as though it hid what one didn't want to see, didn't want to think about. She went to stand at the wide window that looked out over the back acreage of The Retreat and down the grassy slope to the river channel. The moon was only half full, but she could see it reflecting on the water in the distance. Everything looked so peaceful.

Caroline was anything but serene. She had suffered three shocks today. She had learned that her husband was going to die. She had seen that Steve's affection for Laura Jane went beyond friendship or even compassion. And Rink had come home.

With a long sigh, she moved away from the windows and began to undress. After running a deep, hot bath, she gratefully sank into the scented bubbles and closed her eyes. Only then did she let herself cry. For Roscoe. He had been frustrated by his illness yet stubbornly refused to see his doctor. A man of his vitality couldn't tolerate being ill. Perhaps it was better that the end would come soon. Forcing a man of Roscoe's spirit and ambition to lie useless and ailing in a hospital bed for months would be inhumanly unkind.

She lay in the tub for a long while until her tears dried and the water cooled. She prepared for bed. The house had grown quiet. When the gentle knock came on her door as she was pulling back the bedcovers, she jumped in a startled reaction.

Opening the door only a crack, she peered into the shadowed, silent hallway. "What do you want?"

"To talk to you."

Rink pushed his way through the door. Unless she wanted to create a scene, she had no choice but to let him in and close the door behind him. He stood in the middle of the floor and pivoted slowly, taking in the furnishings of the room. He crossed to the window and trailed his hand down the draperies, as though remembering the feel of them from long ago. He surveyed the items on the antique dressing table. He stared at himself in the beveled mirror over it. Was he looking for the little boy he had once been?

"This was my mother's room," he said at last.

Caroline's hands found each other at her waist and clung together moistly. "Yes, I know. It's a lovely room. One of my favorites in the house."

"It suits you," he said, studying her reflection behind his in the mirror. "Just as it did her. It's a totally feminine room."

As he continued to stare at her, Caroline became uncomfortably aware of her attire. The nightgown and robe were no competition for the burning gaze Rink subjected her to. She was conscious of her nakedness beneath her nightclothes, even though she was covered from chest to toes. And most unnerving of all was the knowledge that Rink was conscious of it, too.

His venturing eyes made pointed stops at her breasts, her waist, below her waist. As though responding to some silent summons, those erogenous places awakened and stirred to life. Her nipples tightened. Her womanhood flowered. Caroline condemned them, condemned herself, yet was powerless to stop the currents of arousal that flowed through her with each glance of those dark gold eyes.

He was holding a tumbler of bourbon in his hand and took an appreciative sip. He savored it as the liquor slid like silky fire down his throat and into his stomach. "Daddy still likes expensive whiskey," he remarked. "And pretty women. You look very pretty in this room, Caroline, with the lamplight on your hair." He gave her one more thorough going-over in the mirror, then turned away.

He walked to the chaise in the corner of the room and stretched out on it. It was made for a much daintier figure than Rink's. His boots hung off the end. He balanced the tumbler on his stomach, holding it with one hand while he put the other arm beneath his head, watching Caroline like a hawk. She stood nervously in the same spot where she had been standing when he'd entered the room.

"Mother and Daddy never shared this bedroom," he said idly, but Caroline wasn't deceived. Rink never said anything just for the sake of conversation. "I remember like it was yesterday the day he told her not to bother moving back into his bedroom after Laura Jane was born. Mother cried for hours. He never slept with her again." He sipped the whiskey and laughed harshly. "I don't think he ever forgave her for Laura Jane."

"He loves Laura Jane," Caroline protested. "He's always done what he thought was best for her."

He laughed again, more scathingly this time. "Oh,

yeah, he's good at that. Doing what he thinks is good for somebody.''

Caroline forced herself to move. She went to the bed and sat down on the edge of it, twisting the cord belt at the waist of her robe through her fingers. ''Is this what you wanted to talk to me about?''

''About husbands and wives sleeping together?'' he asked, one black brow arching. ''Or about Laura Jane?''

He was being deliberately provoking. Where had all his sweetness gone? All that tenderness he had showed her when they'd met in secret and poured out their hearts to each other? He was someone she didn't know, yet was so very familiar with.

His shirt was unbuttoned and lay open. His chest rose and fell with each breath. She remembered how he had looked the first time she'd seen him, river water streaming down that muscular chest and matting the dark hair. His stomach was just as hard and flat now, corded with muscle. A black stripe of hair divided it into two perfect halves before disappearing into the waistband of his jeans. Behind the fly of the snug-fitting jeans was profound evidence of his sex.

Flustered, Caroline's eyes flickered away from him. ''Why do you want to talk to me about any of it? I don't want to get involved in the argument between you and your father.''

He found that extremely funny and chuckled for long minutes while he leisurely finished the whiskey. Then he got off the chaise and stalked toward her. The single lamp cast shadows on his dark features. He was satanic, dangerous and illicitly appealing as he stood there, looming over her. His knees were almost touching hers, he stood so close. She forced herself not to shrink away from him in fear. Not fear for what he might do to her, but fear of how she would respond if he did.

''I'll need a car in the morning. I came to ask if I might borrow yours.''

"Of course," she said on a breath of relief. "I'll get you the keys." She moved off the bed, avoiding brushing up against him as best she could. But as she squeezed past him, for one heart-stopping moment her thigh rubbed his and she felt the hard muscles contract. She moved away quickly and went to the dresser where her purse was. With shaking fingers, she fumbled for the keys, finally extracted them and dropped them into his palm. "Where are you going in the morning?"

"I want to see the doctor before I see my father. I'll come back midmorning to drive you and Laura Jane to the hospital if you like."

"Yes, that will be fine. I have some business to attend to here first thing in the morning."

"Cotton gin business?"

"Yes. I do the bookkeeping."

"So I understand from Granger. He said you became indispensable to Daddy before you married him." He came a step closer. His breath was warm and fragrant with expensive bourbon as it wafted over her face.

"Granger often goes overboard with his compliments." She tried to move aside, but he merely followed her with a matching sideways movement of his own. If anything, her avoidance tactic had brought them closer.

"I doubt that. I bet you're indispensable to Daddy in a lot of ways, aren't you?"

Her eyes flashed like lightning as she glared up at him. "Why do you insist on making these snide innuendos, Rink?"

"'Cause it just tickles hell out of me to get a rise out of you, that's why. Caroline, so young, so sweet, so demure, so . . . pure." He snarled the word.

She lifted her hand, but he grabbed it and twisted her arm behind her, hauling her against him. Her breasts were flattened against his hard chest. She stubbed her bare toes on the toes of his boots. His face came down to within an inch of hers. When he spoke, each word was pushed from behind clenched teeth.

"I let you get by with that once, but if you ever slap me again, you'll wish to God you hadn't."

"What would you do? Slap me back?"

He smiled with evil mischief. "Oh, no. That's not how I'd get retribution. I'd do something you wouldn't like at all." He pulled her tighter against his aroused body so she would understand his implication. He brought his head down closer. "Or would you like it very much, Caroline? Hmmm?" His belt buckle gouged through her nightclothes to bruise her stomach. "You may be Mrs. Roscoe Lancaster to everybody else, but you're still just Caroline Dawson to me, a girl walking through the woods in the summertime on her way to work . . . and driving me into a slow madness in the meantime."

Caroline stared up at him. Her expression was one of defiance. Her eyes were dark, like a storm cloud blowing up from the Gulf that carried with it rain and wind and lightning. The hair he had complimented earlier fell away from her face to hang down her back in a rich cascade. "Then you *do* remember, Rink. I was wondering if you had any memory of it at all."

Rink's eyes went wide for an instant before they narrowed. They scanned her face hotly, lingering long on her mouth, sliding down her throat to her breasts, which swelled in the opening of her robe, then going back up again. In those eyes was turbulence, the sign of an internal battle being waged.

"Yes," he said roughly. "Yes, goddammit. I remember."

She was released so suddenly that she reeled and caught herself against the dressing table. By the time she had regained her balance, he had stridden angrily from the room.

Damn! He wished he didn't remember.

Back in his room, he tore off his shirt, refilled the tumbler from the bottle he had pilfered from the liquor cabinet in his father's study and flung himself down into the leather easy chair that had always stood next to the windows. He took a swig of the whiskey, but it had lost its charm and he set it aside in distaste. He bent down and pulled off his boots, dropping them with soft thuds onto the rug.

Leaning back, he rested his head on the chair's deep cushion and let his mind go back, back to that summer day when he had taken all he could of the gin, his father's harping and the humid Mississippi heat. He had gone to the river, stripped to the skin and plunged into the stream where it ran cold. It was after he had gotten out, shaken himself dry and pulled on his jeans that he had seen her. . . .

"God Almighty!" Rink exclaimed. His fingers fumbled to zip up his jeans quickly. "How long have you been standing there?" He almost laughed out loud at her expression. If he was surprised at seeing her, the girl was absolutely paralyzed at seeing him.

He didn't think she was going to answer; then she stuttered, "I . . . I just got here."

"Well it's a damn good thing, because I've been skinny-dipping. If you had come along any sooner, we would both have been embarrassed."

His grin was wide and confident, with more than a trace of conceit. She was still shaking in her bobby socks and penny loafers, but she managed a timid smile. "I hope I didn't disturb you," she said with a politeness that, under the circumstances, amused him.

"No. I was finished. It's been so hot, I had to take a swim."

"Yes, it is hot. That's why I was walking down here by the channel. It's cooler than on the road."

He was curious about her from the beginning. Not only was she a strikingly beautiful girl, she was different. Her skirt was cotton, clean and pressed, but unfashionable. Her white cotton blouse smelled of laundry soap and starch rather than Youth Dew, which was what all the girls seemed to be wearing these days.

Beneath the blouse he could see the outline of a white brassiere that must have been as confining as a straitjacket. Most of the girls he knew wore something called a demicup push-up bra, which did just that, he was certain, with the sole intention of driving their dates crazy.

He dragged his eyes away from her chest, ashamed of himself for imposing on her the analysis he gave to every woman he met. She was just a kid. Fifteen? Sixteen? At most. And she still looked scared half to death of him.

But God, she was a looker. Clear skin; eyes the color of the fog that rode low over the bayous; a neat, trim body with a softness about it that was all female. Her hair gleamed darkly, like polished mahogany wood. Every time a breeze stirred the limbs of the trees overhead, dappled sunlight shot sparks of fire through the heavy strands.

"Where are you going?"

"Into town. I work at Woolworth's."

He didn't know any girls who actually worked during the summer. Most lay out by the swimming pools, private or public, cruised the main drag until they saw someone they knew and organized parties for the evenings.

"I'm Rink Lancaster."

She was looking at him strangely and it occurred to him that her fascination was with his state of undress.

She was fighting her curiosity, but her eyes kept flickering to his chest, his stomach and to the as yet undone snap of his jeans. Normally that would have boosted his confidence that this was going to be an easy conquest. He would have taken such an appraisal as an announcement that the woman was willing and available. But the innocence in this girl's eyes made him irritatingly self-conscious. With her eyes constantly returning to his fly, Rink was dismayed to feel unwelcomed arousal enlarging him.

Trying to keep an air of propriety, he stepped forward to offer her his hand. She flinched momentarily, then shyly placed her palm in his. "Caroline Dawson," she said tremulously, lifting her eyes to meet his.

They stared.

Time ticked by, insects hummed around their heads, an airplane whined high overhead, the channel water lapped the mossy rocks lining its banks. It was long moments before they moved and dropped their hands.

"Dawson?" Rink asked at last and wondered why his voice sounded as it had ten years prior when it was "changing." "Pete Dawson's daughter?"

Her eyes dropped to the ground and he saw her shoulders sag. Damn! Why had he asked in that incredulous tone of voice? Everyone knew Pete Dawson. He played dominoes all day in the pool halls, begging money off anyone dumb enough to stop and talk to him, until he had enough to buy a bottle of cheap whiskey to get him through to the next day.

"Yes," she said softly. Then, shaking slightly and raising her head with an air of pride that made Rink's chest feel warm and full, she said, "I've got to be going or I'll be late for work."

"It was nice to meet you."

"Nice to meet you, too."

"Be careful walking through the woods." She laughed. "What's funny?"

"You telling me to be careful when you just went swimming in there." She pointed at the channel. "There could be water moccasins and Lord knows what else in there. Why didn't you go to the swimming pool in town?"

He shrugged. "I was hot."

He was hot. God, was he hot. When she had laughed, her head had gone back, making her throat look white and vulnerable and inviting. Her hair had shimmered over her neck and shoulders. Detergent and starch were beginning to smell better than any fancy perfume his nose had ever come in contact with. The fragrance blended so well with the clean fresh scent of her skin. Her laughter, husky and genuine, had seemed a tangible thing that reached out and stroked him. It stroked him right where it felt damn good and right where it hurt like hell.

Yes, he was hot. Burning up with heat. "What time do you get off work?" He was as surprised as she by his question.

"Nine o'clock." Cautiously she began to back away.

"After dark? You walk home after dark?"

"Yes. But then I don't go through the woods. Only in the daytime."

He pondered that. This girl was like none other he had ever met, here in Winstonville or at Ol' Miss.

"I'll be late for work," she repeated and backed away farther, though he sensed in her a reluctance to part, too.

"Yeah, sure. Don't be late. Be seein' you, Caroline."

"Good-bye, Rink."

There was more said in that parting than either had verbalized. He counted on their meeting again. She never thought they would.

He had walked back to his convertible and vaulted behind the wheel without opening the door. He made the drive to The Retreat in record time and went immediately to his room, bounding up the stairs two at a time, and . . .

Now, as then, thoughts of Caroline swirled through his mind. He could see himself entering this very room that summer afternoon twelve years ago. He had tossed his discarded clothes onto the floor and fallen into this same chair. He had sat in the same slumping posture then as he did now, the same woman filling his mind. She was still a mystery, still elusive and haunting and obsessive.

And now, as then, he knew that no matter what he might do, there was little hope of easing his aching, throbbing desire.

Chapter 3

It was early when she awoke. She had hoped to sleep longer, to put off waking up and facing the crises of Roscoe's illness and Rink's return to Winstonville.

From downstairs she heard the front door open and close quietly. Throwing off the covers, she went into the hall and out onto the second-story balcony. The sun wasn't yet up over the tops of the trees, though a peachy glow painted the eastern sky. One star and a half-moon were still vividly bright against a vermilion sky. Mist rose from the dewy grass in trailing wisps. It would be another humid day.

Below her, Rink stepped off the porch. He lingered on the bottom step and studied the landscape that Caroline knew he loved. This land was as vital to him as breath. She pitied him for all the years he had banished himself from the home he loved.

Slowly he walked to the car parked in front of the house. He had on jeans and a sportcoat, a pretentious combination for drugstore cowboys but exactly right for him. The jeans were fashionably faded but had been starched and pressed to knife-blade creases down the front of his legs. Caroline watched as he dug into the front pocket for the car keys.

He swung open the car door. That was when he accidentally caught sight of her standing there watching him from the balcony. Propping his arm on the top of the car, he stared back up at her.

She stood perfectly still, didn't speak, didn't greet him, except with her eyes. They locked with his and held. And held. For long moments, in the pinky gold of the dawn, they stared at each other. The hazy morning light surrounding them seemed unreal, outside of time. In that silent moment of intimacy they could let down their defenses. They could indulge themselves. There existed nothing else in the world save the two of them.

Then at last, without speaking a word, he got into her Lincoln and drove away. Dejectedly Caroline returned to her room and dressed. She looked at herself in the mirror and asked, "How could this have happened?"

The only man she had ever loved, or had ever come close to loving, was Rink Lancaster. For only a short while they had shared something special and rare. At least to her it had been. She had allowed herself to dream that the implausible might be possible. She had been duped into believing all he'd told her that summer. His words had been meaningless. She had been nothing more to him than a novelty.

Now, by some whimsical twist of fate, she was married to his father. His *father!* When Roscoe had asked her to marry him, it had seemed the answer to all her dreams. She would have respectability, money. People who had looked down on her all her life would treat her with deference.

Rink had been gone, never to return. Why hadn't she considered that he might come back and how she would feel if he did? Had she been completely honest with

herself? Had she married Roscoe not because she'd
wanted to make him happy and help him with his
business, to be a friend to Laura Jane, but because she'd
wanted to make Rink jealous and sorry that he had
deserted her? Was she trying to pay him back for the
heartache she had suffered when he left? Had she
secretly hoped that he would hear about the marriage,
remember that summer twelve years ago and be outraged?

She smiled sadly at her reflection in the mirror. "He's
merely amused, Caroline. Amused and disgusted."

Haney was already in the kitchen when Caroline came
down a short time later to pour herself a cup of coffee.
"Good morning."

"You're up bright and early," the housekeeper remarked over her shoulder.

"I have to get the payroll out and I want to do it early
and leave the rest of the day free." She sipped the coffee.
"You're up earlier than usual, too."

"I want to cook a fine breakfast for Rink."

"He's already left, Haney."

She whirled around and confronted Caroline to verify
what she'd heard. "Already?"

"Yes. About an hour ago."

Haney shook her head, making *tsk*ing sounds. "He's
not eating right. Here I was wanting to make him his
favorite breakfast and he's hightailed it out of here
before I even got a chance."

Caroline placed a comforting hand on her arm. "Why
don't you fix it for Laura Jane? Call Steve over to share it
with her. I'm sure they'd like that."

"Okay," she mumbled. "But it won't be the same
without Rink. Nothing in this house has been the same
since he married that gal and left town."

Haney was right about that, Caroline thought as she
made her way toward the back of the house and into
Roscoe's study. Painfully, she remembered the day Rink

hadn't showed up at their rendezvous. Disconsolate, she had gone on to work only to overhear the town buzzing with gossip that Rink Lancaster was going to marry Marilee George, one of Winstonville's prominent debutantes. Caroline's world had never been the same.

She whipped through the bookkeeping without having to think too much about it. When she telephoned the gin, the morning shift foreman told her things were running smoothly.

"Got one machine that's being ornery, but it's nothing you need to worry about at a time like this."

"I'll count on you to carry on as though nothing's out of the ordinary, Barnes. As long as he's alive, Roscoe is still in charge and I report directly to him."

"Yes, ma'am," the foreman replied before he hung up.

She was sure some of the men balked at the idea of taking orders from a woman, especially ol' Pete Dawson's daughter. But if they did, they never vocalized their feelings. They feared Roscoe too much. But what would happen when he was gone?

"Problems?"

Her head jerked up to see Rink lounging against the door frame. She realized that her brow was creased with worry and she relaxed it. "Minor ones. You know how it is at the gin."

"Actually, I don't." He sauntered into the room. His sportcoat was hooked over his index finger and slung over his shoulder. The first three buttons of his plaid shirt had been left undone to reveal a tanned throat and a wedge of dark hair. "I left town before I had much to do with the running of the gin." By now he was at the edge of the desk. He leaned far over it until his face was on a level with hers. "Why don't you tell me what it's like, boss lady?"

Seething with anger, she surged to her feet, sending her chair rolling backward on its casters. They faced each other like adversaries in a boxing ring waiting for the bell to begin the round.

"Rink, Haney sent me in here after you. Breakfast is just now ready and she wants you to eat." Laura Jane happily skipped into the room to hug her brother. "Good morning. Caroline, I'm supposed to bring you, too. And Haney said no excuses."

Another argument had been thwarted, but Rink wasn't going to let her off easily. He extended his hand to her. "Caroline." She had no choice but to place her hand in his and let him lead her around the desk. Nor did he release her hand until they reached the dining room. That he was also holding Laura Jane's hand didn't matter. Where his palm touched hers, where his fingers curled possessively through hers, Caroline's skin tingled.

Despite Haney's sumptuously prepared brunch, it wasn't a pleasant meal. Rink didn't seem too happy to find Steve sitting next to Laura Jane. Steve cast uneasy glances around the table, as though he might be asked to leave at any moment.

The hostility between Rink and Caroline was palpable, though they went out of their way to be polite to each other. Haney couldn't figure it out and she was huffy because the tension between them was ruining all her efforts to make this a special homecoming for Rink.

"Why is everybody mad?" Laura Jane asked suddenly.

They all looked at her, dumbfounded. She alone was happy, enjoying the presence of those she loved. But her perception was keen and she had picked up on the antagonism that crackled around the table.

It was Caroline who finally spoke. "We're all just worried about Roscoe," she said gently, reaching across the table to pat the young woman's hand.

"But Rink's here. And Steve." She blessed him with a look radiant with love. "Let's all be happy."

She shamed them into it. Rink stopped staring suspiciously at Steve and tensing every time he looked at Laura Jane. He and Caroline stopped glowering at each other and even got into a conversation about the townsfolk that Rink had known years ago. She informed him about who had married whom, who was divorced, who was prospering and who wasn't.

When they were done, Steve stood and thanked Haney, then headed toward the kitchen. "Just a minute, Steve," Laura Jane announced. "I'm coming with you to see the filly."

"We're going to the hospital, Laura Jane," Rink said curtly.

"But I want to see the foal. I promised Steve I would come to the stables this morning."

Steve shifted self-consciously from one booted foot to the other. "Laura Jane, your daddy will be disappointed if you don't go see him. That filly's not going anywhere," he teased. "You can come see her another time."

"All right, Steve," she acquiesced softly. "I'll come see you as soon as I get back."

Steve nodded, thanked Haney again and left quickly. He didn't look directly at Rink before going.

Caroline stood hastily. "I'll be ready in a few minutes, Rink. Laura Jane, do you want to freshen up before we go?"

"I guess so."

They came back downstairs a few minutes later. Rink was waiting for them in the foyer. Haney stood beside him, holding a vase of fresh-cut roses. "Haney wants to follow us in her car and take Daddy the roses. Then she'll come on back. Laura Jane, why don't you ride with her and hold the flowers so they won't spill."

"I'll do that," Caroline offered hurriedly. Rink's hard look said otherwise.

"I'd like to talk to you on the way." Imperiously he helped her into the Lincoln while Haney drove the station wagon that belonged to The Retreat but was left at her disposal.

"Did you see the doctor this morning?" Caroline asked to break the tense silence.

"Yes. He told me what he'd told you and Granger."

"Did . . . did he say when it—"

"Any time."

They were on the highway, heading toward town, before Rink said another word. "Who is this Steve?"

"Steve Bishop." Caroline was automatically on the defensive. She thought she knew what was coming and she wasn't going to like it.

Irritation thinned Rink's lips. "Can you elaborate on that a little?"

"He's a Vietnam War veteran."

"Is that why he limps? A war injury?"

"He lost his left leg from the knee down." She turned to him as she imparted that piece of news. He continued to stare out the windshield, but she saw his hands grip the wheel and the muscles in his arms bunch. His face was set in hard lines that bespoke an iron will and dogged determination. And pride. So much pride.

She knew he wanted to dislike Steve. Knowing he was permanently handicapped wasn't going to make it easy to do. "He was bitter and surly when he applied for the job. I believe his attitude was a defense mechanism against being rejected. He's conscientious, hardworking, honest."

"I don't like the attachment Laura Jane has for him."

"Why?"

"You have to ask?" he demanded, swiveling his head around. "It's unhealthy and dangerous, that's why. She has no business hanging around a single man all the time."

"I see no harm in it. She's a single woman."

"And innocent about sex. Totally. I doubt if she even

knows the difference between men and women and why
the difference is there.''

''Of course she does!''

''All right, then, all the more reason why she doesn't
need to spend so much time in his company. Because I
can guarantee that he knows the difference.''

''I think he's good for her. He's kind and patient. He's
been hurt and not only physically. He knows what it's
like to be an outcast and feel rejected as Laura Jane
always has been.''

''What if he took advantage of her fondness? Sexu-
ally.''

''He wouldn't do that.''

Rink scoffed. ''He damn sure would. He's a man and
she's a beautiful woman, and plenty of opportunities
present themselves.''

''You ought to know all about that, shouldn't you?''

The heated words were out of her mouth before she
could halt them. He braked the car jarringly in the
parking space at the hospital and swung around to face
her. His face was as angry as hers. She had gone to the
water's edge, she might as well plunge in.

''You should know all about taking advantage of an
innocent girl, lying to her, making promises you don't
intend to keep.''

''Are you referring to that summer?''

''Yes! I've never understood how you could be with
me the way you were and still get Marilee pregnant. You
must have exhausted yourself. Or was I merely the
warm-up act for your big finish?''

He broadened her vocabulary by several choice words
before he shoved the car door open and slammed it
behind him. Only then did Caroline realize that Haney
and Laura Jane were already at the hospital entrance and
were watching them expectantly. Caroline's fingers were
icy as she clenched them, but she forced herself to relax

when Rink opened her door and helped her out. Her features were schooled into a mask of composure by the time the group traversed the lobby of the hospital and entered the elevator.

The nurse at the desk on Roscoe's floor informed them that they could go in together if they didn't stay too long. "He had a rough night. A lot of pain," she told them sadly.

"Maybe I'd better go first and tell him you're here," Caroline said. No one objected. Rink was rigid and remote. Haney was uncharacteristically subdued. Laura Jane was wide-eyed and looked like she might bolt at any moment.

Caroline pushed open the heavy hospital room door and went into the room. It was the largest, most expensive private suite the hospital had to offer. Florists' arrangements already lined the window ledge and TV table. Much as she hated to admit it, Roscoe inspired little love in the people his life touched. But many revered or feared him, as evidenced by the abundance of cards and flowers.

He didn't look intimidating now as he opened his eyes and saw her. His skin had the gray-yellow, pasty look of death. Dark shadows ringed his sunken eyes. His lips were tinged with blue. But his eyes were as dark and alive as ever.

"Good morning." She bent over him, took his hand and kissed his forehead. "The nurse said you had a rough night. Did you get any rest?"

"Don't patronize me please, Caroline." He shook off her hand. "I'll have a whole goddamn eternity to rest." He laughed wheezingly. "Or to burn, I'm sure some hope. Did you get the payroll done?"

"Yes," she said, stepping away and taking his rejection of her affection pragmatically. He was gravely ill. He was allowed some contrariness. "This morning. I'll deliver the checks to the gin this afternoon."

"Good. I don't want them to think I'm dead yet." He laid a hand on his stomach and winced with pain, cursing viciously.

When he subsided, Caroline said softly, "Are you up to having visitors?"

"Who?"

"Laura Jane and Haney."

"Haney! That hypocritical bitch. She's hated me since the day she first saw me. Thought I married Marlena for her money and for The Retreat. Blamed me for Rink's leaving. Blamed me for every goddamn thing that went wrong with this family."

Caroline played devil's advocate. "Why didn't you fire her years ago?"

He cackled. "Because I liked jousting with her. Kept my wits sharpened. Now she's come to snivel over my deathbed. Ha!"

Caroline had seen him in this kind of mood before, but she had always ignored it until it passed. She regretted that he chose to be this way during their last days together. "Please, Roscoe. Don't be angry. Haney picked some flowers from the rosebeds for you."

He growled his consent to see the housekeeper. "Laura Jane has no business in here. This place'll scare her silly. Does she know I'm not coming home?"

Caroline looked away from the razor-sharp eyes. "Yes. I told her yesterday."

"What did she say?"

"She said you'd go to Heaven and be with Marlena."

He laughed until pain wrenched him again. "Well, it would take a simpleton to think that."

His choice of words offended Caroline greatly, but she held her peace. Few ever argued with Roscoe over anything, even his way of putting things. "Shall I tell them to come in?"

"Yes, yes," he said, waving a thin hand weakly. "Let's get it over with."

"There's someone else, Roscoe."

Her quiet tone brought his eyes snapping back to her. He stared at her hard, searchingly, making her unaccountably uncomfortable. "Rink? Rink's come?"

She nodded. "As soon as Granger called him."

"Good, good. I want to see my son, to say some things to him before it's over."

Caroline's heart swelled with gladness. It was time these two strong-willed men settled their differences. She hastened toward the door, missing the cold, shrewd calculation in Roscoe's eyes as he watched her go.

Laura Jane was first in the room. She ran toward the bed and flung her arms around her father's neck, hugging him hard. "I miss you at home, Daddy," she said. "We have a new filly. She's beautiful."

"Well, that's fine, Laura Jane," he said and gently pushed her away. Caroline watched, wishing just once that he would return the spontaneous affection his daughter showed him. "Been picking the rosebushes, I see," he grunted crossly as he peered up at the housekeeper from under scowling brows.

Haney had been bullied by him for years. She wasn't the least intimidated now. "Yes. These are only half of them, too. The others are on the dining room table."

Roscoe appreciated her spunk. They had waged a cold war for over thirty years and he considered her a worthy opponent. "To hell with flowers. Bring me anything to eat?"

"You know you're not supposed to have anything the hospital doesn't cook."

"What the hell difference does it make?" he roared. "Huh? Somebody tell me."

One by one he treated the women to baleful stares and then turned his head to meet his son's steady gaze. For an interminably long time the two men stared at each other. No one moved. Finally Roscoe's chest began to shake with a low, rumbling laugh. "Still mad at me, Rink?"

"I got over being mad a long time ago, sir."

"Is that why you came back? To make peace with your old man before he croaks? Or for the reading of the will?"

"I don't need anything in your damn will."

Haney stepped forward diplomatically. She had feared the reunion wouldn't be pleasant. "I'm taking Laura Jane home now. Laura Jane, kiss your daddy and let's go." The girl complied dutifully.

Roscoe barely noticed them leave. His eyes were still boring into those of his son. Caroline was left alone with two generations of Lancasters who had far more than years separating them.

"You turned out to be a good-looking man, Rink," his father said analytically. "Hard and mean, too. The meanness doesn't show up in all those smiling newspaper pictures, but I figured it was there."

"I had a good teacher."

That same laugh, a hideous laugh, filled the room again. "You bet you did, sonny, you bet you did. Only way to get on in this world. Be mean as hell to everybody and no one'll ever get the best of you." He gestured impatiently. "Sit down, both of you."

"I prefer to stand, thank you," Rink replied. Caroline sank into an available chair. She'd never seen Roscoe quite this acerbic. No wonder Rink had been forced to leave his home. She had known the antagonism between them was strong but nothing like this.

"From what I read, that airline of yours is making you rich."

"My partner and I had great expectations for Air Dixie from the first. So far all our goals have been exceeded."

"Smart philosophy you've got. Herd the passengers

on, herd them off, low fares, keep the planes flying. You've profited when others are going out of business.''

If Rink was surprised to learn that his father had followed the success of his commuter airline, he gave no indication of it. ''As I said, we've been pleased with our success.''

A nurse came in carrying a stainless-steel tray with a hypodermic needle on it. ''I've come to give you a shot for your pain, Mr. Lancaster.''

''Stick it in your own ass and leave mine alone,'' Roscoe shouted at her.

''Roscoe,'' Caroline said, shocked by his vulgarity.

''Doctor's orders, Mr. Lancaster,'' the nurse said firmly.

''I don't care what that quack said. This is my life, what's left of it, and I don't want any damn shot to relieve my pain. I want to feel everything. Understand? Now get out of here.''

The nurse's lips pursed in severe disapproval, but she left the room.

''Roscoe, she's only doing—''

''Stop mothering me, for God's sake, Caroline!'' The tone of his voice was like none he had used with her before. She shrank back as though he'd struck her. She fell silent, her lips compressed. ''If all I'm going to get from you is insipid pity, don't bother coming back.''

Breathing hard, Caroline hastily grabbed up her purse and left the hospital room with regal dignity. As soon as the door closed behind her, Rink whirled on his father.

''You sonofabitch.'' His golden eyes flashed fire. Each hard muscle in his athletic body was strained with fury. ''You've got no right to talk to her in that way, I don't care how much pain you're in.''

Roscoe chuckled, an evil sound, as evil as his calculating expression. ''I have every right. She's my wife. Remember?''

Rink's hands balled into fists on his thighs. He made a

feral sound deep in his throat before he spun on his heels and stormed from the room.

At first he didn't see Caroline. Then he spotted her at the end of the corridor, slumped against the wall, gazing sightlessly out a window. He came up behind her. He raised his hand to touch her, paused to reconsider, then thought, To hell with it, and placed his hand on her shoulder. She reacted instantly, stiffening reflexively.

"Are you all right?"

Oh, God, she thought. Why had he asked that, in that particular tone of voice? It was exactly the way he had asked her that same question another time. The same words, the same inflection, the same gentle concern in the husky timbre of his voice.

She turned slightly to look up at him over her shoulder. Tears formed in her eyes. They could have been put there by the humiliation she had suffered at her husband's hands. But that wasn't the reason for them. They were tears of remembrance. She gazed into his eyes and was transported back, back to that first night. . . .

The car lights came up behind her and she hurried her footsteps. She didn't particularly like walking home alone. Of course, she could wait for Papa, but Lord knew when he'd likely start home. Besides, in his condition he would be of no help if she were to be attacked.

She had almost died of shame that afternoon when Rink Lancaster had figured out that she was the town drunk's daughter. He would know that they lived in an old ramshackle house and that her mama took in laundry to keep food on the table and secondhand clothes from her customers on Caroline's back.

She had recognized him instantly. Everybody knew the Lancasters. She had seen Rink many times from afar, driving like a bat out of hell in his shiny red sports car with the convertible top down, the wind whipping his black hair around his head. Usually there was a girl with him, her left arm draped over his shoulders. The radio would blare. He would honk and wave at everybody he knew, including the sheriff's deputies, who overlooked his flagrant disregard of the speed limit. Everybody knew Rink Lancaster, football hero, basketball team captain, track star, heir to The Retreat and the largest cotton gin in five counties.

He had occupied her thoughts during the hours she worked at Woolworth's. Now she hurried home so she could crawl into bed and think about him and all he had said to her that day. Of course he probably wouldn't even remember—

"Hi, Caroline." The car that had been cruising behind her crept to her side. Incredulously she looked into Rink's smiling face as he leaned over the passenger seat and opened the door. "Get in. I'll drive you home."

She glanced up and down the road as though she had been caught doing something she shouldn't. "I don't know if I should."

He laughed. "Why?"

Because boys like Rink Lancaster didn't drive girls like Caroline Dawson around in their sports cars, that's why. But she didn't say that. She didn't say anything. Her heart, pounding in her throat, left no room for words.

"Come on, get in," he said with an irresistible smile. She slid into the leather seat and pulled the door closed behind her. The seat swallowed her in luxury and it was all she could do to keep from running her hands over its softness. The dials and gadgets on the dashboard winked at her in myriad colors.

"Do you like chocolate milk shakes?"

She had only had one in her life. One day after Mama got paid they had stopped at a lunch counter in town and bought one to share as a special treat. "Yes."

"I stopped at the Dairy Mart. Help yourself." He tilted his head and indicated the paper cup propped between the seats on the console. It had a lid on it, but the straw was sticking up out of the hole in the top.

"Thank you," she said timidly, picking it up and sucking on the straw. It was cold and rich and delicious and she smiled her pleasure. He smiled back.

The radio wasn't playing loudly and the canvas top was up on the car. He didn't want anyone to see her with him. She understood and didn't mind. He had come to pick her up; he had bought her a chocolate shake. That was enough.

"How was work?"

"I sold a set of dishes."

"Yeah?"

"They were ugly. I don't think I'd like eating off them."

He laughed. "Then you don't plan to sell dishes all your life?"

"No."

"What do you want to do?"

Go to college, she thought with that desperation of the hopelessly hopeful. "I don't know. I like math. I was on the honor roll two years in a row."

She felt a need to impress him with something, tell him something that would make him remember this night, because she knew she would never forget it for as long as she lived. She, Caroline Dawson, riding around with Rink Lancaster! Why had he bothered? He could have his pick of girls, girls older and far more worldly than she. Girls who wore pretty clothes and went to club meetings, girls whose mothers served on committees and drove long cars, girls who would never deign to speak to Caroline Dawson.

"Math, huh? Maybe I could have used your help up at college. I barely squeaked through my math courses."

"Did you like college?"

"Sure. It was a blast. But I'm glad to be out."

"You graduated?"

"Six weeks ago."

"What's your degree in?"

"It was a toss-up between agriculture and engineering. I thought I already knew a lot about agriculture, so I majored in engineering."

"That should be helpful at the gin."

"I guess." Without asking directions he turned off the highway onto the county road that led to her house.

"You don't have to take me all the way," she said hastily.

"It's darker than pitch out here."

"I'm not scared to walk the rest of the way, honest. Please stop."

Without an argument, he braked the car. She didn't want him to drive her all the way home. There would then be explanations to make to her mother. This day was too special. She didn't want to share it with anyone. Mostly, she didn't want him to come face-to-face with the squalor she lived in.

After the motor had been cut, everything went silent. He turned off the headlights and let the convertible top down. The moon bathed them with a silvery-white glow. A breeze flirted with their hair.

He propped his arm on the back of her seat. His knee bumped into hers as he turned to face her. He didn't move it away. She could smell the cologne he was wearing, see the faint shadow of a beard. He wasn't a boy, he was a man. She had never had a date before, never been alone with a man of any age.

Self-conscious because he wasn't saying anything, she continued to suck on the straw. He watched her intently. With every pull of her lips on the straw, she was aware of his eyes on her mouth. The straw made a loud slurping sound when she reached bottom and she looked up at him in mortification.

He was smiling. "Enjoy the milk shake?"

"Very much. Thank you." She handed him the empty cup and he bent to shove it beneath his seat.

When he straightened, he leaned forward slightly so that they faced each other. As it had that afternoon, conversation gave way to ravenous curiosity. She studied him as intently as he did her. She could see his eyes roving over her face and hair and neck and chest, and it made her feel warm and funny on the inside, weightless. Yet there was a gathering heaviness in the lower part of her body. A heat, unfamiliar and delicious, forbidden and heavenly, began to pump through her veins.

He placed his thumb lengthwise under her lower lip, touching the border of it with his well-trimmed nail. She thought she might die of suffocation. Suddenly she couldn't breathe.

"You're very pretty," he said huskily.

"Thank you."

"How old are you?"

"Fifteen."

"Fifteen." He muttered a curse under his breath and looked away from her. Then, as though he couldn't control them, his eyes came back. "I thought about you all day after I saw you in the woods." His hand was lying along her cheek now and his thumb was hypnotically stroking her bottom lip.

"You did?"

"Mmm," he murmured. "All afternoon you were on my mind."

"I thought about you, too."

That seemed to please him. He grinned lopsidedly. "What did you think?"

Her cheeks flamed and she was grateful to the darkness for hiding her girlish blush. To avoid his eyes, she looked down at his throat in the open collar of his shirt. "Things," she said hoarsely, shrugging with feigned indifference.

"Things?" He smiled. But it was a slight, fleeting smile, not one that distracted him from his intent perusal of her face. "Did you think about . . ." He seemed to search for the proper words.

"Making out" was what came to her mind. That was what kids did when they went on dates, wasn't it? Wasn't that what they whispered about in groups that she was never invited to enter?

But that was not what Rink said. He said, "Did you think about us . . . together? Maybe touching?"

"Touching?" she repeated breathlessly.

"Kissing?"

Her lips parted, but no sound came forth. She heard nothing but the beating thud of her own heart.

"Have you ever been kissed?"

"A few times," she lied.

"You're so damn young," he groaned, squeezing his eyes closed momentarily before opening them quickly. "Would you be afraid if I kissed you? Would you like it if I kissed you?"

"I'm not afraid of you, Rink."

"And the other?" he prodded gently, touching her hair.

"I . . . I think I'd like you to . . . kiss me."

"Caroline," he whispered, moving closer. She felt his breath on her face first and her eyes closed. Then his lips touched hers—soft, still, hesitant. When she didn't pull away, he tilted his head to one side and pressed more firmly. Again and again his lips collided with hers in brief, light kisses, soft pecks that made her hungry from the bottom of her soul for something she couldn't name. Even "making out" didn't apply. Because anybody could do that and this was something she knew no one had ever experienced before.

He cupped her face with both palms and laid his mouth, lips open this time, firmly over hers. She felt the moistness of his tongue just a breath away from her lips, then on them, flicking lightly.

He moaned softly before he pressed his tongue against her lips. Caroline's eyes went wide with shock. She froze. Then the pleasure of what he was doing vanquished her resistance and her lips parted. His tongue slid between them. It touched the tip of hers, rubbed, stroked, pushed deeper.

When his arms closed around her, she grasped handfuls of his shirtfront and clung. Her insides were in chaos, tossed about and tumbling with what she didn't know yet was arousal. She knew a compelling urge to gravitate toward him. The need to touch his body with hers was an obsessive desire she could barely keep under control. She both craved and feared the impulses he had awakened her to.

He pulled back regretfully, kissed her moist lips tenderly, then separated himself from her and put hateful space between them. His hands returned from her back to rest on either side of her face. Her eyes were closed and when she raised the heavy eyelids, it was with a lassitude that had invaded her entire body.

"Are you all right? . . ."

Now, in the chilly hospital corridor, she answered him as she had twelve years ago on a warm balmy night after that first kiss. "Yes, Rink, I'm all right."

Rink, too, seemed caught up in a memory. He gazed down at her for a long time before he brusquely turned away and said, "We'd better go."

Chapter 4

"SHE'S SO PRETTY."

"So are you."

Laura Jane's hands stilled on the filly's neck as she lifted her dark liquid eyes to Steve, who had spoken with soft fervency. "Do you really think I am?"

Her expression made him curse himself. She was vulnerable, took everything literally. He shouldn't speak aloud the things he thought. Her feelings were fragile and could be easily shattered.

He levered himself up from the hay-strewn floor of the stall, bracing his weight on his good leg. "You're very pretty," he said tersely and turned away from her, leaving the stall.

Putting space between them was becoming necessary more frequently. She had no idea what her nearness, her flowery scent, the warm smoothness of her skin did to his senses. Had she known the responses she elicited from his body, she would have been terrified of him.

He hauled a saddle from the tack room wall. Rink had

told him that afternoon that he wished to ride the following morning, and Steve wanted everything to be perfect. He knew the reason for Rink's apparent dislike of him. The man wasn't blind. Nor was he insensitive. Rink would recognize longing when he saw it. Steve knew his desire for Laura Jane was as evident as a neon billboard hanging around his neck.

He didn't blame Rink for his suspicions. Laura Jane was his sister, a very special sister who had required special care all her life. If Steve had had anyone in his life like her, he would have been as fiercely protective as Rink was.

Still, he couldn't help loving her, could he? Love wasn't something he had gone looking for. He hadn't expected to ever love anybody. But he did and he missed Laura Jane every moment of the day that she wasn't with him. She was standing close beside him now as he applied saddle soap to the saddle. Each time his elbow moved with the sawing motion of his cloth, it almost touched her breast.

He bent to his task with renewed vigor and tried not to think of what her breasts would feel like beneath his callused hands or how soft her throat would be beneath his lips.

Laura Jane, vaguely disappointed that Steve hadn't gone on talking about how pretty she was, had patted the foal farewell and followed him. "Is your leg hurting?"

Without looking up, he answered. "No. Why?"

"Because you're frowning, the way you do sometimes when your leg hurts."

"I'm just working hard, that's all."

She moved closer. "I'll help you work, Steve. Let me help you."

He moved away from her, ostensibly to get another rag. His blood was pounding. She was so sweet, so sweet, but the feelings she aroused in him were far from sweet. Around her he felt like a slavering savage within

touching distance of the sacrificial virgin. "No. You
don't need to help. I'll be through in a minute."

"You don't think I can, do you? No one thinks I can
do anything."

His head came up quickly and he dropped his polish-
ing cloth. "Of course I think you can."

He saw the hurt on her face, the pain in her dark,
fathomless eyes. She shook her head and her soft brown
hair swished over her shoulders. "Everybody thinks I'm
stupid and useless."

"Laura Jane," he groaned miserably and placed his
hands on her shoulders. "I don't think any such thing."

"Then why won't you let me help you?"

"Because this is dirty work and I don't want you
getting messed up."

With a childlike need to trust, she peered up at him.
"That's the only reason? Promise?"

"Promise."

He didn't release her as he should have, but kept his
hands on her shoulders. Her upraised face was bathed
with the soft amber glow of the stable lights. She looked
like an angel except for the flame burning steadily in her
eyes. If he hadn't known better, he would have thought
that flame had a carnal origin.

"I know I'm not bright. But I'm smart about some
things."

"Of course you are." God! Her lips were soft and
moist and pink as they formed her words. He wanted to
taste them. What he'd give to press her close, to feel that
beautiful dainty body against his hulking, scarred, deformed one. It would be like applying a healing balm to
his aching body, his aching spirit.

"I notice things. For instance I know Rink isn't
happy. He laughs and tries to act happy, but his eyes are
sad. He and Caroline don't like each other. Have you
noticed that?"

"Yes."

"I wonder why." Her face wrinkled with concentration. "Or maybe they like each other very much, but are trying to make everyone think that they don't."

Steve smiled at her perception. That had been the conclusion he had drawn after eating brunch with them that morning. They looked ready to either fight or love. He thought the scale tipped strongly in favor of the latter. He chucked Laura Jane under the chin. "You may be right."

She smiled up at him and moved closer. "You think I'm smart? And pretty?"

His dark eyes roamed her face. "You're beautiful."

"I think you're beautiful, too." With fingers as flawless as china, she reached up and traced his hard cheekbone, then trailed her fingertips down to his chin.

He felt her touch on more than his face. The sensations it created rocketed straight to his loins. He sucked his breath in sharply and stepped away from her, dropping his arms to his sides. "Don't," he said with unintended harshness.

Laura Jane recoiled as though he'd slapped her.

"Oh, God, Laura Jane, I'm sorry. I'm sorry." He reached out to touch her comfortingly but couldn't bring himself to. She had covered her face with her hands and was weeping softly. "Please don't cry."

"I'm a terrible person."

"Terrible? You're far from terrible." He had never felt so wretched in his life. He was damned if he touched her and damned if he didn't. It was suicidal to show her any affection; Rink would kill him if he found out. On the other hand, how could he hurt her this way, make her feel rejected, unloved, unwanted? "You're wonderful," he whispered urgently. "You're all that everyone should be."

"No. I'm not." She lifted her tear-streaked face to his. "I've loved Rink for as long as I can remember. I thought that if he came home, everything would be all right. I thought he was the strongest, most beautiful man in the world. But now that he's home, I see that he's not." She wet her lips with her tongue. "You are." Her small breasts trembled beneath her summer dress. Teardrops rolled down her cheeks. "Steve, I love you more than I do Rink!"

Before he could react, she flung herself against him, kissed him swiftly on the lips and ran from the stable.

He could count the racing heartbeats as they thudded in his eardrums. He was both elated and miserable. God, what could he do about this?

Nothing. Absolutely nothing.

He turned off the lights in the stable and went into his well-maintained but painfully lonely apartment at the back of the building. Flopping down in his narrow bed, he covered his eyes with his forearm. He hadn't felt this kind of despair since he had awakened in the army hospital to learn that he was going home . . . with half of one leg missing.

"Oh, I'm sorry, Rink. I didn't see you out here."

"It's all right," he said from the shadows. "This is your house."

Caroline let the screen door close behind her and sat down on the wicker glider. She breathed deeply of the cool evening air. Her eyes closed tiredly as she leaned her head against the wicker back. "This is your house, Rink. I'm only a visitor for as long as—"

"As my father lives."

"Yes."

He didn't make a reply. He was weary of arguments. "You didn't go back to the hospital."

"I called. They had finally talked him into a shot and it put him to sleep. The doctor said there was no reason for me to be there. Roscoe wouldn't know one way or another. I felt I could be more useful here at home doing some business for the gin. It'll soon be picking time and we need to make sure we're ready.''

"I'd hate to be at the hospital when Roscoe wakes up and discovers he's lost a day."

Caroline rubbed her forehead as though she already had the headache his angry shouting would bring on. "So would I."

"Does he often treat you the way he did today?"

"No. Never. I've seen him lose his temper with other people. I've gone behind him and placated them. Today was the first day I've been the target."

"You've been lucky, then," Rink said. "He was that way with my mother, constantly on her case about some trivial something he had trumped up. God"—he slammed his fist against the arm of his chair—"there were days when I wanted to smash his foul mouth as hard as I could with my fist. Even as a little kid, I used to hate him for making her unhappy when she had given him everything. Everything."

He glanced up at her and she got the impression that he was embarrassed by revealing so much emotion to her. "Can I make you a drink?" he asked shortly.

"No thank you."

He sighed in the darkness. "Sorry. I forgot. You don't drink, do you?"

"After growing up in Pete Dawson's house? No," she said with a soft laugh. "I don't drink."

"Then I won't, either." He leaned over the arm of the chair where he was sitting and set his highball glass on the floor.

"No, please. I don't mind. It doesn't smell on you the way it did on him."

It was far too personal a comment to make. She looked at him to see if he had read anything into what she had said. His golden eyes captured hers from across the darkness that separated them. She was the first to look away.

"Haney told me that your daddy died," Rink said at last. He left the glass untouched on the porch.

"Yes. They found him dead one morning in a ditch on the highway. The coroner said it was a heart attack. I think he finally succeeded in poisoning himself."

"And your mother?"

"She died a few years ago." Her eyes were unseeing as she stared into the twilight. Her mother had been barely fifty. Yet she was a stooped, wrinkled old woman when she gratefully died of exhaustion and despair.

Rink got up from his chair and came to sit closer to her on the top step of the porch. Crossing his ankles, he leaned back and propped himself up on his elbows. His shoulder touched the frame of the glider, dangerously close to her calf. "Fill me in, Caroline. What happened to you after that summer, after I left?"

She yearned to reach down and touch his hair, to sift through the thick dark strands with her fingers. His body was long and lean, the male power within it just as evident in repose as in movement.

"I finished high school and got a scholarship to college."

"A scholarship? How?" He yanked his head around and bumped against her shinbone with his chin. He pulled back quickly.

"I don't know."

He sat up and looked at her inquiringly as he turned slightly. "Don't know?"

She shook her head. She couldn't organize her thoughts. They had scattered like autumn leaves in a whirlwind at his touch. He was now sitting with his knees raised, his arms looped loosely around them. The dangling fingers of his left hand had but to extend to touch her leg.

He was waiting for an explanation, so she collected herself and spoke, haltingly at first. "One day the high school principal called me into his office. It was just a few days before graduation. He said I had a scholarship from a donor who wished to remain anonymous. It paid for everything. I even got an allowance of fifty dollars a month for mad money. To this day I don't know who was responsible.''

"God Almighty," he said under his breath. Haney had told him in one of her gossipy letters that "the Dawson girl" had gone to college ("You probably don't remember her. She was several classes behind you. Old Pete Dawson's girl. Anyway, she's left town to go to school and everybody's wondering how she managed it."). And much later he had received a letter from Laura Jane ("Daddy told me today that somebody named Caroline Dawson has married a boy at college. He said she used to live here and that you might know her.").

"After I got my degree, I moved back to town," Caroline continued.

"Your marriage must not have lasted long."

His studiously casual observation baffled Caroline. "Marriage?"

"The guy you met at school."

She stared at him as if he had lost his mind. "I don't know what you're talking about, Rink. I didn't even *date* anybody, much less get married. To keep the scholarship, I had to maintain a B average. I studied all the time. Where in the world did you get the idea I'd been married?"

Rink, too, was shocked. Had Laura Jane made that up? No. Laura Jane hadn't even known Caroline until she'd started working for Roscoe.

Roscoe.

A worm of suspicion entered his mind. What occurred to him was too diabolical even to contemplate. But where Roscoe was concerned . . . "I heard that you'd gotten married. I forget who told me."

"Whoever it was told you wrong. I didn't marry until I married . . ."

"My father."

After a long awkward silence, Caroline asked what had been on her mind for years. "What happened between you and Marilee?"

"World War Three," he said with a short laugh. Caroline didn't say anything. She sat stiffly, her fingers knotting together. "It was doomed from the beginning. She didn't want that baby any more than I did. She used it as a means to trap me into marrying her, and after Alyssa was born, we started divorce proceedings."

"Do you ever see the child? Alyssa?"

"No. Never," Rink said. His face was inscrutable, but the tone of his voice indicated clearly that the subject was closed. It hurt Caroline to the quick that he didn't love his child, his only child. How could he be so unfeeling? For years after that magic summer, she had wished she had had his baby. It would have been something of his left for her, some part of him to love since he wasn't there.

"After the divorce was finally settled—it took years— I began to concentrate on getting the airline started."

"I'm very proud of it for you, Rink," she said in a voice so soft and sincere that it brought his eyes up to hers.

His smile was wry. "Yeah, well, I worked like hell to make a go of it. It was something to occupy my mind and keep it off . . . other things."

"What other things? Home?"

His eyes remained pinned on hers for a long moment. They were hard and piercing. "Yes," he said shortly and stood. Giving her his back, he propped his shoulder against one of the pillars. "The Retreat. Laura Jane. My father. The gin. Winstonville was home. I never intended to leave it."

"You made a new life for yourself in Atlanta."

"Yeah." Such as it is, he could have added. His house

was too new, too ostentatious. It had no character or gentility. The parties were too raucous. The women . . . The women were too glitzy, too cosmopolitan, too phony. He saw through them just as they did him.

The life he led now was a charade. Not that he wasn't happy with Air Dixie. He was. The airline was certainly something to take pride in because it had taken years of hard work to get it where it was.

But the accoutrements of success had never meant a damn to him. His roots were here, in this town, in this rich bottomland, in this house. Any other life was just pretense. He would never forgive his father for driving him away. Never.

Suddenly he whirled on Caroline. "Why did you marry him?"

She almost cowered at his fury. "I won't discuss my private life with your father with you, Rink."

"I don't want to know about your private life. I only asked why you married him. He's almost old enough to be your grandfather, for God's sake." He strode forward and leaned over her, bracing his hands on the arms of the glider and imprisoning her between them. "Why? Why did you even come back to this town after you graduated from college? There was nothing for you here."

Her neck hurt as she arched it back to look up at him. "My mama was still alive. I came back, got a job at the bank and within a few months had saved up enough to get us out of that pigsty and into a rented house in town. I met your father in the bank. He was nice to me. When he asked me to come to work for him at the gin, I did. He doubled the salary I was making at the bank, which allowed me to bury my mother with some semblance of dignity."

His breath came in rapid gusts on her face. Dark locks of wavy hair fell over his forehead. His shirts seemed never to remain fully buttoned for long. This one wasn't now. Her eyes were on a level with his muscular chest. He was male; he was virile; he was attractive, dangerously so. She wanted to close her eyes against his appeal.

"After a while I started coming here to The Retreat to work rather than going to the office at the gin."

"I bet you loved that, being invited to The Retreat."

"I did," she cried defensively. "You know how I've always loved this house. For that naive girl walking to work through the woods, it was like the castle in a fairy tale. I don't deny that, Rink."

"Go on with your story. I'm fascinated. Was my father the Prince Charming of this fairy tale of yours?"

"Of course not. It wasn't anything like that. After Mama died, I spent more time here. He came to rely on me in business matters. Laura Jane and I became friends. Roscoe encouraged that since she didn't have any friends her age."

Hurriedly she wet her lips. Greedily his eyes charted the action of her tongue. "It was something that happened gradually. It seemed right since I was already spending so much time here. When he asked me to marry him, I said yes. He could give me everything I'd always wanted and never could have any other way."

"A new name."

"Yes."

"Clothes."

"Yes."

"Money."

"Yes."

"A beautiful house."

"The one I'd always loved."

"For all that you sold yourself to my father!" he hissed.

"In a way I suppose I did." His repulsion made her

feel dirty. She groped for justifications. "I wanted to be the constant friend Laura Jane needed. I wanted to help your father."

"So your motives were purely unselfish."

"No," she confessed, lowering her eyes. "I wanted to live in The Retreat. I wanted the respect that would go with being Roscoe's wife. Yes, I wanted all that. And you'd have had to grow up in a shack, lived hand to mouth every day of your life, worn shabby clothes when other girls had dyed-to-match sweaters and skirts, worked every day after school and on Saturdays when all the other kids were riding around in convertibles and going to the Dairy Mart and football games, been the daughter of the town drunk before you'd understand that, Rink Lancaster!"

On speaking his name she bolted off the glider, but he didn't budge. She was brought up soundly against his body. His hands closed firmly around her upper arms and secured her against him. Their breathing was harsh and labored as though they had both been running hard.

She wouldn't lift her head and look at him. If she did, she didn't know what she would do. So she stared into the V at the base of his throat, at the rapid pulse beating there. Her lower body felt heavy and thick, weak with passion. Her lips were rubbery as she tried to form words on them. "Please let me go, Rink. Please."

He ignored the plea. Instead he buried his face in the side of her neck. Helplessly, her head fell back. His lips rubbed back and forth over her skin, leaving behind the moist vapor of his breath to cool and excite.

"Knowing that you're my father's wife, knowing the reasons you married him, why do I still want you?" With frantic desperation his head moved to the other side of her neck. Her head tilted to accommodate him.

Feebly she protested her own responses. "No, no, Rink, don't."

"I want you so much I hurt." He kissed her neck with hot urgency. His teeth nipped her lightly. "I want you. Why, damn you, why?"

Caroline groaned. "Oh, God, help me," she breathed. More than anything, she wanted to surrender herself to him. She needed him as he needed her, to ease the years of misery they had both suffered. For a few precious moments, they wanted to forget everything but each other.

But it was impossible. That knowledge gave her strength to resist and she renewed her efforts to get away from him.

Just as quickly as he had embraced her, his hands released their grip and fell to his sides. He stepped backward, breathing rapidly and hard. Hastily she went to the front door.

"Caroline." His voice halted her and commanded that she turn around. "I've always had difficulty accepting things I didn't like. I had no right to grill you that way. It was none of my business."

His image blurred through her tears. She knew the pride it had cost him to admit that. She smiled at him softly, a smile that said much that couldn't be spoken aloud. "Wasn't it, Rink?" she asked quietly. Then she let herself in and went upstairs.

Lying on her bed, still clothed and too apathetic to undress, she stared up at the ceiling. And remembered. She hadn't known whether to expect to see him the next day or not. But he had been there. . . .

"Hi."

"What are you doing here?"

"Fishing." He cocked his head toward the cane pole that was stuck in the mud near the riverbank. The line trailed in the water. He wasn't fishing very ambitiously. "You're earlier than yesterday."

She blushed and looked away from his dazzling smile.

When she had left home half an hour early, she had sworn to herself that it wasn't on the outside chance that he might be in the woods and that she would have some time to spare with him if he were. She had taken great care in dressing, wearing her best skirt and blouse, brushing her hair after she washed it until her scalp tingled, inspecting her fingernails.

She had run home in the dark after leaving his car the night before. He had kissed her. And he had been tender afterward, asking if she were all right. But she hadn't anticipated ever seeing him again.

Only now he was here, sitting under the willows in short cutoff jeans and a sleeveless T-shirt and looking as confident and handsome as a movie star. The muscles of his athletic arms and legs bulged. The dusting of body hair on his limbs intrigued her, but when she looked at him too long at a time, her stomach began to do flip-flops.

"I had Haney, that's our housekeeper, pack some sandwiches. Do you like smoked turkey?"

"I don't know. I've never eaten it."

"Well, you're about to," he said, grinning. He spread a quilt on the grass and asked her to sit down. Then he opened a hamper and handed her a plastic-wrapped sandwich. They chatted as they ate.

"Are you going to start working in the gin? Smoked turkey is delicious, by the way."

"Glad you like it." He rested his back against the trunk of the tree as he munched. "I guess I will," he said thoughtfully. "If Daddy and I can ever come to terms on some things." She wanted to ask what things but didn't. He would think she was meddling in his business.

But he glanced at her, saw her intent listening posture and went on. "See, Daddy doesn't want to dip into the profits to make the gin better. He's satisfied with it as it is. There are many ways we could improve it, update it, make it a safer place to work for our employees. I haven't convinced him that some expensive investments right now would pay off in the long run.''

"Maybe you could compromise with him on a few for a start.''

"Maybe," he remarked doubtfully. He reached into the hamper and pulled out a can of soft drink. He winked at her. "I'm dying for a cold beer, but I was afraid if I got caught drinking beer with someone as young as you, I'd be arrested.''

If they were caught together, what they were drinking would be the least of their worries and they both knew it. They finished their lunch and Caroline conscientiously helped him put the leftovers back in the hamper. She took his place leaning against the tree trunk and he stretched out on his side and propped his head on his elbow. He looked up at her.

"What are you thinking about?" he asked.

Her eyes found his. "Your mama.''

"Mother?" The surprise in his voice couldn't be disguised.

"I was sorry to hear when she died, Rink. She was a very nice lady.''

"When did you meet her?''

"I never did, but she used to come into Woolworth's now and then. I always thought she was the . . . cleanest person I'd ever seen.''

Rink laughed. "Yes, she was. I don't ever remember her being less than immaculate.''

"She was beautiful, and always dressed up so nice.'' Her expression was soft. "What did she die of, Rink?''

He studied the hem of her skirt, ran his index finger along the row of tiny handmade stitches. "A broken heart,'' he said in a low voice.

Caroline saw the sadness on his face and it tugged at her heart. She wanted to press his head into her breasts, to comfort him, to run her fingers through his hair.

"How could anyone be brokenhearted living in a house like yours?"

He ignored her question and asked one of his own. "You like The Retreat?"

Her eyes sparkled. "It's the most beautiful house in the world," she said worshipfully and he laughed. She blushed. "Well, at least it's the most beautiful one I've ever seen."

He seemed surprised. "You've been inside?"

"Oh, no, never. But I've walked past it many times. I love to just stand and look at it. I'd give anything to live in a house like that." She looked away self-consciously. "You probably think I'm crazy."

He shook his head. "I love The Retreat, too. I never get tired of looking at it either. I'll invite you to see the inside sometime."

They both knew he wouldn't, and for the next moment they couldn't meet each other's eyes. Finally Caroline said, "Your little sister is pretty. I saw her with your mother a few times."

"Her name is Laura Jane."

"I've never seen her at school. Does she go to a private school?"

Rink plucked a blade of grass and bit into its stem. His teeth were very straight and very white. "A school for retarded children. She's not severely retarded, but her mind was slow in developing. She doesn't learn as quickly as other children."

Caroline's cheeks burned. "I'm . . . I'm sorry . . . I didn't—"

"Hey," he said, taking her hand. "It's all right. Laura Jane is a wonderful little girl. I love her very much."

"She's lucky to have a brother like you."

He propped his head on his hand again and looked up at her roguishly. Sunlight glistened on the black fringe of his eyelashes. "You think so?"

"Yes."

They lapsed into one of those staring spells when words were superfluous. His eyes fell to her hand resting on her thigh. He lifted it, turned it over and lightly examined the faint lines etched in the palm. His finger trailed from her palm to the sensitive hollow in the bend of her elbow. His touch made her tingle all over. There was an uneasy fluttering in her chest and she marveled at her nipples, which were becoming hard and swollen.

"I've got to go soon," she said breathlessly.

"I wish you didn't have to," he said huskily. His eyes traveled slowly up to meet hers. "I wish we could spend the day here, like this, talking."

Her heart was thudding. There was a roaring in her ears that blocked out all other sound save his voice. "I'm sure you could find plenty of your friends in town to spend the day with. They talk to you, don't they?"

"They outtalk each other," he said. "No one listens, just listens, like you do, Caroline."

With his golden eyes locked onto hers, he sat up slowly. His hand lifted her hair off the back of her neck and closed around the slender column. He drew her close and she went without a hint of resistance until his mouth met hers. They melted together, murmuring their harmonizing groans of gratification.

His lips were as gentle as the night before, but her sweet acceptance of them aroused him quickly. The kiss became more fiercely insistent.

Caroline was carried along by his passion. Her soul spun crazily, caught up in his taste, his smell, the pressure of his body against hers. Soon she was lying across his bare thighs and he was bending over her. His tongue thrust madly into her mouth while her fingers tangled in the wild mass of his hair.

He raised his head, panting for breath, dropping hot kisses on her face. "Caroline, fight me, say no. Don't let me do this." He moved the collar of her blouse aside and slipped his hand inside. Her skin was warm and silky against his palm. He toyed with the strap of her brassiere. His fingertips brushed against her flesh and he moaned. "You're just a kid. A *kid*. God help me. You're not old enough to know better, but I am. We're playing with fire, sweetheart. Stop me. Please." He kissed her again, deeply and thoroughly.

A restlessness deep within claimed her. Her legs shifted in agitation. Her breasts throbbed achingly and she wanted to cover them with her hands. With his hands. She looped her arm around his neck and strained upward.

But he pulled away, gulping for air, his eyes squeezed tightly shut. "This can't go any further, Caroline. If we don't stop, things are going to get out of hand. Do you understand what I'm talking about?"

Dumbly, she nodded, wishing he would hold her again, kiss her some more, touch with his hands all the places on her body that were feeling swollen and warm.

He pulled her to her feet. She swayed against him and he held her close, stroking her back, whispering lovely words in her hair. Unashamedly, naturally, her arms went around his waist. When he pushed her away from him, his smile was rueful. "I would never forgive myself if I got you fired from your job," he whispered.

"Oh, my goodness!" she exclaimed, slapping her palms to her flaming cheeks. "What time is it?"

"You've got time if you leave right now."

"Bye," she said, stuffing her blouse back into her waistband and shaking her hair to straighten it.

He clasped her hand. "I won't be able to pick you up tonight."

"I didn't expect you to, Rink," she said earnestly.

"I *want* to, but I already had plans for tonight."

"It's all right. Truly." She began backing out of the clearing. "Thanks for the lunch." Turning, she dashed through the trees. He went tearing after her.

"Caroline!" He called out so masterfully that she stopped in her tracks and turned around.

"Yes?"

"I'll see you tomorrow. Here. Okay?"

Her face rivaled the sun for brilliance as she smiled at him. "Yes," she had called back, laughing. "Yes . . . yes . . . yes . . ."

He had come the next day and the day after that and the day after that and for most days for the next few weeks. And when he could, he picked her up at some point on her walk home.

Caroline rolled to her side and stared at the moon through the branches of the trees outside her window. How glorious those days had been! She had lived in a haze of excitement, savoring the feelings his kisses generated and miserable because she yearned for something more. He shared his dreams of the future with her and she confided her secrets. They communed on a level that neither had known with anyone else.

Every stolen hour they had spent together had been golden and only partially because of the summer sun. Because one day when they met, it had rained.

That day had been the most golden of all.

Caroline hiccuped a sob and let the tears stream unchecked from her eyes. She prayed for forgiveness but didn't think she was absolved. Because she tried to weep for Roscoe, her husband, but her tears were all for Rink, her love.

Chapter 5

CAROLINE SLEPT LATER THAN SHE HAD INTENDED. SHE put on a robe and went down to the kitchen for a cup of coffee before going into the library to work. Haney was humming as she stood at the sink washing dishes. She disdained the automatic dishwasher.

"Good morning. You sound happy."

"Rink ate a good breakfast," she said, beaming.

Caroline smiled. The housekeeper talked about him as though he were a four-year-old. "He's already up and about?"

"Yep." Haney nodded at the back door and Caroline wandered toward it, sipping her coffee as she went. Rink was standing beside one of the Lancaster prize horses talking to Steve. As she watched, he vaulted into the saddle, swung his long leg over it and secured his booted foot in the stirrup. The stallion pranced arrogantly before Rink pulled sternly on the reins. The horse responded immediately and after Rink nodded his thanks

to Steve, horse and man went bounding across pasture-
land toward the road.

Caroline watched for as long as she could see him. His
hair was as black and shiny as jet in the early morning
light. Thigh and back muscles rippled as he effortlessly
jumped a fence and guided the horse into the trees.

When Caroline turned away, Haney was staring at her
curiously. Nervously Caroline's hand went to her throat.
"I need to make some calls, so I'll be in the library,"
she rattled off before hastily leaving the kitchen. She
couldn't help her absorption with Rink, but she would
have to guard against anyone else becoming aware of it.

The nurse's station at the hospital had little to report
when she telephoned. "He isn't awake yet. He slept
through most of the night. He woke up once but we
immediately gave him another sedative."

"Thank you," she said before breaking off the call
and dialing Granger. "Is there anything I should be
doing that I'm not?" she asked the attorney. "I don't
want to presume that I have anything to do with Roscoe's
professional or private dealings, but I want to be useful if
I can be."

"I would never think you presumptive," Granger said
kindly. "And it's your right to be concerned."

"I'm not concerned for myself. I just want to make
certain that Laura Jane's affairs are taken care of. And
Rink's, of course."

The attorney remained silent and Caroline knew he
was reminding himself of professional discretion. "I
don't know all of Roscoe's intentions, Caroline. Swear
to God I don't. He made up a new will several years ago,
but he's asked to see me about it. I'm sure some
provision will be made for you. I don't think there will
be any surprises."

She fervently hoped not, too, but didn't express her
anxiety that there might be. After discussing a few minor
business items, they said their good-byes.

As soon as she hung up, the telephone rang again. "Hello?"

"Miz Lancaster?"

The racket in the background told her the call was originating at the cotton gin. "Yes."

"This is Barnes. 'Member that gin stand I was telling you about the other day? This morning she sounded like she was grinding her guts out, so we shut her down."

Caroline rubbed her temple. This was a breakdown they couldn't afford with cotton picking time approaching. The gin stands separated the lint from the seeds. With even one breakdown during harvest, hours of production time could be lost.

"I'll be right there," she said briskly.

Hurriedly swallowing what was left of her cooled coffee, she dashed upstairs. Within half an hour, she had bathed and dressed efficiently in a poplin skirt and pullover knit top. Her shoes were low-heeled. She had pulled her hair back into a ponytail at her nape and tied a bright printed scarf around it. She never went to the gin dressed in her finest. One reason was because it wouldn't be practical. The other, the main one, was because she wanted the workers to consider her one of them and not merely the boss's wife.

She called out her good-bye to Haney, explaining where she was going. Then, catching up her purse, she ran out the front door. Rink was just reining in the stallion. When he saw her, he handed the stallion over to a waiting Steve and jogged over to her.

"Where are you going in such a hurry? The hospital?"

By his expression, Caroline knew he thought the cause for her haste was that his father had taken a turn for the worse. Despite the antagonism between them, she thought, Rink cared for his father and hated the agony he was suffering. She relieved him quickly. "No. I called earlier. Roscoe wasn't awake yet, but they said he had a fairly peaceful night. I'm going to the gin.''

"Problem?"

"Yes. With one of the stands."

He nodded. "Bad?"

"I think it might be. The foreman had to shut it down." She could all but see the wheels of his brain whirring and before she could weigh the wisdom of her impulse she asked, "Would you come with me, Rink?" His eyes flew to hers and she swallowed hard. "Maybe if you looked at it, you could tell what's wrong. I would trust your judgment. Anyone else might try to take advantage of me right now."

He stared at her so long and so thoroughly that she thought he was going to refuse. Then he held out his hand. "I'll drive."

She dropped the keys to the Lincoln into his palm and they each ran to the car, getting in on opposite sides. He drove as he did everything else, aggressively. The car roared out of the curved drive, leaving behind it a shower of gravel and a cloud of dust.

"Have you been having problems with this machine?" he asked her.

"Some, yes."

"Recently?"

"Yes."

She wished they could keep the conversation going. His nearness was wreaking havoc on her senses. He smelled of fresh morning air, of wind, of horseflesh, of a brisk cologne and of man. The image of him on horseback kept creeping back into her mind.

With stark clarity, she remembered the day he had showed up at their rendezvous riding bareback. She had shrunk from the horse, which had looked enormous to her. Rink had laughed away her timidity and insisted that she ride with him. He had easily hoisted her across the horse's back. Luckily she had worn a full skirt that day so she had been able to sit astride.

Even now she remembered the feel of the horse's bristly hide against her bare thighs, of Rink's middle against her hips as he pulled himself up behind her, the bunching and flexing of his thighs against hers, the strength of his arms as they went around her to hold the reins. His body had been warm and faintly damp with healthy sweat. He had rested his chin against her hair. She could even now feel his breath on her cheek, on her eyelids. He smelled the same today as he had that day twelve years ago.

She didn't remember much of that horseback ride beneath the canopy of low-hanging trees, only the pounding of her heart as his hand rested just beneath it. She remembered being afraid of nothing save that he might not like the way she felt when his hand brushed against her breast. She couldn't afford the lacy confections the other girls wore for underwear. Her lingerie was basic, white, functional and unattractive. She had wanted to feel soft and alluring and sexy beneath his hand. She had feared she didn't.

Now, she looked at his hands as they steered the car. Beautiful hands. Dark and strong, lean and tapered. His nails were bluntly clipped straight across. Dark hairs bristled on his knuckles, the back of his hand, the wrist bone.

"Let me help you down," he had said, raising those hands up to her.

She had swung her leg over the horse's back and leaned down to rest her hands on his shoulders. His hands had cupped her underarms as she slowly slid from the animal's back. But long after her feet touched the ground, he kept his hands there, the heels of them pressing into the fleshy sides of her breasts. And he had spoken her name.

"Caroline. Caroline."

Now, she jumped, realizing that his voice wasn't a part of her mental meanderings but reality.

"What?" She looked at him, her agitation evident. Her eyes were smoky and dilated with remembrance of the heady kiss that they had shared then. Her chest was rising and falling rapidly, just as it had that day when his hands had moved to cover her breasts, to massage them with slow, rubbing circles that had brought her nipples to peaks.

Rink looked at her strangely. "I asked if there's any special place you park."

"Oh. Y-yes. By the door. It's marked."

He steered the car into the space where her name was stenciled on the concrete and cut the car's motor. She was treated to another analyzing stare. "Ready to go in?" He didn't sound certain that she was.

But she had to escape the car, the memories. Almost shouting her yes, she shoved open the car door and nearly fell out of it in her haste to leave.

The din and dust of the gin were welcome familiarities. She entered with Rink and led him toward his father's office.

Rink saw that little had changed. Most of the workers who clustered around them were familiar.

"Barnes!" he exclaimed. "Still here?"

"Till they bury me." He pumped Rink's hand. "It's good to see you, boy."

Others greeted him just as enthusiastically and he inquired after family members by names that another man might have forgotten. But these people were part of Rink's heritage. They would be as much a part of him as his life's blood for as long as he lived.

"What's the problem?" he asked Barnes, walking toward the broken gin stand that stood in a row of many.

"Age, mostly," the foreman replied uneasily. "Been patching up these machines for years, Rink. Don't know how much more rigging they'll stand. Especially if this year's crop is as good as it's supposed to be. We'll be going day and night.''

Rink picked up the cotton fibers that were the last out of the machine and rubbed them between his fingers. There were bits of leaves and burrs enmeshed in the fibers. Both Barnes and Caroline avoided his eyes as he looked at them sharply. "What grade cotton is this?"

"Middling," Caroline finally admitted when Barnes remained silent.

"Lancaster gins have always produced good-to-strict middling. What the hell is going on here?"

"Let's go into the office, Rink," Caroline suggested softly. She turned and led the way, hoping that Rink would follow her and not make her appeal to him in front of the men.

She was seated in the leather chair behind the desk when he came through the office door and slammed it behind him, rattling the frosted glass in its top half.

"This used to be one of the finest spot markets in the state," he began furiously and without preamble.

"It still is."

"Not if that's the best grade of cotton we can produce, it isn't. If I were a planter I'd sure as hell take my crop to some other gin. Why aren't we producing better than that?"

"I told you we're having some trouble with the equipment. It's—"

"Ancient," he cut in. "Dammit, hasn't Daddy done one damn thing to improve or update?"

"He didn't see the need," she replied softly.

"The need!" he shouted. "Look at this place. It's a dinosaur compared to modern gins. We're not being fair to ourselves or to the growers. It's a wonder they haven't started taking their crops to other—" He broke off suddenly and his eyes narrowed. "Or are they?"

"We lost a few last year, yes."

He hooked the toe of his boot around a chair leg and pulled it toward him. Sitting down, he leaned across the desk and said in a voice she couldn't disobey, "Tell me about it."

"A few of Lancaster Gin's dependable planters have started taking their cotton to other gins, paying the fee to have it ginned and then selling it to the merchants directly."

She squirmed uneasily in the squeaky leather chair as he studied her. "So they'd rather go to all that trouble and expense rather than let us buy their crop, gin it, bale it and sell it to the merchants." She nodded and he vocalized the rest of what they were both thinking. "They can make more money doing it that way than by letting us gin it, because we're paying them for a lesser grade of cotton."

"I suppose they think so."

He got out of the chair and went to the window. He turned his hands palms out and slid them into the back pockets of his jeans. He seemed to be studying the landscape, but Caroline knew that he wasn't seeing it at all. "You knew all this, didn't you? Didn't you?" he repeated, spinning around when she didn't answer him immediately.

"Yes."

"But you didn't do anything about it."

"What could *I* do, Rink? At first I was only the bookkeeper. I learned about the ginning process and the marketing by listening, studying, making a nuisance of myself around the workers. I don't make executive decisions."

"You're his wife! Doesn't that give you a vote in anything?" He held up both hands. "I take that back. Wives of Roscoe Lancaster don't criticize him or anything he does, they just remain meekly at his beck and call and administer . . . wifely comforts."

Her chin went up as she balled her hands into fists and crossed her arms at her waist. "I told you once that I wouldn't discuss my relationship with Roscoe with you."

"And I told you once that I don't give a damn what you do in his bed."

They both knew that wasn't true. Rink almost looked embarrassed for telling such a bald lie. Caroline wisely chose not to challenge it. "If insulting me is the best you can do by way of helping, then I'll ask you not to bother."

He spat an expletive and raked frustrated fingers through his hair. Their eyes battled until they tacitly declared a truce. "I'll do whatever I can," he grumbled.

"Can you repair the stand?" she asked, putting aside her pride.

"I'll need some tools, but I think I can. I've torn airplane engines apart and repaired them. Surely this can't be any more intricate than that. But I'm not promising anything, Caroline. What repair I do won't be an answer to your problems."

"I understand that." She softened considerably, letting her rigid posture relax as she smiled that shy, apologetic smile of hers. "Whatever help you can give me, I'll appreciate."

This time his curse was even more vile, but silent. And it was aimed at himself for his own culpability. He wanted nothing more at that moment than to hold her, protect her, meld her lips to his, graft his body to hers. What a damn fool he was. It drove him to distraction to think of her body entwined with that of his father. God! Sometimes he thought he'd go mad thinking about it.

Yet, he couldn't despise her, much as he wanted to. Every time he looked at her, he wanted her more. He should leave. Immediately. Before he did something to disgrace himself. He couldn't do that, either, for so

many reasons. Laura Jane. His father. But mostly
Caroline. Seeing her after twelve years, he couldn't
bring himself to voluntarily leave so soon.

"You'll know where to find me," he said on his way
out the door.

Caroline worked in the office doing paperwork while
Rink commissioned the workmen's help in seeking out
the necessary tools. An hour later, she came up behind
him where he was studying the entrails of the huge
machine. "Rink, I'm going to the hospital for a while.
You can ask one of the men to drive you home if you get
done before I get back."

He smiled wanly. "Not a chance. I'll be here for a
while yet." She grinned and he had the notion that her
half-raised hand was going to touch his arm. Instead, she
muttered a rapid good-bye and left.

The hospital was cool and quiet after the noise and
confusion in the gin. Roscoe was lying in bed, his eyes
glued to the television screen, though he had turned the
sound off. Tubes were feeding him and ridding his body
of wastes. Monitors blinked and beeped and recorded his
vital signs. He was pitiable to behold, but Caroline
smiled brightly and bravely as she came in.

By an act of will, she forced yesterday's encounter
from her mind. He was in tremendous pain. He couldn't
help his behavior. She had been merely a convenient
scapegoat for the terrible frustration he felt.

"Hello, Roscoe." She kissed his chalk-white cheek.
"How are you feeling?"

"It's too crude to say to a girl of your sensibilities,"
he growled. Eyeing her attire, he asked, "Have you been
to the gin?"

"Yes. All morning in fact, or I would have been here
sooner. We have a problem with one of the stands."

"What kind of problem?"

"I'm not certain. Something mechanical. Rink's taking a look at it. These flowers from the Sunday school class are lovely.''

''What the hell do you mean, Rink's taking a look at it?''

She had been looking over the flower arrangements delivered in her absence, collecting the cards so she would know whom to acknowledge. But at his words she spun around in alarm. From their dark sockets, Roscoe's eyes gleamed fiendishly. She had never seen him look so menacing. Or was it merely his illness that gave him that malevolent expression?

''Answer me, damn you!'' he roared with far more strength than she had expected. ''What is Rink doing anywhere near that cotton gin?''

She was flabbergasted and had difficulty getting the words out of her mouth fast enough. ''I . . . I asked him to look at the broken equipment. He's an engineer. He could tell—''

''You took it upon yourself to ask my son back into the gin?'' He struggled to sit up. ''He gave up any rights he had to Lancaster Gin when he left here twelve years ago. I don't want him in the gin, *near* it. Do you understand me, woman?'' Sweat had popped out on his brow. His eyes bulged with fury.

Caroline was afraid, both of his ire and for his life. ''Roscoe, please calm down. All I did was ask Rink to look at a broken machine. He's not asserting any rights over the business.''

''I know him. He'll start finding fault with everything down there, telling you how to spend my money.'' He pointed a gnarled finger at her and said stridently, ''You listen to me and you listen good. You're not to spend one damn cent on that gin without my approval.''

She wanted to slap down that finger, which unfairly accused her. ''I never have, Roscoe,'' she said levelly.

''Rink's never been around, either.''

''And whose fault is that?''

Her unwise question reverberated off the sterile walls of the room and came back to assail her. For several seconds she failed to breathe, only glared back at the wasted form of her husband, who in his weakness appeared dangerous, like a normally tame animal who had been wounded and would now destroy anyone trying to help him.

He laughed that horrible laugh as he collapsed against the pillows. "Is that what he told you? That I sent him away in disgrace for knocking up that George gal?"

Caroline's eyes dropped to her hands. Her fingertips were frigid and the hospital's air-conditioning was only partially responsible. Her palms were slick with perspiration. "No. We didn't discuss it," she said honestly.

"Well, just so you don't go getting the wrong notion, I'll set it straight. I didn't ask Rink to run off and stay away for twelve years. He knew I was mad as hell at him, but not for getting that gal pregnant." He chuckled. "I expected mischief like that. Boys will be boys. They'll take it where they can get it, won't they?"

She turned away. His words were like lances stabbing into her. "I suppose so."

His laugh was snarling. "Oh, believe me. A man will do anything, say anything, to get under a girl's skirt. Especially if she's halfway obliging."

She closed her eyes, willing away the tears, willing away his words, willing away her own shame.

" 'Course, they don't like getting caught at it the way Rink was. When Frank George came to me and said Rink had knocked up his Marilee, I told him right off Rink would marry her. That was the honorable thing to do, wasn't it?"

"Yes." It hurt to speak the word.

"Well, that scoundrel said he wasn't having any of it. That was the real disgrace. Not that Rink had been caught with his pants down, but that he wouldn't face up to his careless mistake. He told me then that if I forced him into marrying that girl, he'd leave and never come back.''

He sighed as though the memory pained him. "I had to do what was right, didn't I, Caroline? I had to make him marry that gal. It was his choice to stay away after that, not mine. So don't go feeling sorry for Rink, no matter what he tells you. He made his bed, and for the rest of his life he'll have to lie in it.''

He fell silent and for a long while she remained staring out the window. If she turned around, he would see her despair, he would know. When she had collected herself, she returned to his bedside. His eyes were closed as she leaned over him and she thought he was asleep. Softly she made to leave, but his hand shot out with uncanny speed and strength and clamped around her wrist. Startled, she gasped.

"You're still behaving like a wife, aren't you, Caroline?''

His smoldering eyes terrified her, as did his question. "Of course. What do you mean?''

"I mean that you'd regret it if you did anything that wasn't in keeping with a grieving, inconsolable wife watching her husband die.'' His fingers twisted over the fragile bones of her wrist until she thought they would crack. Where did he get the strength?

"Please don't talk about dying, Roscoe.''

"Why not? It's a fact. But you remember this.'' Again he tried to sit up. Spittle gathered in the corners of his blue-tinged lips as he hissed at her. "Until I'm dead, you're my wife and you'd damn well better act like it.''

"I will,'' she vowed frantically, trying to pull her hand free. "I mean, I do.''

"I never put much stock in religion, but one thing I do believe. Thinking of disobeying a commandment is the same as doing it. Did you learn that in Sunday school?''

"Yes,'' she cried desperately, terrified of him and not knowing why.

"Have you been thinking of disobeying any commandments?"

"No."

"Like committing adultery?"

"No!"

"You're my wife."

"Yes."

"You'd better remember it."

All the strength went out of him then, and he fell back onto the pillows, struggling for air. Caroline wrenched her hand free from his death grip and ran to the door. She was bent on escape but remembered herself just in time and went for a nurse. "It's my husband," she panted. "I . . . I think he needs a shot of something. He's terribly upset."

"We'll take care of him, Mrs. Lancaster," the nurse said kindly. "If I might say so, you look in bad shape yourself. Why don't you go home for now?"

"Yes, yes," Caroline said, trying to restore her wits. Her heart was racing. She was trembling with fear. Why had she become so afraid of her own husband? "I think I will."

Granger was getting off the elevator as she got on. "Caroline, is something wrong?" He was alarmed by the state she was in.

"No, no. I'm going back to the gin. Trouble there, but please don't mention it to Roscoe. He's upset." Breathing raggedly, she backed against the wall of the elevator as though it were a hiding place from some unnamed terror that stalked her.

"Can I help—"

"No," she said, shaking her head furiously as the doors began to close. "I'll be fine. Go to Roscoe. He needs you."

The doors closed between them and she brought her hand up to her mouth, covering it to stifle the whimpers she felt welling up in her throat. "God, God," she repeated, wondering how he could have frightened her so. Her stomach was churning. Her body was flashing hot and cold.

She forced herself to walk through the first-floor lobby without a visible sign of her distress. By the time she reached her car, the most violent of her trembling had subsided. Lowering the car windows, she drove out of town along the river road. The wind beat through her hair, carrying with it all the scents of summer. There was little traffic and she drove fast, ridding her mind of the fears of moments ago.

She had let her imagination get the best of her. Roscoe couldn't possibly have known about her and Rink that summer. Rink wouldn't have told him. She certainly hadn't. No one had ever seen them together or there would have been gossip all over town. No, Roscoe couldn't know. Nor would he guess they were attracted to each other. To his mind, they had only met a few days ago.

His veiled threats and warnings were products of her own imagination and guilty conscience. Maybe his carefully chosen words hadn't been threats at all. No, she shook her head. They had been, much as she would like to think otherwise. But why had Roscoe made them?

How else could he occupy himself? He had nothing more to do than to think, to speculate, to become paranoid and suspicious. A man with a brain as active as Roscoe's would loathe lying in bed all day. He would despise that kind of inactivity. So mental power was the only thing he had left and his mind was working overtime to compensate for his wasting body.

Pain and anguish were magnifying everything in his mind, building mountains out of molehills. He had a wife more than thirty years younger than he. He had a strong, good-looking, virile son. For the time being they were living in the same house. He had put together a combination of facts that added up to a horrible suspicion.

He was wrong! She'd done nothing a wife shouldn't.

On the other hand, he was right. Thinking about making love to Rink was as grim a transgression as the act. And she never stopped thinking about it.

She must force that thought from her mind. Maybe if she treated him more like a friend, as ludicrous as it seemed, more like a friendly stepmother trying to keep peace in the family, memories of times past would fade. She had to put things into a new perspective, into the here and now and forget all that had happened before.

When she returned to the gin, the afternoon sun was slanting across the floor from the windows high on the walls. She looked around her in dismay. The place was deserted save for Rink, who was lying on his back, one knee bent, inspecting the workings of the gin stand. He was banging against the metal with a wrench. The ringing sound echoed loudly and drowned out her footsteps. "Where is everyone?"

The racket ceased. His head came out from under the piece of equipment and he sat up. He wiped his sweaty forehead with a handkerchief. "Hi. I didn't hear you come in. I took the liberty of sending everyone home an hour early. There was nothing much to be done while I was trying to get this back in shape." He hitched a thumb over his shoulder to indicate the machine. "Dust was flying everywhere. With some of the faulty wiring in this place, that could create a dangerous situation."

She should have berated Rink for closing early when it wasn't his place to do so, but she didn't. On her long drive, she had decided that Roscoe's decision-making ability had been affected by his hospitalization. The thought of doing something he wouldn't approve of behind his back was loathsome, but she had reasoned that what he didn't know wouldn't hurt him. In the long run, what was good for Lancaster Gin was what he would want her to do.

She squatted down next to Rink. "How's it going? Find the problem?"

"Yes, and it's a doozy."

"Can it be repaired?"

"Temporarily." He sighed and made a swipe across his brow with his sleeve. "How is Daddy today?"

The reminder of the scene in the hospital room made her shiver. "Not so well. About the same." He studied her closely, but she didn't give anything away with her composed expression. Changing the subject quickly, she asked, "Have you had anything to eat?"

"No. I'm too hot and dirty to eat." It was true he was dirty. His face was grimy and sweat-streaked. It made his teeth look even whiter when he smiled. "Besides, I didn't want to take the time."

She smiled and reached into the white paper sack she had carried in with her. "I brought you a late lunch. You won't have to stop working—you can drink this lunch." She poked a straw into the plastic lid on the paper cup.

"What is it?"

She thrust the tall frosty cup into his hand and stood up. "A chocolate milk shake."

Chapter 6

WHAT DID IT MEAN?

Damned if I know, Rink answered his own question as he reached into the shower stall to turn on the taps. He peeled off the sweaty, oil- and dirt-streaked clothes. He sipped his drink and set it on the dressing table.

First there had been the chocolate milk shake. It was as obvious a friendship-making token as a peace pipe. All afternoon she had remained at the gin. She had said she had paperwork to do in the office, but more often than not she was kneeling down beside him asking if there were anything she could do to help, if there were something she could get him. With the efficiency of a surgical nurse, she had passed tools to him when he'd extended his hand.

They talked about inconsequential things. Most of those topics they agreed on. They talked about family matters. On none of those did they agree.

"Did you see Laura Jane today?" she asked him.

"No. Did you?"

"No. Yesterday she seemed depressed. I wonder if she's just now realizing the severity of Roscoe's condition."

"Maybe. But it could have something to do with Bishop."

"Why do you say that?"

"Hand me that screwdriver again, please."

"The one with the red handle or the yellow?"

"Red. Because this morning when he brought that horse around for me, he was as touchy as a hungry crocodile."

"Maybe you just intimidate him."

"I hope to God I do."

He expected an argument. Though he could tell she didn't like what he'd said, she didn't comment. Since the floor of the gin was dusty, she had pulled a stool near him—too near. Even when his head was buried in the machinery, even when he wasn't looking at her, he was constantly aware of her presence. Her fragrance was as all-pervasive as the afternoon heat. Beneath his clothes, perspiration beaded and formed pools and trickled down his body in rivulets. But when his hand came in contact with hers, it was cool and dry. He wanted to press it to his face, his neck, his chest.

Cursing his recollection of the afternoon, he took another sip of his drink. That had only been the beginning of where he would like her hands to be.

On the way home, she had been chatty. As soon as they'd come through the front door she had turned to him and said, "Take your time in the shower. I'll tell Haney to hold dinner until you've had time to cool off and relax. Let me fix you a drink to take up with you. What would you like?"

What he would like was for her to explain what the hell she was up to with this friendly camaraderie routine.

Was this something Roscoe had put her up to? Or had she thought of it all by herself? Why all of a sudden was she acting like a new stepmother trying desperately to win the approval of the stepchild?

Well, whatever her game, it wasn't going to work, he thought as he stepped under the shower's spray. He was never going to think of her as a stepmother, and if she thought he ever could, then she didn't remember anything that had happened that summer. That summer. The merest thought of it set his heart to pounding.

He scoffed at himself. Twelve years later and he was still acting like a besotted moron. He, Rink Lancaster, heartbreaker. Ha! He had never had problems with women except how to get rid of one once he was tired of her. Was it any wonder that his feelings for Caroline had come as a rude awakening?

That summer was a time of conflict. He was both happier than he had ever been and more miserable than he could remember. When he wasn't with Caroline, he counted the minutes until he could be. When he was with her, he cherished every second but dreaded the time they would have to say good-bye. He was frustrated because he couldn't take her somewhere on a normal date and terrified that someone would see them together. He was starving all the time but wanted nothing to eat. He went around in a perpetual state of sexual arousal, but there was no appeasing it. He wouldn't with Caroline and he didn't want another girl as a substitute.

He wanted Caroline Dawson. He couldn't have her.

Night and day he had argued with himself. She's a little girl, for God's sake. *Fifteen!* You're asking for trouble, Lancaster. Big trouble.

But every day had found him waiting for her in the woods, holding his breath out of fear that she might not come. His anxiety wouldn't leave him until he saw her standing among the trees in a shower of sunlight.

But one day, that last day, the sun didn't shine. It had rained . . .

It was sunny when he left the house. That day, even more than most days, he was anxious to see her. He and his father had had an argument that morning. Roscoe was bending the regulations of the cotton exchange. What he was doing wasn't so much illegal as unethical. When Rink had hesitantly pointed that out to his father, Roscoe had flown into a rage. How dare his still-wet-behind-the-ears son presume to tell him how to run his business or live his life? He hadn't brought Lancaster Gin to where it was by being Mr. Nice Guy.

Rink was heartsick over the things he saw happening but was powerless to do anything about. He needed to talk to Caroline. She listened.

She was already there, sitting under a tree with her legs primly folded beneath her. Her face lit up when she saw him rushing toward her. Without a word he dropped to his knees in front of her, cradled her face between his hands and kissed her. His tongue plowed deeply into her mouth, finding a wellspring of sweetness there so different from the ugliness between him and his father. Her kisses always took him far from the gloom that shrouded his beautiful home.

When at last he released her mouth, he muttered, "God, it's good to see you." Then once again his mouth came down hard on hers. Gradually and without preliminary, he lowered her to the ground, onto a bed of soft fern and moss. Compliantly she lay down and he stretched out beside her, pressing one thigh over hers.

He raised his head and gazed down at her. Her gray-blue eyes were languorous behind sooty lashes. Her lips were dewy and full from the ardor of his kisses. Her hair was fanned out behind her head like a dark silk mantle on the green undergrowth. A rising wind flirted with the wisps on her cheeks.

"You're beautiful," he whispered. He bent down and kissed her eyelids.

"So are you."

He shook his head in denial. "I'm a selfish bastard. Who do I think I am, coming on to you like this, kissing you, taking for granted that you want to be kissed, without even so much as a hello? Why do you let me?"

A graceful hand came up to brush back the hair that was falling low over his eyebrows. "Because you needed me this way today," she said.

He laid his head in the curve of her shoulder and her arms folded loosely around his neck. "You're right. Daddy and I had a helluva shouting match this morning."

"I'm sorry."

"So am I, Caroline." His voice had the ragged, tearing sound of desperation in it. "Why can't he and I love each other? Or even like each other?"

"Don't you?"

He took his time, considering the answer carefully. He knew then how important it was. "No. We don't. Not even a little. I hate it, but that's the way it is."

"Tell me."

"He married my mother for her family name and her money. He didn't love her and she knew it. He's to blame for her unhappiness in life and her premature death. I meant it when I said she died of a broken heart. And he doesn't like me because I see him for what he is and he can't stand that. He's got so many fooled, but he can't fool his own son and that galls the hell out of him."

Her comforting fingers continued to sift through his hair. "Perhaps you judge him too harshly. He's a man, Rink, not a god. He has faults. Are parents supposed to be without flaws?" She stroked down his cheek and applied light pressure to his jaw until he lifted his head and looked at her.

"I think you're a bit intolerant. Forgive me for saying

so. You demand perfection and can't abide failure within yourself. But you expect the same from everyone else and that's unfair, Rink. It's unjust to impose your standards on the rest of us. We're all no more than human.''

She stroked his lips with her fingertips. "I'm so sorry that the relationship between you and your father isn't what it should be. Despite what my father is, I can't help but love him. Mainly because he needs love so much.'' She smiled up at him. "Go slow, Rink. Don't be so impatient. Your father has lived one way for a very long time. It won't be an easy conversion.'' Her eyes filled with unshed tears. "But I admire you so much for the uncompromising stand you take on what's right, even if it means angering your father.''

His smile was slow and infinitely tender. "You're something, you know that? How do you make everything seem better? Hmmm? Why is it that when I'm with you things don't look so dark, so hopeless? Why do I feel like I have all the answers when you're around? At the same time you're slapping my hand, you restore my self-confidence.''

Her pleasure in what he said was evident. Her eyelids lowered with unintentional coyness. "Do I do all that for you?''

The gold in his eyes turned molten. He moved closer and lifted himself over her. He was hard and full. "You do a lot of things for me,'' he said thickly, rubbing his front against hers. Her eyes went wide and she shivered. Cursing himself, he moved away from her. "Damn! What's the matter with me? I shouldn't do things like that with you. I'm sorry.''

Reaching for him, she said, "It wasn't that.'' She held her arm up and showed him the gooseflesh. "It's turned cooler. I think it's going to rain.''

The words had no sooner left her mouth than raindrops began to fall lightly on her face. He rolled off her onto

his back and watched as the clouds opened up. The
rainfall rapidly increased to a downpour and they
laughed like carefree children as they lay on their backs
and let it deluge them. The fury of the sudden summer
storm was soon spent and the rain once again subsided to
a gentle shower.

Rink raised himself on an elbow and looked down at
Caroline. Her complexion hadn't suffered from being
washed of the frugal amount of makeup she wore. It was
glowing with youthful loveliness. His eyes moved down
her neck, farther. The breath caught in his throat. Her
white blouse was wet and clung to her breasts. Today she
hadn't worn a brassiere.

He looked at her in stunned inquiry.

Her voice was low and husky with embarrassment. "I
don't have anything pretty to wear. I thought . . . if I
didn't wear anything, it wouldn't be so ugly . . .
I . . . oh . . ." She made a whimpering sound and
crossed her arms over her breasts. "I didn't mean—"

"Shhh," he said, slowly lifting her arms aside. For a
long moment, while the only sound around them was the
dripping rain, his eyes appreciated her. The wet blouse
detailed everything, the soft mounds, the puckering
areolas, the peaked nipples.

"I think I hear thunder," she whispered tremulously.

He lifted her hand and laid it against his own wet shirt.
"No. That's my heart beating."

He bent over her and placed his mouth on hers. The
kiss was soft and sweet, exquisite in its tenderness. His
tongue lightly flicked the corners of her lips, delicately
traced their shape. From her throat a low purr reached
his ears. "Oh, Caroline," he rasped.

The kiss changed character. It was no longer gentle.
His lips slanted over hers, opening them. He pressed
home with his tongue and it sank into the recesses of her
mouth. His hand settled on her waist, squeezed lightly,

then inched up slowly, slowly, until it covered her breast.

Nothing in his life, nothing, had ever felt so good and right as having her breast, still immature but already full, beneath his hand. He plumped the tender mound, pressed soothing circular motions into it. He explored with enough finesse not to alarm her but with enough technique to coax all the sensuality in her into play. She moved against him, each movement inadvertently seductive and inviting.

When his fingers found her nipple, her back arched off the soft grass. The sensitized flesh beaded with passion. His fingers played with it gingerly until it hardened more. And what his fingertips were doing to her nipple, his tongue was doing to the tip of hers. Sounds he wasn't even aware of issued out of his throat and his breath was hot and quick on her face and neck.

His hand went to the buttons of her blouse and he undid them swiftly. Caroline gasped softly and clutched at his hand and the wet fabric he was loosening. "Rink. No," she whispered, meaning yes. She flung her head from side to side. Her teeth made tiny dents in her lower lip.

"Baby, baby," he murmured. "I won't hurt you. I just want to see you, touch you."

His mouth fastened onto hers again with a sweet suction. He drew life and love from her as he parted the blouse and slid his hand inside to cover the soft globe of her breast. When he felt her flesh against his palm, he exploded with new fire, hotter and more rampant than any sexual stimulation he had known in his life.

And he knew then that no other woman in the world would ever complement him as this one did. He had found her, the woman who would make him complete.

He fondled her, pushing her breast high with his hand, rubbing the nipple with his thumb. He inched down her body dropping light, quick kisses on her throat and chest. Then he took one rosy pearl into his mouth and sucked gently. Caroline sobbed. She grabbed handfuls of his hair and held his head fast. His heart burst with love at the moans of pleasure his loving elicited from her.

Her knees were raised, instinct having placed them so with no conscious thought from Caroline. He laid a hand on her bare knee and caressed it. Her thighs were long, silky, as his hand smoothed its way up. The full cotton skirt she was wearing didn't deter him. He didn't stop his quest until he touched the elastic leg of her panties.

Her back arced still higher and she gripped his shoulders. "Rink, Rink." Her cry carried both rapture and panic and he understood both.

"It's all right, sweetheart. I'd never do anything to hurt you. I swear I won't."

His touch was feather light. The strokings continued on and on until there was no longer cloth between them. His fingers touched the soft hair, the soft flesh, her feminine mystery.

"Oh, my God," he groaned, burying his lips in her neck. "You're so sweet. Oh, God."

His fingers strummed, parted, discovered. When she quickened beneath him, he knew he had found the source of the magic. Deftly he applied just the right pressure as he circled and stroked until her throat arched, her head went back, the petals of flesh closed around his fingers and her cries mingled with the rustling wind in the rain-drenched trees.

He studied her face, gloried in its sublime expression. He watched as her eyes blinked open, as she righted her world and gradually returned to reality from that realm where all is bliss.

With the reality came confusion. She shoved down the skirt bunched around her waist. "Rink?" she asked on a high note. "Rink, what happened to me? Hold me. I'm frightened."

He lowered himself over her, sheltering her with his body. He held her close, hands on each side of her head. His lips nuzzled soft kisses over her face as he reassured her. "Don't you know what happened to you, Caroline?" Emotion roughened his voice.

She searched his eyes, pondered his mouth, touched it, as though she marveled over the miracle he was and what he had brought about. "But you didn't . . . I mean . . . you weren't . . . inside me."

Groaning, he pressed his forehead against hers. "No I wasn't. But I wanted to be. I wanted to be deep inside you, filling you with myself, giving you everything that I am." He kissed her, making love to her mouth with his tongue, pressing it deep inside her mouth. But the kiss was too evocative a reminder of what he couldn't do and he raised himself off her.

She was weeping. Her tears mingled with what remained of the rain. He wiped them off her cheeks with his thumbs. "Don't cry." He got to his feet and pulled her up with him, holding her close. Still she cried. "Why are you crying, Caroline?" God, if he had broken his promise and hurt her in some way, he would never forgive himself. Would she despise him now, be frightened of him? "Please tell me why you're crying."

"You won't be back. Not after today. After what I did . . . you'll think I'm trashy."

Relief flooded through him. "Oh, sweetheart," he whispered fiercely and gathered her even closer to him. "I love you."

Slowly she lifted her head to look at him. "You love me?"

"I love you," he vowed, because he knew it to be true. If he didn't love her, they would still be lying in the grass and he'd be doing what his loins ached to do. "I love you and would risk hell or high water to come back tomorrow." He hugged her hard, kissing her breathless. Then, as he held her with fierce possession, he whispered directly into her ear, "We're in a helluva mess, Caroline." Pushing himself away from her, he searched her eyes. "You see that, don't you?"

"Of course!" she cried softly. "I've always known that anything between you and me was hopeless."

"Not hopeless. I'm going to do something about the situation. Tonight."

"Tonight? What?"

"I'll see to it that we can go on proper dates, be with other people and stop all this hiding."

She gripped his upper arms. "No, Rink, don't do anything. Let's just keep on as we are for as long as we can."

"I'll die if we keep on as we are."

"Why?"

"When we're all alone like this, it's too hard for me not to finish what we start."

She was still and silent for a long moment, staring at the base of his throat as her fingers lightly trailed up and down the collar of his shirt. She wet her lips. "Rink, I wouldn't mind if you . . . I'd let you if you wanted to . . . uh . . ."

A finger tilted her chin up. "No." His voice was quiet but adamant. "I don't like the back street flavor of all of this. There's no way I'll complicate matters, risk hurting you, by making love to you." He lowered his face to within kissing distance of hers. He closed his eyes tightly and released a breath between clenched teeth. When he opened his eyes he said, "I want to. God, I want to. But I told you, didn't I, that I would never do anything to hurt you?"

"Yes. And I believe you."

"Then leave everything to me. Don't worry about

anything. I'll get this straightened out and then we won't have to meet in secret like this ever again.''

"Are you sure, Rink?" The worry was still stamped on her face and he knew the worry was for him, not herself.

"I'm sure. Tomorrow I'll have good news. Tomorrow, baby. Here. In our place." His hands folded around her face. "Oh, God, Caroline, kiss me again." His lips seared hers, but it wasn't a lengthy kiss. He didn't trust himself to uphold his promise. He wanted to take her and damn the consequences.

"Tomorrow, tomorrow," he repeated as he backed away, stretching his hand to reach her outstretched one until the tips of their fingers finally fell apart. He ran through the rainy woods to where his car was parked, anxious to get home. . . .

"You fool," Rink said to the fogged mirror as he stepped out of the shower. His image was blurred, which he thought appropriate to describe what he had been like since that day twelve years ago. "Whatever made me so naive as to think that it would all go as I planned?" He threw the last of his drink down his throat with no regard for its mellow taste. He only regretted that the ice had diluted the bourbon's punch.

Thinking of that night when he had gone into his father's study asking for an interview still turned him inside out. Like a residual poison, hate and resentment crept through his body every time he remembered how stupidly confident he had been. What a sap. What an idiot. He had been a young David facing Goliath. Oh, he had had the courage. But he hadn't had the slingshot and stones. And Roscoe had had a cannonball.

He had stridden into the study and announced, "Daddy, I've found the girl I'm going to marry."

"You're damn right you have," Roscoe had growled,

rolling his fat cigar from one corner of his lips to the other. "Frank George called me this evening. Marilee's pregnant. Three or four months gone. According to him she's bawling her eyes out because you haven't been around to see her. Congratulations, son. You're about to become a husband and father."

Even now his father's words made his gut feel as tight as a steel spring. That bastard. That hateful, manipulative, conniving bastard.

And Caroline, *his* Caroline of the river and the rain, was his father's wife. Now it was he she listened to, talked with, gave solace and encouragement to. With Roscoe she shared that sweetest of mouths, those breasts, those thighs.

Rink dug into his eye sockets with the heels of his hands as image after image of them together flickered like an obscene slide show across his mind. Thinking about it was almost more than he could bear.

Everything inside him hurt. And there wasn't one damn thing he could do for the pain.

"Thank you, Steve."

"You're welcome."

"Rink said that toaster was done for and Haney should just buy a new one. But she said there was no use getting a new one when this one could be fixed. Rink was going to fix it but he's been busy at the gin. I said for him not to worry about it. I'd ask you to. You didn't mind, did you?"

"Of course not. I'm glad I could get it working again." He busied himself with straightening up the worktable in the garage where small tools were kept.

"Are you mad at me, Steve?"

He stopped what he was doing and looked down at Laura Jane. She was wearing a halter sundress and her skin looked as soft and creamy as a magnolia blossom.

Desire hit him like a sledgehammer. He turned away brusquely. "Why would I be mad at you?"

She drew in a shaky breath and perched on the top level of a stepladder. Restlessly her fingers fiddled with the tie belt at her waist. Her head was bent so low her chin almost touched her chest. "Because I kissed you the other day," she said softly. "Ever since then, you've been mad at me."

"I said I wasn't mad."

"Then why won't you look at me!?"

He did then. Her shouted, angry demand brought his shaggy head around and he stared at her in speechless awe. He had never known her to lose her temper or raise her voice for any reason. There was little of the child in the face that was defiantly staring back at him. Her expression was that of a woman scorned.

He swallowed with difficulty. "I look at you."

"Your eyes slide over me. They never stop to look anymore. Why, Steve?" she asked, getting off the ladder and approaching him. "Why? Don't you like the way I look?"

His eyes gorged on her, taking in everything from the crown of her soft, heavy brown hair to her slender, sandle-clad feet. When his eyes lifted to hers once again he said huskily, "Yes, Laura Jane, I like the way you look very much."

She smiled, but it faded rapidly. "Is it the way I kissed you? Didn't I do it right?"

He slid his hands up and down the outsides of his thighs, drying his damp palms on his jeans. "You did it just fine."

She drew her face into a worried frown. "I don't think I did. The women on television kiss the men for a long time. They move their heads from side to side. I think they open their mouths when they do it."

His whole body groaned. "Laura Jane," he said on a

hoarse whisper, "you shouldn't talk about this to a man."

"You're not 'a man.' You're Steve."

"Well, you shouldn't talk about kissing to me, either."

She was genuinely puzzled. "Why?"

"Because there are some things that a man and woman who aren't . . . aren't . . . married shouldn't discuss."

"It's all right to do them, just don't talk about them?" she asked quizzically.

He snorted a laugh in spite of the seriousness of the situation. Laura Jane was making more sense than he was. "Something like that."

She glided toward him and laid her hands on his chest. Her head fell back as she looked up at him. "Then let's not talk about them. Let's just do them." Her voice was as light as the breath that landed on his throat.

His hands covered hers. "It's not proper for us to do them, either."

"But why, Steve?"

Anguish tore at his vitals. It took every ounce of discipline he had to pull her hands from him and gently set her aside. "Because it isn't." He went back to the table and picked up the bridle he had been working on when she'd called him from the tack room.

Disconsolately she watched him leave the garage and cross the yard. Taking up the toaster, which had only been an excuse to see him, she headed back toward the house. When she saw Caroline's car turn into the driveway, she paused to wait for her.

"Hello, Laura Jane. What are you doing with that out in the yard?" Caroline asked, gesturing toward the toaster as she alighted.

"Steve fixed it for Haney. I was on my way back to the house."

Something in the girl's tone caught Caroline's attention. "How is Steve? I haven't seen him in several days."

Laura Jane's slight shoulders lifted in a shrug. "He's okay, I guess. He acts funny sometimes."

"Funny?"

"Yes. Like he doesn't want to be my friend anymore."

"I doubt that."

"It's true. Ever since I kissed him."

Caroline stopped in her tracks. "You kissed him?" She glanced around worriedly, hoping that no one else had heard and offering up a small prayer of thanksgiving that Rink wasn't around.

"Yes." Laura Jane's eyes were guileless and calm as she stared into Caroline's dismayed face. "I love him."

"Did you tell him that?"

"Yes. Was that bad?"

"Not bad, exactly." Caroline knew that she must choose her words carefully. This was Laura Jane's first and probably only romance. How did one caution and yet keep from intimidating? "Maybe you were too hasty. You probably took Steve by surprise. He might have wanted to kiss you first."

"I don't think he would have and I couldn't wait."

Caroline smiled. "Given enough time, I think he would have gotten around to it."

"Do you think Rink will get around to it?"

"Get around to what?"

"Kissing you. He wants to."

For the second time within the same sixty seconds, Caroline was dumbfounded. "Laura Jane, you mustn't say such a thing! He wants nothing of the sort."

"Then why does he stare at you?"

Her mouth went dry. "Does he?"

"All the time when you're not looking. And he works so hard at the gin for you."

"Not for me. For everybody, for the workers and the planters who use it, and for your father."

"But you're the one who asked him to. I didn't think he was going to at first, did you?"

Caroline thought back to that night after he had repaired the gin stand. She had tried all afternoon to establish a new rapport with him and thought that she had succeeded. But after they'd returned home, when he'd come down to dinner after his shower, he'd been more hostile than ever. She'd refused to acknowledge it. What little ground she had gained, she wasn't about to surrender.

During the evening meal and later in the living room with Haney and Laura Jane, she had killed him with kindness until he no longer scowled each time he looked at her. Finally she'd garnered enough courage to ask him to check out several more things that she'd thought warranted attention at the gin. He had grudgingly consented. For the past three days he had worked as hard as any of the salaried laborers.

"I'm grateful that he's here to help out while your father's sick. He's working hard."

"So are you. You look tired, Caroline."

She was tired. Very tired. She was still walking a tightrope with Rink, hoping to keep the channels of communication open between them without hinting at intimacy. And Roscoe. His verbal abuse became more vitriolic every time she visited him, which was at least once a day, twice if she could stand it. She didn't tell him about the work Rink was doing at the gin because she knew he wouldn't approve. Nothing else she did suited him. He criticized her on everything from the way she was dressed to the way she took his doctor's orders as law engraved in stone.

"I am tired," she admitted to Laura Jane. "About Steve," she said, returning to the original subject, "maybe he's just in a bad mood. Don't crowd him.

Generally men don't like that. I think the next time you kiss, if you do, it should be his idea, not yours.''

"I guess," she mumbled, her head hanging low.

Caroline thought she knew the reason behind Steve's sudden coolness. Apparently he was in love with Laura Jane but didn't want to do anything to encourage her at the risk of incurring Rink's wrath. Her sympathies were with all of them. "Let's go get some supper," she said kindly, taking the younger woman's hand.

"Where's Rink?"

"I don't know. He said he'd be along—"

She was cut off by the loud honking of a horn, and when she and Laura Jane turned around they saw Rink pulling a shiny new pickup truck to a stop behind the Lincoln. He bounded out of the cab.

"Well, what do you think?"

His exuberance reminded Caroline so much of the young man she had met in the woods that she almost ran to him and heedlessly threw her arms around him.

"Is it yours, Rink?" Laura Jane asked, hopping up and down happily and clapping her hands. "I like the color."

"Cavalier blue," he said, sweeping her a low bow. "I needed my own transportation as long as I'm here and I'd been giving some thought to a pickup. How I'll get it and the airplane both back to Atlanta, I haven't figured out yet."

They all laughed and Caroline's heart melted at the sight of him, hair windblown, eyes dancing.

"I'm starving. Is dinner ready?" He looped one arm around Caroline's shoulders and the other around Laura Jane. "Let me escort you ladies into the dining room."

Before they reached the front porch, Haney came running through the screen door shouting, "Caroline, Rink! Thank God you're here. The doctor just called. Mr. Lancaster's taken a bad turn. He said you two better get to the hospital fast."

Chapter 7

ONLY ONE DIM LIGHT OVER ROSCOE'S BED ILLUMI-
nated the room. It was a directional fixture. The metal
shade was pointed down so that the light fell harshly and
eerily on the man's pain-ravaged features. A nurse was
bending over him when Rink and Caroline entered the
room. With his arms trailing IV tubes, he waved her
away querulously.

"Get out of here and leave me alone. There's nothing
you can do."

"But Mr. Lancaster—"

"Get out," he hissed nastily. "I want to talk to my
wife and son." The titles were slurred in a way that
made them sound like insults.

The nurse left, the rubber soles of her shoes squeaking
faintly on the vinyl floor. Caroline went to Roscoe's
bedside and took his hand. "We came as soon as the
doctor called."

Dark eyes, like iron pellets, bored into her from

blackened sockets as intimidating as the barrel of a gun. His face was ugly. He had a look of decay about him that wasn't physical but spiritual, a rottenness that had eaten at him for years from the inside and was only now making itself manifest on the surface. "I hope I didn't drag you away from anything important," he said snidely and snatched his hand from her grasp.

Caroline refused to be provoked. Calmly she answered him. "Of course not, Roscoe. You know I want to be here with you."

He grinned maniacally. "So you'll know the instant I'm dead? So you'll know the very second you're free of me?"

Her body flinched as though she had sustained a blow to the head. "Why do you say things like that? Do you truly think I want you to die? Didn't I urge you to see the doctor long before you consented to? I've never given you any reason to doubt my devotion to you."

"Only because you lacked the opportunity." His eyes slid to Rink, who stood at the foot of the bed, his shadowed face giving away no emotion.

"W-what do you mean by that?" Caroline stammered, bringing Roscoe's eyes back to her.

"I mean now that the man you really wanted is living under the same roof with you, you might be tempted to be unfaithful to the husband you claim such devotion for."

All the breath left her body. She stared speechlessly at her husband. That sly grin was still riding his lips. His eyes were gleaming like the lights of hell.

"Are you talking about Rink?" she asked.

"Rink?" he repeated, mimicking her. "Rink, *Rink.* Yes, goddammit! Of course I mean Rink."

She wet her lips with her tongue. "But Rink and I . . . we haven't . . . we never—"

"Don't lie to me." He came to a sitting position and

snarled at her like some fearsome demon chained to the bed by plastic tubes. "Don't pretend with me, little girl. I know all about you and Rink."

Caroline backed away from him, hunching her shoulders forward, folding her arms protectively across her midriff. Wildly her eyes sought Rink's. He hadn't moved. He was still standing rigidly at the foot of his dying father's bed, his eyes glowing with hate. He was the first to break that terrible silence.

"You knew about Caroline that night you told me Marilee was pregnant, didn't you?"

Roscoe collapsed onto the pillows. His breathing sounded like paper crackling in his chest. Physically it had cost him to shout his triumphant message, but his face was smug with satisfaction as he directed those malevolent eyes to his son.

He laughed. "I knew. Everything," he sneered. "You should have known you couldn't go sneaking off into the woods every day without arousing my curiosity. I gave you credit for being smarter than that."

"So you followed me one day and saw us together," Rink supplied in a quiet and level voice.

"Hell no." Roscoe sounded amused. "I wouldn't have troubled myself with anything to do with you. I just wondered what mischief you were up to. I sent some flunky after you and what he had to report was very interesting. You were meeting some trashy girl down by the river every day."

Caroline made a pitiful crying sound. Roscoe didn't even look in her direction. His fight was with his son, always had been. She had been a convenient pawn.

"This girl you were sneaking off to see was just a kid, the man said, but as juicy as a ripe peach." Roscoe smacked his lips. Caroline closed her eyes and fought off nausea. Rink rocked back and forth slightly in an effort to control the rage that tore through him. "We had a good laugh when we found out your ladylove was ol'

Pete Dawson's girl.'' He winked at Rink. ''But I had to admire that streak of lust in you, boy. She was jailbait, but you were willing to risk it, weren't you?''

''Let's get on with it,'' Rink snapped. ''You knew that wasn't my baby Marilee was carrying, didn't you?''

''I thought it was just as likely yours as it was anybody's, and you couldn't prove otherwise. Everybody in town knew she wasn't all that discriminating as to whom she took to bed.''

''The child wasn't yours?''

Rink's head snapped around and his eyes met Caroline's full on. Her voice had cracked with a combination of incredulity and . . . something else. Joy? Her eyes were swimming with tears. ''No, Caroline,'' he said. ''The child wasn't mine.''

''You'd been with Marilee, though, hadn't you?'' Roscoe asked from his bed.

Rink kept his eyes on Caroline as he answered. ''Yes. But it was long before she became pregnant. I wasn't with anyone that summer after I met Caroline. Alyssa was not my child.'' He turned back to his father. ''And you damn well knew it. I told you the baby didn't belong to me, that I hadn't slept with Marilee for almost a year. But you forced me into marrying her anyway. Why?''

''How conveniently you forget that you chose to marry her.''

''Because you threatened to put Laura Jane in an institution if I didn't!'' Rink yelled, finally giving vent to the anger that had simmered until it had to boil over.

''Oh, my God.'' Caroline covered her face with her hands. Would this nightmare never end? Roscoe had blackmailed Rink into marrying a girl carrying another man's child? How could he have?

''Why was it so damned important to you that I marry Marilee? Why didn't you laugh in her daddy's face when he suggested that I was that baby's father and send him packing? Surely you weren't afraid of the scandal it might cause. You never cared a fig for social niceties. And I know you weren't intimidated by old man George. Why did you make me marry her?'' His voice had risen to a shout and the question hung in the air a long time after the words had left his mouth.

"Money,'' Roscoe said laconically. "He had money. I needed it. It was as simple as that. I sold you, boy, for twenty-five thousand dollars.''

Rink was stunned. Even knowing the worst about his father, it had never occurred to him that something as commonplace as money had been behind the coercion. "But you didn't stop the divorce once Alyssa was born,'' he said, perplexed.

"There was no time stipulation to the deal. George only wanted a husband for that sorry gal of his and a daddy for her kid. He wanted a respectable name slapped on the birth certificate.''

"Respectable,'' Rink scoffed, throwing his eyes toward the ceiling. He swore. "We reek of respectability, don't we?''

"Besides,'' Roscoe continued smoothly, "it seemed a convenient way to keep you from making a big mistake.''

"What kind of mistake?''

"Taking up with trash, that's what.'' Roscoe cocked his head in Caroline's direction.

"Leave her out of this,'' Rink said threateningly. "This has nothing to do with Caroline.''

Roscoe chuckled maliciously. "It has everything to do with Caroline. I couldn't have you knocking up a little gal like her, now could I? That would have been one helluva fine mess.''

"It wasn't like that.'' The words were forced through Rink's clenched teeth.

"From what my informant told me, it was getting close. He said you could barely keep your hands off her.'' Roscoe's eyes narrowed as he glared at his son.

His lips curled with contempt. "You fool. Do you know how hard it was for me to keep from laughing when you said you'd met the girl you were going to marry?"

Caroline jerked in reaction and her eyes flew to Rink. He glanced at her, but this wasn't the moment to dwell on the fathomless inquiry in her gray eyes.

Roscoe went on relentlessly. "Marilee was a hot little slut. She'd let just about anybody crawl between her legs, but at least she came from a respectable family." His eyes slithered to Caroline. "At least she wasn't the town drunk's kid."

"Then why did *you* marry me?" Caroline demanded, breaking her silence at last. Roscoe was responsible for all the heartache she had suffered. All this time she had believed that Rink had fathered Marilee's child while he had been seeing her. Roscoe's machinations had been skillfully executed. He had gotten away with deliberately ruining both their lives. She had nothing to lose now by fighting back.

"I married you because I wanted to make good on my investment," Roscoe stated bluntly.

"What do you mean?" She had a sinking feeling that she didn't want to know any more. But she had to know. This was a night of revelation. She didn't think she could survive another encounter like this. It would be better to learn everything at once. "What investment?"

"I'll be damned," Rink said softly as the truth dawned on him.

"You figured it out, did you?" Roscoe cackled.

"Will one of you tell me what we're talking about?" Caroline cried.

"I think you've been living with your mysterious benefactor, Caroline," Rink said softly.

She stared at him until the fog of misapprehension began to lift and she saw what had always been apparent if only she had looked for it. "The scholarship?" she asked hoarsely, staring down at Roscoe.

"I wanted to keep you out of town in case Rink, once his divorce was settled, decided to come back for you."

"You paid for my schooling?" She was trying to assimilate what was quickly unfolding. "It was that important to you that I not taint your son and his family name?"

"Oh, it wasn't just that," Roscoe drawled. "You had to be made suitable for the final step of the plan."

"Which was?" she asked on a thread of air.

"Which was that you become Mrs. Lancaster. Mrs. *Roscoe* Lancaster."

Clutching her stomach with both arms, she bent at the waist. Humiliation pumped through her with every agonizing beat of her heart. "You planned all this years ago? You made it happen?"

"How do you think you got that job at the bank so soon out of college? Did you think it was an accident that I met you there? I made available the job at the gin when the time was right. Want me to go on?"

"But why?" she cried. "Why?"

Roscoe said nothing, only slid his cunning eyes from her to Rink. It was Rink who answered. "Because I wanted you. And he knew it. And he would have done anything, no matter how unscrupulous, even marry you, to keep me from having you."

"You always were a smart boy." Roscoe leered.

"You told Laura Jane to write me that Caroline was married."

"That was easy enough to do. She would do anything to please me and then forget it within hours. You could have learned a lot about devotion and respect from your simpleminded sister, my boy."

"Respect." Rink spat the word.

"For years you manipulated all our lives because of some grudge you had against Rink?" Caroline said, still not believing that a man could be so obsessed with hate. "I wasn't good enough for him, but you married me.

You gave me your name, brought me to live in The Retreat. I can't understand it.''

"You were easily seduced, my dear. I knew that coming from your background, we Lancasters and The Retreat would represent all that you'd never had. The house and family name were bait you couldn't resist, weren't they? Even if that house and name belonged to your long-lost love. Actually there were times when I was grateful to you for making it so simple. You were articulate and clean, which was a bonus. You're refined. God knows where that came from, but it was a benefit. You're good to look at, which made it easy for folks to believe that a dirty old man like me could be taken with you. Yeah, Caroline, thank you for making it so easy.''

She turned her back in mortification. She had been used abominably. But oddly it was herself she blamed more than the twisted mind of her husband. If she hadn't been so gullible. If she hadn't been so quick to judge Rink. If she hadn't been so ambitious in her own right. If, if, if . . . What could Roscoe have done to hurt her more than she had hurt herself?

The dying man's eyes were lively as they darted between the two. "What's it been like living in the same house? Torture? This week has been the most fun of all, watching you squirm. You thought no one knew, didn't you? Oh, it's been entertaining watching you trying to hide it, watching you trying to keep from looking at one another and giving yourselves away.''

His eyes lit on Rink. "You've been wanting her again, haven't you, boy? Got a twitch between your legs you can hardly stand, hmmm? Have you been thinking about her in my bed and what we do there?''

Caroline whirled around, outraged and offended. "Stop this, Roscoe!''

"Look at her, sonny. She's got a terrific body, doesn't she?''

"Shut up," Rink ground out.

"All woman. Every silky inch, female."

"Don't talk about her that way, damn you!"

Roscoe chuckled evilly. "I'm not saying anything you haven't been thinking. Have you been thinking about how you'd like to kiss her? Hold her? Undress her? Sleep with her? Been wanting your daddy's wife, boy?"

"Oh, *God!*" Devastated, Caroline ran from the room.

Roscoe laughed as he watched her go.

"You sonofabitch." Rink addressed his father with deadly calm.

"You're right about that." With an effort Roscoe pulled himself up and propped his weight on his elbow. "I'll burn in hell and love every miserable minute of it because you'll be more miserable here on earth. Ever since you were born you've been a thorn in my side."

"Because I saw all the ugliness in you. Because you killed my mother as surely as if you'd put a bullet through her brain."

"Maybe, maybe. She was a weak woman. Never stood up to me. But you did. You did, all right. I never could stand your eyes looking at me with such righteous reproach. And the older you got, the worse it got. You appointed yourself my conscience and I didn't want a conscience."

He pointed a shaking, skeletal finger at his son. "Well, I got you back, son of mine. It took me years, but I've repaid you in full. You'll never have that woman now, Rink. I know you. Your damned stubborn Winston pride won't let you have her." He paused significantly, then added, "Because I had her first. You remember that. She was *my* wife and I had her first!"

The four in the limousine were silent as it glided beneath the trees on the lane that led to the cemetery. Rink and Caroline stared out the windows by which they sat. Laura Jane, sandwiched between them, threaded her handkerchief between her fingers. Haney, on the jump seat, analyzed them all but kept her peace. At least as long as she could.

"Looks like a good turnout," she commented, peering out the back windshield at the procession of cars following the hearse and limo.

No one spoke. Finally Caroline said, "Most everyone in town, I think."

"I don't remember much about Mama's funeral. Do you, Rink?" Laura Jane asked timidly. When Rink's eyes looked as hard as they did now, he frightened her.

"Yes," he said bitingly, "I remember it." Then, realizing he was speaking to his sister, he turned his head and gave her a soft smile. Taking up her hand, he kissed the back of it and clasped it warmly between his. "A lot of people came to it, too."

"I thought so," she said, smiling tremulously, glad that he wasn't staring into space with that cold, foreboding expression on his face any longer.

"Folks are going to talk," Haney said prophetically. "'Cause you aren't holding a funeral service in the church. The preacher was shocked. Everyone else was, too."

"Then they'll just have to be shocked and I don't care if they talk," Rink said bluntly.

"You don't have to live here," Haney snapped. "We do."

"No church service," Rink said gratingly. "All right, Haney?" His spearing eyes and the imperious edge to his voice rendered her submissive.

"Yes, sir." She drew herself up huffily. He turned his eyes out the window.

Caroline's heart went out to Haney and Laura Jane. Innocent as they were to the true nature of Roscoe's spirit, they couldn't understand Rink's remarkable coldness over the loss of his father. For herself, they thought that grief had stupefied her.

Haney had taken her hand and said, "You're a brave

soul, Caroline, but the crying will come. When you're alone and all the hubbub is over, then you will cry.''

Haney was wrong. Caroline would shed no tears for the man who had been her husband. Her eyes had remained dry from the moment she had run from his hospital room in abject humiliation. Rink had followed her out a while later, looking like he had been in hell and visiting with the Devil himself. His visage had been terrible, stony. It had stayed that way.

Through the long night they had kept vigil in the plastic-and-chrome waiting room chairs. They didn't speak. They didn't look at each other. So many times she had wanted to apologize for thinking he could have betrayed her love with Marilee. She had wanted to touch him, to hold him, to grieve with him for all the years they had been kept apart. But they were apart still. Every taut line of his body and tense angle of his face told her so. She kept her distance and held her silence.

Roscoe had been heavily sedated after Rink left his room. Once the doctor had come to Caroline and knelt in front of her, taking her hand. ''It won't be long. You can go in if you wish, but he won't know you're there.''

She had shaken her head. She never wanted to see his face again. When at last the doctor had come to tell them that Roscoe had died, she left the hospital with Rink, dry-eyed and empty-hearted.

Now she must play the role of the bereaved widow. The limousine pulled to a halt. She was helped out of the backseat by the solicitous funeral director and led to the temporary tent that had been set up at the gravesite. She took the chair he indicated and sat stiffly, Rink beside her, Laura Jane next to him. Haney chose to stand behind Laura Jane, her comforting hands on the young woman's shoulders.

Caroline closed her ears to the minister's eulogy. Her eyes stared right through the casket with its blanket of white roses. When the service was over, she accepted the condolences of those who came to speak to her and Rink with formal graciousness.

"Isn't she holding up well?" they murmured to each other.

"Not a tear."

"Of course, since he had that exploratory surgery she's known it was only a matter of time."

"Yes. She's had time to prepare herself."

"Still, she could be carrying on something awful. You know how those people are. They tend to get emotional in public."

"I wonder what will happen to the gin?"

"She'll go on running it, I reckon."

"What about Rink?"

"He'll stay."

"He'll go back to Atlanta."

"I don't rightly know."

She heard the whispered speculations as she returned to the waiting limousine, and she was unmoved by them. The magnitude of Roscoe's deceit was still in the forefront of her mind. If she let any of her control slip, she would lose it all and disgrace herself by screaming like a madwoman. So she let them think her stoic. She would neither pray nor weep for the soul of Roscoe Lancaster. He had hurt not only her, but the only man she had ever loved. There would be no forgiveness in her heart for meanness so profound.

"Thank God that's over," Rink said as he sank into the backseat after shaking hands with the minister one last time.

But it wasn't over. All afternoon The Retreat was filled with people who had ostensibly come to pay their respects to Roscoe's survivors. Caroline thought most of them had come out of curiosity. Did they want to see what changes she had made in Marlena Winston Lancaster's house? She got the impression that most of them were disappointed to find it unaltered. Had they expected scarlet wallpaper and fringed lampshades?

They were insatiably curious about Rink and his life in Atlanta. He was grilled about his business, his private life, the years he had been away from them, his future plans. He handled the subtle inquisition adroitly.

They were equally curious about Caroline. From where she sat in somber dignity, she watched her visitors covertly study her and wondered what they expected. Had they expected her to wear something besides a sedate black dress? Did they expect her to be weeping uncontrollably? Or did they expect her to be laughing now that her rich older husband had died? Just as they were disappointed with the unchanged house, she felt they were disappointed in her. The Dawson girl hadn't given them anything to talk about later.

At last the callers began to leave, until finally the house was empty. Lengthy evening shadows came through the shutters to stripe the hardwood floors. Haney went about clearing up used glasses and paper napkins, emptying ashtrays.

"Will anybody be wanting supper?"

"Nothing for me, thank you, Haney," Caroline responded desultorily.

"No thanks." Rink splashed a draught of bourbon in a highball glass. "Go on to bed, Haney. It's been a long day for you."

She hoisted up her laden tray. "As soon as I get these things washed up, I may take you up on that. Is there anything you need, Caroline?"

Caroline smiled her thanks and shook her head. "Good night, Haney."

"Well, there's plenty of food in the refrigerator if anybody gets hungry. Good night."

She left the two alone in the front parlor. Caroline leaned her head back on the sofa cushions and massaged her temples as she closed her eyes. She unbuttoned the top button of her dress and slipped off her shoes, sighing in relief.

Having taken off the jacket of his dark suit and rolled up his shirt-sleeves, Rink stood at one of the tall windows. One hand was in his pants pocket, the other periodically raised the glass to his lips. This was the first time they had been alone together since they'd left the hospital two nights before. It seemed they still had nothing to say to one another.

Caroline's eyes drifted open and she studied him from across the room. She indulged herself and greedily soaked up the sight of his dark silhouette against the indigo evening.

His black hair was a startling contrast against the white collar of his shirt. His shoulders were wide and she followed the tapering shape of his vested back to his waist. His buttocks were narrow and taut beneath the tailored slacks, his thighs hard and lean and long. She wanted nothing more than to go to him. She could almost feel her arms sliding under his and around that firm torso to a stomach she knew her hands would find flat and corded. Her breasts ached to be pressed against the strength of his back. She wanted to lay her cheek against his shoulder and drink in his scent, every nuance of him.

Then, as she watched, his body tensed and she heard his muffled, "What the hell?" before he slammed the glass down on the antique sideboard and stormed from the room, his face set in hard lines. Alarmed, Caroline jumped from the sofa and hurried to the window.

Steve and Laura Jane were on the lawn. They were making slow progress toward the house. His arm was around her shoulders as he held her securely close to him. Her head was nestled against his chest. His head was bent protectively over hers. Caroline saw his lips moving as he spoke to her softly. Then she saw his lips rest fleetingly on her temple in a gentle kiss.

Spinning on stockinged feet, she raced from the room, knowing now what Rink had seen. She must catch up with him before—

But even as she thought it, she heard the front door screen bang closed behind him and his heels on the front porch. "Laura Jane," he called out.

Caroline ran after him, bounding down the front steps. "Rink, no."

Laura Jane raised her head from Steve's chest, but she made no effort to move away from him. Instead she carried him along with her as she obeyed her brother's summons. Caroline could see the reluctance in Steve's footsteps. He wasn't as naive as Laura Jane and had recognized the rage in Rink's voice immediately. But he didn't avert his eyes from the other man as they came forward.

"Yes, Rink?" Laura Jane asked.

"Where have you been?"

"I've been in Steve's apartment watching television." She smiled up at the stable manager. "He was trying to take my mind off Daddy's funeral."

Fury radiated off Rink like heat from a stove. "Well, it's getting late. You'd better get upstairs to bed."

"That's what Steve said, too." She sighed. "Good night, everybody." She bestowed upon Steve a private smile before she glided toward the front door.

Rink let several seconds tick by after they heard the door close behind her. Then he took a belligerent step forward. "Keep your hands off my sister, understand? If I see you pawing her again, you'll be out of a job and off this place so fast your head will spin."

"I wasn't pawing her, Mr. Lancaster," Steve said levelly. "I was comforting her. She's upset by your father's death and . . . other things."

"Well she doesn't need your kind of 'comforting.' "

"Rink," Caroline interrupted and laid a cautioning hand on his arm. He shook it off.

"What's that supposed to mean?" Steve asked.

"You know damned good and well what it means. You could get by with a helluva lot under the heading of comforting."

Steve gnawed his lower lip and Caroline knew that only fear of losing his job and having to leave The Retreat and Laura Jane prevented him from lashing back at Rink.

"You can think whatever you like about me, Mr. Lancaster, but this you can write down as fact. I've never done anything to hurt Laura Jane, nor will I ever."

Rink glared at him balefully. "Then we don't have a problem, do we? But just to make sure I don't ever misunderstand anything you do, stay away from her." With that he turned away and stamped back into the house.

After casting an apologetic glance in Steve's direction, Caroline rushed after Rink. She caught up with him in the wide foyer and, grasping his arm, spun him around. "You bully! Did taking your anger out on Steve give you any satisfaction? Do you feel better now?"

"Not quite."

He reversed their roles and became the aggressor. Taking both her upper arms in fists of iron, he pushed her into the parlor and slid the door closed behind them. Pressing her into the wall with his body, bending his face close over hers, his breath labored, he demanded, "How could you have slept with him? How, Caroline?"

Chapter 8

THE KISS THAT FOLLOWED WAS BRUTAL. HIS MOUTH twisted over hers and forced her lips to part and admit his tongue. His hips thrust forward and ground into hers. One hand released her arm and covered her breast. He squeezed it without tenderness. It was a caress intended to debase.

She fought him. Her free hand alternately pushed against his unyielding chest and pounded his shoulder. She tried to drag her mouth free of his assaulting lips, but to no avail. Her screams were nothing but high-pitched garbled noises that were muffled by his mouth.

This wasn't Rink. Caroline knew that he didn't want to hurt her this way. He was crazed with an anger that had been building all his life. His enemy was dead and that left him with no one to fight. Frustrated, he was taking out his rage on her, because unwittingly she had been a part of Roscoe's scheme. She understood then that her best defense was not to fight him at all. She went limp in his arms.

It was several moments before Rink came to his senses and realized that she was no longer struggling against him. His lips gentled and the tempestuous kisses became sweet nuzzlings against her mouth. The hand on her breast ceased its insulting groping and after touching her tenderly, apologetically, was withdrawn.

It was this sweetness that she had to fight. The violent caresses of a moment ago weren't from the man she had known and loved but a man torn asunder by deceit and bitterness. Now, his touch was painfully familiar, achingly reminiscent of that summer when every touch had been enchanted.

"Rink." His name was a soft groan, carrying with it yearning and hopelessness.

"Did I hurt you?"

"No."

"I didn't mean to."

"I know."

He leaned forward and placed his arms from elbow to fingertips against the paneled wall behind her. His forehead pressed into the wood as he rested it close above hers. His breath stirred her hair. "Why do I want to make love to you more than I want to breathe? Why haven't I been able to forget you? After all this time, why am I still obsessed by you?"

He inclined toward her until they were touching in one unbroken line. Their position was so blatantly sexual that their hearts hammered against each other. "We could be lying in a bed in this same position, couldn't we, Caroline?"

"Oh, God." She burrowed her nose in his neck. "Don't talk about it, Rink."

"That's what you're thinking. That's what I'm thinking."

"Don't think about it."

"I'll always think about it."

Their bodies heated one another. Her breasts flattened

softly against his hard chest. Their bellies massaged each
other with every shallow breath. He adjusted himself
against her so that she might feel the strength of his
desire. His sex nestled in the receptive hollow of her
femininity. Their thighs pressed against each other.

Fully clothed, standing, not moving, they were intimate. They made love. It was a mental intimacy, not
physical. But each was thinking about the act so potently
that it couldn't have meant more had it been performed.

Rink turned his face into her hair, burying his nose in
it. He whispered her name repeatedly. Their emotions
were so undisciplined that they trembled with them.
Then they were still.

Minutes passed and they neither moved nor spoke.
They just stood there, relishing the nearness of one
another, regretting what had never been and lamenting
that it could never be.

Gradually Rink began to back away until they were no
longer touching. His eyes pored over her face, hot and
compelling. She raised hers to meet them. "How could
you have been with him, Caroline?" he rasped. He
pushed himself away from the wall and ran his hand
through his hair. He didn't ask again, but his stern
expression demanded that she answer him.

"He was my husband." It was a simple statement that
should have explained everything. Instead it provoked
fresh anger.

"How could you have married him in the first place?
How, for God's sake? After what had been between us,
how could you have married *him?*"

"That's not fair, Rink!" she said heatedly. "You
deserted me, not the other way around."

"You know why I married Marilee."

"Not until two days ago I didn't."

He put his hands on his hips and faced her angrily.
"Then you actually thought that I was screwing some-

body else while I was defying everything, even my own common sense, to be with you?"

His vulgarity shocked her into flaring back. "How was I to think otherwise? You were gone without a word. I heard that you were getting married to Marilee George because she was pregnant. What was I supposed to think?"

He cursed and turned away to avoid her sound reasoning. "I couldn't come to you with the truth. You wouldn't have believed me any more than anyone else did."

"I might have."

"Would you?" he asked, rounding on her. Her eyes fell beneath the accusation of his. "No, you wouldn't have," he answered for her. "You would have thought just what everybody else did, that the baby was mine."

He went to the couch and flopped down on it, extending his legs far out in front of him. He rubbed his eyes with his thumb and middle finger. "Besides I was afraid you might become involved somehow if I tried to see you again. I knew the town was buzzing with gossip and that I would be watched like a hawk. Anything I did would be duly reported. I didn't want to risk getting you mixed up in the mess."

She went around the room plucking cards from the numerous flower arrangements that had been delivered before the funeral. "Who was the baby's father, Rink?" Disinterestedly he named the man. Caroline turned to him in surprise. "But that was the man Marilee married after your divorce."

He laughed mirthlessly. "She could hardly wait to run back to him. But first she had to bleed me dry financially. That was my punishment for not wanting her."

"You wanted her at some point," she said in an almost inaudible whisper, remembering what he had said that night in Roscoe's hospital room.

His head snapped up. "Are you going to hold that against me? My God! I was just a kid, Caroline." He was irritated and it showed. "Sewing wild oats. Yeah, I was with her a few times. Every guy in town was. But I had sense enough to take precautions so she wouldn't get pregnant. A couple of romps in the backseat of my car sure as hell didn't mean I wanted to marry her."

She looked down, studying her thumbnail. "And it's true that you weren't . . ."

"Caroline." Her head came up at his soft beckoning. "Do you want to know if I was with her at the same time I was seeing you?" Her eyes brimmed with emotion as she stared back at him. "No," he said with soft emphasis. "I wasn't with anyone else that summer."

"Did you really tell Ro . . . your father . . . that you wanted to marry me?"

"Yes. I told him I'd met the girl I wanted to marry."

Their eyes locked and held and it was a long while before her head fell forward and she turned away. "The baby, Alyssa?"

The corners of Rink's lips lifted in a brief smile before his face became sad. "She was a great little girl."

At his mellow tone, Caroline faced him again. "You loved her," she said with no inquiring inflection.

Unashamed he looked up. "Yeah," he said, laughing softly. "Crazy, isn't it? But once she was born, I wanted to keep her."

Caroline's heart wrenched with love for him. She sat down beside him on the couch. "I'm not prying, Rink. But if you want to talk about it, I'll listen."

His eyes roamed her face. "You always were good at listening. Tell me, did you sit at my father's feet and listen as he poured his heart out to you?"

She uttered a strangled cry as she leaped to her feet. He caught her wrist and checked her retreat. "I'm sorry. Sit down." When she strained to pull her arm free, he gave it a swift, light jerk that brought her back down on the sofa. "I said I was sorry. That was uncalled-for, but habits are hard to break. If you want to know about my ill-fated marriage, I'll tell you. You know about all the other garbage in my life, you'd just as well know about that, too."

"I said I wasn't prying."

"And I believe you," he snapped. "Okay?" When she bobbed her head once in terse agreement, he released her hand. "Marilee didn't love me any more than I did her. Roscoe was right about that. She only claimed the baby was mine to keep her family from disowning her. Anyway, when we left here, which she hadn't bargained for, we went to Atlanta. I had to find work because I wouldn't take a cent from my father. The marriage deteriorated, but I loved Alyssa. As soon as she was born her real father showed up and he and Marilee picked up where they had left off."

"You didn't mind?"

"Hell no. I couldn't wait to get her off my hands. But I worried about the baby. Marilee wasn't the most conscientious of mothers. When she filed for divorce on the grounds of mental cruelty, I didn't contest it, but she wasn't done yet. She demanded an outlandish settlement. At one point I was actually supporting her and her lousy boyfriend. To make a long story short, I had to work day and night for years to buy her out of my life. I hated losing Alyssa, but Marilee insisted on having custody of her."

"Did Alyssa ever know that you weren't her father?" Caroline couldn't bear the thought of the little girl pining away for a father who never saw her.

"Oh, yes," he said with disgust. "Alyssa was about three when the divorce became final. She was crying, clinging to me while Marilee pulled her out of my arms. They were coming back to Winstonville and I was staying in Atlanta. Alyssa was calling me Daddy, crying that she wanted Daddy. Marilee told her that if she

wanted her daddy she'd have to go to Winstonville to
find him because I wasn't her daddy.''

"Oh, Rink," she murmured, shivering at the thought
of such a terrible scene.

"She's eleven now and I hear she's as wild as a March
hare, the scourge of Winstonville Junior High." He
shook his head sadly. "It's a shame, because she was
such a sweet little girl. As you know, she's had a
succession of 'stepfathers.' I doubt if she even remem-
bers me."

After a long silence Caroline said, "Had Air Dixie
started by this time?''

"Not quite. I had gotten my pilot's license my first
semester at college. By the time I moved to Atlanta I had
gotten in enough flying time to hire on as a charter pilot.
I kept logging hours, upgrading my classification to fly
larger airplanes. I met my partner and we started
thinking about a charter service of our own. When one
went bankrupt and was selling cheap, we managed to
scrape enough together to make a down payment on it.
We began doing so much business we paid off our loan
years ahead of time and couldn't keep up with our
demand. We bought a larger plane, then another, then
another.''

"And it went from there.''

"Yes.''

The lamplight formed a halo around them. Her dark
hair fell to her shoulders and blended with the black
dress she wore. Only her face and throat shone creamy
and pale in the golden light. Her eyes were shadowed but
luminous as they gazed back into his.

"Caroline?" he asked softly.

Her heart began to thrum behind her breasts. It was
disgraceful to feel the way she did on the day of her
husband's funeral, but she knew that if Rink made one
overt move, she would flow toward him and there would
be nothing she could do to stop herself. She still loved

him, had never stopped. But she no longer worshiped him as an adolescent does an idol. She loved him as a woman loves a man. Despite his temper, his intolerance of human weakness, his fury over her relationship with Roscoe, she loved him.

"Yes, Rink?"

"Did you ever think of me when you were making love with my father?"

He couldn't have hurt her more if he had plunged a dagger into her heart. She cried out in agony and bolted off the sofa. "You bastard! Don't ever say anything like that to me again."

He came off the couch to stand facing her. His proud chin jutted forward. "I want to know. Didn't it prick your conscience just a little to marry my father when we had come so close to being lovers ourselves?"

"I was willing to be your lover, remember. You weren't willing to be mine. You weren't willing to take the risk."

"That's right. I wouldn't risk hurting you."

"I wanted you to hurt me." She spoke with so much emotion it sounded like a sob.

He gnashed his teeth and his voice lowered to a rumble. "I wanted to hurt you that way, yes. I wanted to be the first, to give you that instant of pain that would make you mine forever." He came a step closer, seething with pent-up emotions. "But I had some misplaced sense of nobility. More the fool, I wanted you to be set apart from the other girls I'd been with."

"And there were many, weren't there?"

"Yes."

"Before and since."

"Yes."

"Then how can you blame me for marrying Roscoe?"

"Because you said you loved *me!*"

"Did you love all those other women, Rink? Did you?" He turned away abruptly but not before she saw the guilt on his face. "You weren't here, Rink. You were married to someone else. For all I knew I had only been a casual plaything for you to while away those lazy summer hours with. You could have written, called, anything. I doubted that you even remembered me except perhaps because I was so unsophisticated compared to the women you were used to."

"You know why I couldn't contact you. I didn't want to involve you in that mess with Marilee. By the time it was over you were in college and I was informed that you were married. I gave up the hope of ever seeing you again. Then the next thing I know you're sharing my father's bed!"

She covered her face with her hands. She could feel his resentment coming toward her in incessant waves. Her hands fell from her face and she bravely met his angry eyes. "We can't go on this way, Rink," she said softly. "We're destroying each other."

His shoulders sagged and again his hair was punished by raking fingers. "I know. I'll be leaving in the morning."

Her heart dropped to her feet like a lead weight. She hadn't intended to run him off, she had merely wanted to make peace between them. "You don't have to leave. I will. This is your house. My residence was temporary. I knew that after Roscoe's death I wouldn't belong here."

"If you left and I stayed, how would that look to everybody? It would look like I had run off my daddy's widow. No. I'll return to Atlanta tomorrow."

"But the reading of the will and the cotton gin . . ." She groped for a plausible reason for him to stay. It was hopeless between them, but she couldn't stand for him to leave her again. Not yet. Later, but not now.

"I'll come back for the reading of the will. We'll decide then on the living arrangements. I'll feel better knowing you're here with Laura Jane. As for the gin"—he smiled sardonically—"carry on as you did under Roscoe's supervision."

The bleak look on her face vexed him. He took the steps necessary to bring them together. He wrapped his arms around her and hauled her against him. Her head fell back as he bent low over her face.

"Don't look at me like that. Do you think I want to leave? My home? My house? Laura Jane and Haney?" His voice dropped significantly. *"You?"* He pulled her closer and moaned as her body molded to his. "Damn you. Damn you, Caroline."

His mouth came down hard and demanding on hers, but she was waiting for it. Her lips opened and invited him inside. His tongue burrowed into the hot sweetness of her mouth. He kissed her long and deeply, his head tilting first to one side then another to taste all of her. His hands closed about her face as his mouth fused intimately with hers.

Then he broke it off with a suddenness that made her dizzy. His voice was gruff, torn from a throat constricted with the pain of wanting. "Damn you for belonging to him first."

A heartbeat later she was alone.

"Laura Jane?" Steve knelt down in the hay and touched her shoulder. "What the hell are you doing here?"

"Hmmm?" She stirred in her sleep and rolled from her side onto her back. "Steve?" she murmured. Her eyes blinked lazily, then came slumberously awake. "Is it morning?" she asked softly, stretching languidly, arching her back and lifting her breasts toward him.

"Barely morning," he said, tearing his eyes away from her chest. "What are you doing in here?"

She sat up and shook hay from her hair. Faint sunlight shone into the stable onto her bare shoulders. The air was still night-cool, but the hay on which she had slept was warm and pungent. Horses in the various stalls were nickering, hungry for their morning ration of oats. Dust motes floated in the air, catching the sun's first rays.

Laura Jane's sleepy eyes focused on Steve. She smiled and touched his cheek, which was pink and shiny after his recent shave. "Last night Caroline and Rink argued. I could hear them shouting all the way in my room. Haney was already asleep so I couldn't go to her. I had to get out of the house. Why are Caroline and Rink always so angry with each other? I don't understand it, Steve."

She leaned forward, laying her head on his chest and wrapping her arms around his waist. "Anyway, I came out here. The door to your apartment was closed and all the lights were out. I knew you were already asleep, too, and didn't want to bother you. I curled up here in the empty stall and went to sleep. I felt better just being close to you."

She snuggled closer to him and his insides were pitched into chaos. He had cursed Rink Lancaster and his threats after the scene in the yard. Did Lancaster actually think he meant any harm to come to Laura Jane? Couldn't that bullheaded brother of hers see that he loved this woman/child, that to him she embodied everything that was pure and good in a world he had thought rancid with hate and killing and blood and war?

He had sworn last night never to be alone with her again, never to touch her. Because to be caught at it would mean that he would have to leave for good. That he couldn't have borne.

Now, however, he knew that he would not be able to heed Lancaster's warnings. The nearness of Laura Jane's soft body was blotting them from his mind. Without his planning it or weighing the consequences of such a move, his arms closed tightly about her.

"I'm sure they were both upset by your father's

funeral. They'll iron out their differences. It's natural for a household to undergo some stress when someone in it dies."

"I love them both so much. I want them to be friends."

He laid his cheek against her hair. His large, scarred hands smoothed her back. She had on a soft cotton nightgown with a daintily smocked bodice across her breasts. Thin straps tied it onto her shoulders. The light robe she had covered herself with had been cast aside when she sat up. Her skin was warm and soft.

"When things settle down, they'll be friends. They won't argue anymore. I promise."

She lifted her head from his chest to look at him. Her brown eyes were trusting and loving. "You're so good, Steve. Why can't everybody be as good as you are?"

"I wasn't good," he said thoughtfully, trailing a finger down her cheek. "Not until I met you. Whatever goodness I have, you gave to me."

"I love you, Steve."

His eyes closed with internal anguish and he drew her close, pressing her head under his throat. "Don't say that, Laura Jane."

"I want to. Because I do love you. I think if you love somebody you should tell them, don't you?"

"I suppose so, yes," he whispered. The dike behind which his emotions were dammed was cracking up. The pressure was getting to be too much. He would have to find an outlet for them and when he did, God help him.

She pulled back and stared at him compellingly. Lashes as long and luxurious as a feather brush surrounded the eyes that had cured a man as hard and cynical as he of all callousness. She stared back at him expectantly and the choice was taken from him. He had to speak the words aloud.

"I love you, too, Laura Jane."

Smiling, she launched herself at him, throwing her childishly thin arms around his neck and hugging him hard. "Oh, Steve. I love you. I love you." She covered his face with kisses as soft and fleeting as the beat of butterflies' wings. "I love you." She came to his mouth and hesitated, remembering Caroline's words of caution.

He inhaled her breath, felt the trembling excitement in her body so close to his. He was like a drowning man going down for the third and final time. What the hell? he asked himself. Lancaster couldn't do anything to him that hadn't already been done. When one has faced death a hundred times, one comes to mock it, dare it.

And besides all that, he loved this woman.

His mouth met hers gently and held. The tiny tremors that shimmied from her breasts up to her throat matched the flutterings in his own body. The way he felt about her was like nothing in his life before. He was well acquainted with women, but not this kind of woman, not one who was loving and trusting, innocent and eager, sincere and unselfish.

Quite naturally her lips parted beneath his and he groaned. His tongue tentatively ventured between her lips, tested, tasted. She pressed her mouth more firmly against his and edged closer until he felt her breasts and their small pointed nipples against his chest. His embrace became stronger as his tongue deflowered her mouth.

They swirled together in an orgy of discovery. It was as significant a learning experience for Steve as it was for Laura Jane. Together they fell back onto the hay. He laid his good leg over her thighs and her slender legs twined around it.

"Laura Jane." He sighed into her neck. Valiantly he tried to get a grip on his rioting sexual impulses, but her breast was beneath his hand and it was firm and ripe with passion. The peak responded with such enthusiasm that he couldn't keep from loving it with his fingertips.

"Steve, Steve," she panted. "Oh, Steve, make love with me, Steve."

His head jerked up and he looked down into her shining face. "I can't," he said softly. "Do you know what you're saying?"

"Yes." Her fingers moved adoringly over the blunt features of his face. "I know about what men and women do together. I want us to do it."

"We can't."

She wet her lips and her eyes filled with uncertainty. "You don't love me?"

"I do. That's why I can't. I couldn't do that with you unless you were my wife."

"Oh." She was vastly disappointed. Her eyes went to his mouth. Her fingers touched it. "Do we have to stop kissing?"

Smiling, he bent down and brushed his mouth against hers. "Not yet," he whispered. "Not yet."

"Good morning." Caroline entered the kitchen and headed straight for the coffee maker. She poured herself a generous cupful. As she carried it to the table, she avoided looking directly at Rink, who was already there.

"I'm calling the doctor this morning," Haney said, stirring the scrambled eggs in the skillet.

"Doctor? Why?"

"You look terrible, that's why," the housekeeper said without compunction. "I know you didn't sleep well. Look at those circles under your eyes. Can't you see them, Rink? You need a sleeping pill or tranquilizer or something."

"No I don't," Caroline said, sitting down across from Rink. Even though he had been included in the conversation, she didn't look at him and he remained silent.

"Don't be so brave," Haney said chastisingly. "No one is handing out prizes for the most courageous widow of the year. No one would blame you if you broke down and got all that grief out of your system. It's natural to grieve when you lose your husband.''

At that point Caroline hazarded a glance at Rink. He was staring at her over the top of his coffee mug. She was the first to look away. "I don't need a doctor."

Haney sighed, not bothering to hide her exasperation. "Well, eat a good breakfast, at least." She piled the eggs onto a plate and set it in front of Caroline. "Go on and start. I'll go up and wake Laura Jane later. I thought it best to let her sleep."

"She's not sleeping," Caroline said, stirring cream into her coffee. "I stopped by her room before I came down." She had wanted the girl to accompany her downstairs, to act as a shield against Rink's mood, whatever it might be this morning. "She wasn't there."

Rink lowered his fork to his plate. Haney turned from the countertop, a plate of toast in her hand. "Where is she? You haven't seen her this morning?" he asked Haney.

"Didn't I just say I thought she was still asleep?"

Rink tossed his napkin down on the table and stood up. He stamped to the back door and tore it open. "Rink!" Caroline shot out of her chair and went after him. By the time she had run down the back porch steps, he was striding purposefully toward the stable. "Rink!" she called after him and increased her pace.

At the door of the stable he turned on her. "Be quiet!"

"You can't spy on them, Rink," Caroline objected, though she kept her voice to a whisper.

"Stay out of it."

She was interfering when she knew it would be wiser not to, but she couldn't let him destroy Laura Jane's chance at happiness. "She's not a child."

"With what he has in mind, she is." He eased the door open. Thanks to Steve's careful maintenance, it didn't make a sound. Rink stepped into the dim building with Caroline following close behind him. His boot made a grinding sound on the floor as he reached the stall where Steve and Laura Jane lay.

They heard it and, seeing the enraged expression on Rink's face, sprang apart. Unfortunately Rink had already seen the intimate way Steve was kissing his sister, the way her body was curved into his, the way his hand was caressing her breast.

Rink's cry of outrage curdled Caroline's blood. He lunged at Steve, grabbed him by the front of his shirt and yanked him jarringly to his feet, a maneuver that Caroline knew must have nearly torn the prosthesis from his stump.

Rink plunged his fist into the veteran's stomach and sent him falling backward against the side of the stall. Then, before he had a chance to recover, Rink's fist slammed into his chin.

Laura Jane screamed and scrambled to her feet. She flung herself toward the fighters, but Caroline grabbed her and pulled her out of the way. Steve's instincts as a guerrilla fighter had been awakened and he came back at his attacker with a vengeance. When a well-aimed fist brought blood to Rink's nose, Laura Jane screamed again and ran from the barn.

"Stop it!" Caroline shouted. "Stop it, both of you."

Fists and feet were flying. They grappled against the stall, striking stunning blows at each other.

Caroline rushed into the two-man melee and wedged herself between them. "Stop it now. Both of you. My God, have you both lost your minds?" At last she was standing between the two fighters, who were panting for breath and swabbing at bleeding cuts.

When Rink had finally regained his breath, he glared malevolently at Steve. "I want you gone by noon."

"He stays." Caroline turned her back on Steve and

resolutely faced Rink. "He stays until I fire him. Roscoe told me to hire him and I'm the only one who can fire him. At least until the will is read and you take possession of The Retreat. In the meantime, as Roscoe's widow, I make the decisions concerning the estate."

"Like hell you do," Rink snarled. "This has to do with Laura Jane, not The Retreat. She may be your stepdaughter, but she's my sister."

"I agree. This has everything to do with Laura Jane." Caroline's breasts were heaving with exertion and emotion. As she faced him defiantly, she loved him fiercely and ached for the bleeding bruises on his face. But she wouldn't back down. "Steve wasn't taking advantage of her. He was loving her, Rink. She wanted him to."

"She doesn't know what she's doing."

"Yes, she does. She loves him. Are you so hard-hearted and immune to human emotions that you can't see what's so plainly obvious? If you send Steve away, how do you think she'll feel about you? You're her god. She worships the very ground you walk on. It will destroy her if you break her heart by doing this. I beg you not to. Please."

"It's for her own good."

"How do you know what's best for her?"

"I know."

"Just like Roscoe knew what was best for you? Would you keep them apart the way he did us?"

Rink reacted as though she had landed a blow better placed and more dreadful than any of Steve's. His eyes bored into hers, but she held her ground. Finally he sliced his eyes toward Steve, who was unconsciously rubbing his aching thigh. Rink glared at him but said nothing before he strode from the stable.

All the life and spirit went out of Caroline then and her body sagged. She stood for a long time, staring at the hay-strewn floor through blurred eyes. She had backed Rink into a corner and he would hate her for it. Sighing, she raised her head and turned to Steve. His face was distorted with rapid swelling.

"Will you be all right?"

He nodded, dabbing at a disfigured lip with a handkerchief. "I've had worse." He tried to smile but grimaced with pain.

"I'll send Haney out to tend to you."

He nodded and Caroline turned. When she reached the door of the stable he called out to her. "Mrs. Lancaster." She faced him, and he took two limping steps toward her. "Thanks. No matter how it turns out, I appreciate your taking up for me."

She smiled wanly and headed toward the house. When she reluctantly went through the back door, Rink was sitting at the kitchen table holding Laura Jane on his lap. Her face was buried in his neck and she was crying uncontrollably. "You're mad at me. I know you are."

"No," he said gently, stroking her back. "I'm not mad. I just don't want anything bad to happen to you, that's all."

"What Steve was doing wasn't bad. I love him, Rink."

Rink's eyes met Caroline's over his sister's head. "I'm not sure you know what it is to love a man, Laura Jane. Or what it means for him to love you."

"I do! I love Steve and he loves me. He would never do anything to hurt me."

Rink wasn't going to concede that he had been wrong. "We'll talk about it later. I'm sorry I lost my temper."

But Laura Jane wasn't going to be placated, either. She raised her head and gripped Rink's shirtfront. "You won't fight with Steve anymore. Promise me you won't."

Rink couldn't hide his surprise. He stared into his sister's determined eyes and finally said, "I promise I won't fight with him anymore."

Slowly she released his shirt and sweetly kissed his

cheek. "I'll go help Haney find the bandages." For Laura Jane the crisis was over. She left the kitchen and skipped up the stairs.

"I won't be leaving today after all," Rink said in measured tones when they were alone.

Caroline's heart jumped with gladness, but it was a momentary reaction. Her chin went up defiantly. "What changed your mind? Are you afraid that in your absence I'll corrupt your sister and ruin the family's reputation?"

He gave her body a deprecating, leisurely inspection before saying, "Something like that."

Her eyes smarted with unshed tears. He knew how to hurt her. "To you I'm still that white trash girl, aren't I, Rink? I'm good enough to kiss when you feel like kissing, but not good enough to be a part of your family."

"I'm not leaving."

That was all he said before he sauntered from the room.

Chapter 9

"MORNING, MIZ LANCASTER."

"Miz Lancaster, nice day, ain't it?"

Caroline acknowledged the greetings called to her as she entered the gin. Harvesttime was upon them. The men were already working overtime to handle the first crops brought in. The hours were long, the shifts tiresome, dusty, hot and noisy. Yet there was a spirit of pride among the gin workers that hadn't existed for years. It was no secret where this feeling of unity came from.

Rink.

There was no denying that all the equipment, due to a recent overhaul, was operating in prime condition. Farmers who in seasons past had been seeking other spot markets for their cotton were returning to Lancaster Gin. There was no secret why that was so, either.

Rink.

In just the few weeks he had been around, the gin had

undergone a radical change. Most of its employees had welcomed him back. Those who wanted to work hard were given a raise in pay. Those who were habitually late or shirked duty were fired. Caroline recognized those who had been fired as perpetual agitators. They were men Roscoe had employed for specialized jobs, jobs she surmised she was better off not knowing about. The one and only time she had suggested that Roscoe get rid of a certain employee, she had learned not to venture into the no-man's-land of Roscoe's private affairs.

"He's a troublemaker," she had said.

Roscoe had smiled benignly. "He does . . . errands . . . for me, Caroline. If he makes trouble with one of the gin workers, do me a favor and look the other way."

"But he's a gin worker, too."

"That's the way it's supposed to look." At her disbelieving expression he had diplomatically added, "I'll speak to him if he causes you any more problems."

She realized now that such a man must have been sent to spy on Rink that summer.

Rink, with her sanction, hadn't wasted a minute cutting off the dead wood and raising the salaries of trusted, loyal workers. They respected him. Rather than working for Rink out of fear, as they had his father, they stayed on because they liked the man. He had a knack for motivating them. He criticized constructively. He praised when it was deserved. He worked and sweat right along with them. It was no wonder to her that he was such a successful businessman.

Ten days had gone by since the eruption in the stable between Steve and Rink. Rink spent most of his time at the gin. Caroline loved having him there. He gave her confidence. She knew that a few of the men had been fired because of their criticism of her.

Though they hadn't specifically laid down the terms, a peaceful truce existed between the two of them.

One morning at the gin she was working on the endless stream of business correspondence when he entered the office without knocking. "Caroline, there's someone out here I'd like you to meet if you're not busy."

She smiled up at him and spread her arms wide over her littered desk. "Oh, no, I'm not busy."

He grinned lopsidedly. "It's important or I wouldn't have interrupted you."

Standing, she asked curiously, "Who is it?"

"A surprise."

With his fingers riding lightly on the small of her back, he ushered her through the teeming gin and out onto a loading dock where five-hundred-pound bales of cotton awaited delivery to the warehouse.

A rotund man in a startling white suit and Panama hat—he looked like he belonged in a Tennessee Williams play—was pinching samples of cotton off the bales and stretching them between his thumbs and fingers. He was chomping on a cigar that fleetingly and unpleasantly reminded Caroline of Roscoe. But there was nothing of Roscoe's dominating personality in the man who looked up and smiled congenially when he saw her coming toward him with Rink.

"Mr. Zachary Hamilton, this is Mrs. Caroline Lancaster."

"Mr. Hamilton." She extended her hand. It was swallowed by his and heartily shaken. Had she ever known a grandfather, she would have wanted him to look like Mr. Hamilton.

"It's a pure pleasure to meet you, Miz Lancaster. A pure pleasure. Your . . . uh . . . er . . . stepson, Rink, here, was telling me that under your careful management Lancaster cotton has improved considerably."

Her cheeks flushed becomingly as she glanced first at Rink, then back to their guest. "Rink is giving me more than my due, I think. But I'm proud of the product we're producing now."

"Mr. Hamilton is a buyer for the Delta Mills in Jackson."

Caroline was looking at Rink, so only he saw the instantaneous lift of her eyebrows and the small circle of surprise her mouth formed. His eyes were dancing mischievously. It was with difficulty that he didn't burst out laughing.

"I . . . I see," she stuttered and turned back to the cotton merchant. Everyone in the South who grew cotton or sold it knew about the Delta Mills. They supplied the world with textiles of the highest quality.

"We'd be privileged to have you sample our cotton, Mr. Hamilton," she said as calmly as she could. She was beside herself with nerves and excitement. Adrenaline had begun to pump through her. If she and Rink could sell to Delta Mills, it would be a business coup.

"Thanks to Rink's hospitality, I've been sampling it." He pinched off a wad of cotton from the bale and began the stretching process until he could determine the average length of the fibers. "This is prime cotton," he said musingly. "Has a good staple length. I think you could sell us some."

Both Caroline and Rink had to force themselves not to whoop with glee. "We've got a lot already committed to other buyers," Rink said with shrewd evasiveness.

"I can appreciate that, Rink," the buyer said. "How many compressed bales can you sell me?"

As Caroline stood by, shifting anxiously from one foot to the other, Rink bargained with the man. Finally they settled on the number of bales to be delivered and the price per bale. It was the best deal Lancaster Gin had ever made.

"Of course, we'll be delivering the cotton by air," Rink said offhandedly as he escorted Mr. Hamilton to Caroline's office to sign a contract.

"By air?" Mr. Hamilton stared up at Rink in awe. But he was far less astounded than Caroline.

"A service we provide only for our most preferred customers." Rink's teeth flashed whitely and when Mr. Hamilton turned to go into the office, he winked at a stunned and speechless Caroline.

After Mr. Hamilton had left, she was still staring at Rink with dismay. "By air?" she asked in a thin, high voice. "Whatever happened to the railroad?"

He laughed and began opening desk and file cabinet drawers in a mad rush to find something. "Nothing happened to it," he said absently. "Ah-ha! I knew it had to be here." He pulled a bottle of bourbon from the bottom drawer of a file cabinet. "Got any glasses? Oh, to hell with glasses." He uncapped the bottle, threw his head back and took a long pull from the bottle. He made a face as the burning liquor went down. "I've got an old freight airplane that I've reconditioned myself. We want to impress Delta Mills, don't we? Do you think they'll forget the company that delivered their cotton by air?"

"But the fuel costs alone . . . Rink, it'll be incredibly expensive."

"Not if I load the cargo and fly it myself," he said, flashing her a broad grin. "It'll cost us fuel and a few hours of my time. But a standing contract with Delta Mills will be well worth the investment, I think. To us." He saluted her with the bottle before taking another swig of the bourbon, then pushed it toward her. "Here."

Caught up in the spirit of his celebration now, she eyed the bottle, tempted. "I couldn't," she said with false coyness and glanced nervously over her shoulder toward the door.

"Of course you could."

"What if someone comes in and finds us drinking?"

"They'd understand. We just pulled off a helluva deal. Besides I've put the word out that no one comes through that door without knocking."

"You do it all the time."

He assumed an annoyed stance. "Are you going to drink some of this or not?"

Boldly, she took hold of the bottleneck and, imitating him, threw back her head and took a large swallow. She came up coughing and sputtering, her eyes tearing and her insides flaming. Rink took the bottle from her as she bent at the waist to cough. He thumped her back with his open palm, laughing uproariously.

"Better?" Slowly she straightened, drying her weeping eyes with the backs of her hands.

"I think so," she croaked and they both laughed at the unfamiliar hoarseness of her voice.

"God, Caroline. My heart was in my throat," he said with boyish enthusiasm. "I was so afraid he was going to say no or leave us hanging without a firm commitment."

"Why didn't you tell me he was coming?"

"I didn't want to get your hopes up."

"I'm glad you didn't. I loved the surprise."

"Did you?"

"Yes." She smiled up at him and her smile widened when she realized again what they were celebrating. "Yes, yes, yes."

It was unplanned. Entirely unplanned. He caught her about the waist, lifted her several inches off the floor and whirled her around. They were both laughing. His head was thrown back as he looked up at her. She smiled down on him from her elevated position and put her hands on his shoulders.

"We did it! We pulled off the best deal ever in Lancaster history. Do you realize what that means, Caroline? New buyers will come snooping around. Planters will check us out," he said, answering for her. "Not this year, but next. We may have to expand." He held her, spinning her around in an impromptu waltz.

When he set her down it seemed perfectly natural for him to kiss her. His mouth met hers firmly and squarely. It wasn't a lover's kiss. It was a kiss between friends, a celebration of a job well done.

But the instant their lips made contact, that changed. They couldn't touch without it being the touch of lovers. When he felt the soft, moist acceptance of her lips beneath his, desire shot through him like lightning. He raised his head to judge her reaction.

His eyes greedily toured her face, taking in every feature. The high color in her cheeks, her auburn hair, the sparkles that made her eyes look like glistening raindrops on slate, her mouth, all caught his attention.

She waited expectantly, feeling his breath accelerate, watching his eyes grow hot.

He wanted her. God, he wanted her. He wanted to devour her, to make her his finally and everlastingly. But she had pledged faithfulness to his father till death parted them. And Rink knew that dead as his father was, his influence reached beyond the grave. She still belonged to Roscoe and for that reason he wouldn't take what he longed for so badly. Desire smothered him, yet he clawed free of it and released her.

He didn't want to. First his hands moved from the back of her waist to the sides, then fell away completely. As though an invisible adhesive held them together, their bodies pulled apart slowly before he took a severing step backward. Last to release her were his eyes, which stayed on hers until he forced them away.

She was disappointed and shaken but tried not to show it as he turned back to her before opening the door.

"I thought I'd invite the whole crew out for a beer in celebration. It'll be an incentive for them to produce the cleanest cotton possible for the Delta Mills."

"I think that would be a wonderful gesture, Rink. I'll see you at home?"

He nodded. "I won't be late."

It was at the supermarket that she got her first inkling that people were talking.

Haney had called the gin and asked if Caroline would stop at the store on her way home. Caroline made a list of items as Haney reeled them off. "Thanks. I'll appreciate it."

"No problem," Caroline said. "I'll be home shortly. Rink is going out after work, so you might want to plan dinner a half hour later than usual."

She was pushing her grocery basket down the aisle, checking off the things on her list when she spotted two townswomen eyeing her with undisguised interest. She recognized them. One was touted to be the most malicious gossip in town. She had a daughter the same age as Caroline, who was now married to a factory worker. It was said that because of a drinking problem, he had difficulty keeping a job. The daughter had been popular, one of the "in crowd" from which Caroline had always been excluded. How it must rankle that the Dawson girl had married so well! The other woman ran the dry cleaning store and dealt out gossip with each exchange of dirty clothes for clean.

There was no avoiding them, though Caroline wished she could. Her chin went up a notch and she deliberately steered her basket so she would have to pass right in front of them.

"Hello, Mrs. Lane, Mrs. Harper."

"Mrs. Lancaster," they said in unison. The effusiveness of their greeting was transparent. "You poor dear," one said. "How are you making out now that Mr. Lancaster is gone?"

"I thought it was a lovely funeral. Lovely," the other said.

"Thank you. I'm doing fine." She would have pushed on then, having satisfied the dictates of politeness, but one of them rushed to engage her in conversation.

"It must be such a comfort to you to have Rink home at a time like this."

Careful, Caroline, she warned herself. These are piranhas and they'll tear anything you say to shreds. "Rink's return to The Retreat meant a lot to Laura Jane and Haney, our housekeeper. Despite the circumstances, they were glad to have him at home again."

They virtually smacked their lips at every morsel she doled out. "How long will he be staying, now that he's a bigshot in Atlanta and all? We must seem like hicks to him."

"Rink loves Winstonville. The town is named after his mother's family, you know. The Retreat will always be his home."

That seemed to whet their appetites even more. They moved in closer, like beasts of prey anxious for a kill. "But what about you? Since you married Mr. Lancaster, isn't The Retreat *your* home? Or do y'all plan on living there together? Like one big happy family?"

"That's what we are," she said, smiling coldly. "One big happy family."

"Oh, of *course*," they agreed enthusiastically.

"Give my regards to Sarah," Caroline said to her classmate's mother as she moved off. "I hear she had another baby."

"Her fourth." Colorless eyes enviously raked Caroline's slender figure in her trim linen dress. "It's a shame Mr. Lancaster didn't leave you with a baby. A child would provide such a comfort to you in your grief." It was the most insincere display of pity Caroline had ever seen. If she weren't shaking with anger, she would have laughed at the inept performance.

"What does she need with a baby, Flo?" Another pair of eyes, just as mean, just as prejudiced, slid over her.

"She's got Rink living in that big house to keep her company and give her all the comfort she needs."

"Oh, yes, Rink. We mustn't forget that he's there with her."

"Good afternoon, ladies," Caroline said quickly. She forced herself to pick up the last items on her list before going through the checkout and leaving the store. Tears of humiliation burned her eyes.

As long as Roscoe was alive no one would have dared speak to her that way out of fear of reprisal. Roscoe Lancaster's wife had commanded their respect, no matter how grudging. Apparently his widow did not. She had gone back to being Caroline Dawson and it seemed that the stigma of her background would live with her forever. It didn't matter how cleanly you lived; if you grew up poor trash, your morals were suspect.

Why didn't she leave this place of small-minded, bigoted people?

For the same reason Rink couldn't. Their roots went too deep. He was at the highest echelon of society and she the lowest, but her place here was as solidly entrenched as his. It was infuriating to be assigned a place at birth, with no hope of changing it. Didn't it matter that she was managing one of the finest, certainly one of the largest, cotton gins in the region? Didn't it count that she had gotten a college degree? Or did her accomplishments only feed their jealousy?

Why punish herself this way? Why not go somewhere where she wasn't known?

The Retreat.

For as long as she could remember, she had dreamed of living in The Retreat. And now, when Rink claimed it as his inheritance, what would she do? Leave town? Never come back?

No. She would find another house in Winstonville and

go back to dreaming of The Retreat. But she could never leave it entirely. Never.

She was quiet throughout the evening meal. They ate the fried chicken dinner in the formal dining room, Rink having declared this an official celebration of the Delta Mills deal. Haney and Laura Jane shared his gaiety. Caroline was finding it hard to be festive after the subtle persecution she had been subjected to in the supermarket.

She noticed Rink looking at her quizzically and roused herself from her disturbing musings. For the rest of the meal, she doubled her efforts not to let her distress show.

After dinner she went for a stroll around the grounds. The evening was cool and clear. A rare breeze fanned the full summer leaves of the trees overhead. She went to sit on the bench swing hanging from the huge pecan tree in one corner of the property. It was one of her favorite spots at The Retreat. The river channel gurgled nearby. Moss dripped almost to the ground from the trees. The undergrowth was lush. With the toe of her shoe barely pushing against the soft grass, she idly rocked herself in the swing.

But her indolence reversed itself when she saw a long, lean shadow separate itself from the trunk of a tree and move toward her on silent feet. He pushed aside draping wisteria vines and bent to walk under the sprawling arms of a live oak until he stood just in front of the swing.

"What's wrong, Caroline?"

"You must have Indian blood. You're always sneaking up on me."

"I didn't come down here to discuss bloodlines. Answer me. What's wrong?"

"How did you find me?"

"I found you." Taking hold of the swing's ropes in each hand and stilling it, he bent over her. "Now, dammit, I'm asking you one last time. What's wrong?"

She shifted uncomfortably. "Nothing."

"Something. What?"

"It's nothing."

"I'm not budging from this spot and neither are you until you tell me. And the mosquitoes can get ferocious around here after dark. So unless you want to be carried off by a swarm of the bloodthirsty little suckers, tell me now what's bothering you. Something at the gin? Me? What?"

"This town!" she exploded and stood up. Rink was forced to let go of the ropes. Her burst of temper was so sudden that he moved aside and gave her room. The swing rocked crazily behind her. She went to the massive trunk of a tree, crossed her hands on it and laid her forehead against them.

"What about this town?"

"It's full of petty people."

He laughed softly. "Are you just finding that out?"

"No. I've known that since I was old enough to walk behind my mama pulling her wagon as she delivered fresh laundry. I've always known they were prejudiced and judgmental." She turned and braced her shoulders against the stout tree trunk. "It's just that I thought a college degree, a good job, a new name would elevate me enough in their eyes so that I wouldn't be considered trash anymore."

"You should have known better. Whatever you're born to around here, you're stuck with."

"How well I know. And lest I forget, I was reminded today."

"What happened?"

She pushed her hair back and let her eyes flicker toward him before looking away again. "It's too silly and insignificant to get upset about."

"So tell me and we won't get upset together."

Sighing, she named the two women who had spoken

with her in the supermarket. Rink made a rude sound. "I don't like it already. Go on."

"They . . . they commented on how lucky I was to have you around after Roscoe's death, living in the same house with me. They made a point of stressing that. They intimated . . . well, you can guess what they intimated."

"They intimated that there was more to our living together than sharing an address. Is that it?"

She looked up at him. "Yes."

He cursed softly. "They hinted that all might not be proper."

"Yes."

"That something illicit might be going on."

"Yes."

"That we might be more than stepson and step-mother."

She didn't reply but merely nodded. Stillness surrounded them. Cicadas sang cheerily. Bullfrogs croaked mournfully. They found it impossible to drag their eyes away from each other. Her breasts vibrated with pounding heartbeats. She could swear the pulse in Rink's temple matched the tempo of hers.

"Forget what those crows said, Caroline. Gossip is their favorite form of entertainment. If it weren't us, it would be somebody else they were raking over the coals. As soon as the newness of Roscoe's death wears off, they'll find something else to occupy their busy little minds."

"I know that. Rationally I know it. But I still can't stand their nasty innuendos. I don't like being the subject of their vivid imaginations." Their eyes met again briefly, hotly, before they darted away. What the gossips had suggested wasn't all that vividly imaginative.

"It would be ridiculous for one of us to move out until all the legalities are settled," Rink reasoned. "Wouldn't that cause even more talk?"

"I suppose so. Everyone would wonder who had driven whom off. They would say you hadn't approved of me."

"As my father's wife, you mean."

Caroline could have bitten her tongue for bringing that up. "Yes."

"Why would they think I don't approve of you?"

"Because of who I was when I was growing up." She shifted uncomfortably against the tree. The bark snagged her dress. "Because of the age difference between Roscoe and me."

When their eyes met this time, there was no pulling them apart. "They would be right," he whispered, leaning close to her. "I would never have approved of you as his wife."

"Don't, Rink." She wanted to back away, but escape was blocked by the tree.

"Why do you worry about gossip, Caroline?" he asked smoothly, coming even closer. "Your conscience is clear, isn't it? You know there's nothing improper going on at The Retreat."

"Of course."

Closer still. "There's nothing illicit going on between us, is there?"

"No."

"Liar."

The last word came out raggedly. He placed his thumbs lengthwise along her throat and enclosed her neck with eight strong, lean fingers that interlaced at her nape. With the pads of his thumbs, he tilted her head up.

"Tell me there's no chemistry between us." Moaning softly, she tried to turn her head aside. He wouldn't permit it. "Tell me that every time you look at me you see only a stepson. Tell me you don't remember what it was like with us. Tell me you don't remember that day it rained. Tell me never to kiss you again. Tell me you never want to feel my touch. Can you tell me that,

Caroline?'' Her only reply was a whimper. ''That's what I thought,'' he growled.

His mouth clamped hard and sure over hers. Her arms flailed uncertainly until the heels of her hands came to rest on his shoulders where she made feeble attempts to push him away. His body only pressed more intimately against hers. Like the pieces of a puzzle designed to lock in place, he fit them together. His mouth moved over hers, willing her lips to obey his command. His tongue probed the seam of her mouth.

''Kiss me back, Caroline. You want to. You want to.''

And she did. With a slight murmur of surrender, her arms circled his neck tightly. Her lips yielded to the persuasion of his tongue. It entered her mouth with no resistance and met only a welcoming warmth and entrapping sweetness. He stroked her mouth, dipping into each recess with so sexual a cadence that Caroline felt the last vestiges of her resistance melting.

Mercilessly he aroused in her a desperate need for him. His kisses were evocative and thorough. The pressure of his virility between her thighs created in her such a hunger that she couldn't bear it. She wanted him to fill that aching void. It was of his making and only he could make it whole.

He freed the buttons of her dress and slipped his hands inside the bodice. Her breasts were covered with a lacy camisole. His senses roared as he slid his hands over their full warmth. He massaged them with lazy motions that hypnotized and seduced.

From his lips flowed curses and prayers in a thrilling litany that fell like love songs on her ears. She heard in his voice the desperation of her own soul, the hunger, the agony of unfulfilled desire. He fondled the lace and satin-covered breasts, sought and teased the crowns with his fingertips. The caress gave her immense pleasure. The sensitive flesh grew hard in response. He dipped his head and touched one nipple with his lips.

Caroline felt the kiss in her womb, deep in her innermost self. Her whole body contracted with an intense need and she made an anguished sound. She knew if she didn't stop now, she would be lost.

She pushed herself free of his embrace. "No, Rink, no," she cried. She covered her breasts with her hands, willing her heart to stop its erratic racing. "I can't. We can't."

His chest rose and fell alarmingly with each breath. His hair had been mussed by her pillaging hands. His eyes, dilated with passion, blinked back into focus. "Why? Because of my father?"

She shook her head, sending her hair flying wildly. "No, no," she protested miserably, pulling her dress together. "Because of the people in town. Because I don't want to be what they expect me to be. I can't do what their sordid minds accuse me of doing, seducing first Roscoe, now his son."

"I don't give a damn what they think."

"I do!" She realized she was crying. Tears were rolling down her cheeks. "Just as you said, we remain what we're born as. You were a Winston and a Lancaster. No matter what you do, it would be considered above reproach. They wouldn't dare criticize you. But me, I came from trash and that's what I'll always be to them. I have to care what they think."

While the seconds ticked by, they stared at each other. Rink was the first to turn away and when he did, it was with a blasphemy. "I can't live in the same house with you and not want to make love to you."

"I know."

"Well, I've admitted it. Isn't that what you wanted to hear?" he shouted.

"No, Rink. I didn't need to hear it to know it." When he whirled around and looked back at her she said softly, "It's the same for me. Did you think that it wasn't?"

It may have been a trick of the moon, but she thought

his eyes looked suspiciously moist. His mouth worked but no words came out. At his sides, his fists clenched and released reflexively. His body was taut with suppressed emotions. He looked barely capable of containing them.

She swiped at the tears on her face. "Do you see why I can't be with you, Rink? They're right. I do want you. But just as you can't forget it, neither will they. I was Roscoe's wife."

He turned, giving her his back for several minutes. When he faced her again, his expression was hard, bleakly resolved. "What will you do after the will is read?"

She made no effort to conceal the tears that filled her eyes. "The only thing I can do, what I always knew I must do. I'll leave."

He nodded his head once, jerkily, before he turned and thrashed his way through the woods. Caroline sank onto the swing and buried her face in her hands. She wept.

Neither of them saw the shadow flitting through the trees as it moved away from the site.

Chapter 10

"STEVE?"

There were no lights on in his apartment, but the portable black-and-white television was shedding flickering silver light on the walls.

"Laura Jane?" he said incredulously.

"I wasn't sure you were here. Were you asleep?"

Self-consciously Steve pulled the plain white sheet over his naked chest. He was lying on his back in the narrow bed. When she squeezed through the door, opening it only wide enough for her thin frame to slip through, he propped himself up on his elbows. "No I wasn't asleep, but what in the world are you doing here? If your brother finds you here—"

"He won't. I just saw him driving away in his new truck. He and Caroline . . . Oh, Steve. I don't understand anything!" She flew across the room and flung herself over him. Automatically his arms went around her. Crying, she buried her face in the hollow of his neck.

"What's the matter? What happened? What don't you understand?"

"Rink. I don't understand him at all. He got in a fight with you because you were kissing me. He made me feel like we'd done something shamefully wrong. But if it's wrong, why do he and Caroline do the same thing? If it's wrong for us, why isn't it wrong for them? They're not married either."

"You saw them together? Kissing?"

"Yes. Down by the old bench swing. They didn't see me."

He combed his fingers through her hair. He didn't want to upset her any more than she already was, so he answered carefully. "I think you saw something you weren't supposed to see."

Laura Jane raised her head. "I shouldn't have stayed and watched, should I? Haney said you're not supposed to watch people and listen to them when they don't know you're there."

"It's impolite, yes."

She plucked at the edge of the sheet like a contrite child. "I know it was wrong. But I heard them, so I followed the sound of their voices. When I got there, Rink was kissing Caroline. They were standing against a tree so close together that I couldn't tell them apart."

As her fingers filtered through the dense hair on his chest, he became increasingly aware that he was wearing only his underwear beneath the sheet. Laura Jane was sitting on the edge of the bed, her hip fitting into the slight indentation of his waist.

She told him how Caroline had ended the kiss. "She said they weren't supposed to be kissing because people would think they were bad. Rink listened to her, standing very still. He looked like he wanted to hit something, not Caroline. He looked like he wanted to go on kissing her."

Laura Jane's voice wavered. "Caroline said as soon as

the will was read, she'll leave.'' Leaning from the waist, she laid her head on Steve's chest. "I don't want her to leave. I love her. I love Rink. I want us all to go on living the way we are now forever.''

With one hand he cupped the back of her head comfortingly. With the other he rubbed her back. He had pieced together the whole story. Hadn't he heard Caroline remind Rink about Roscoe keeping them apart? At some point in time, they had been important to each other. But Rink had left and she had married his father. Now, still attracted in spite of themselves, they were trapped in an untenable situation. "It's a helluva mess all right,'' he murmured against Laura Jane's hair.

She lifted her head and gazed down at him. "Do you know what I wish?''

He touched her face with exploring fingertips, marveling over the unspoiled beauty of it, the purity of her mind, the lack of guile and meanness. Such qualities were precious to him because he had seen so little evidence of them. Until he had met Laura Jane, he'd thought human nature was putrid, including his own. "What do you wish?'' he asked softly.

"That they could love each other the way we do.''

He longed to laugh, he longed to cry, he longed to kiss her. He thought about the two former, he did the latter. Pulling her down gently, he pressed a tender kiss onto her parted lips.

"Steve?'' she whispered.

"Hmmm?'' He kissed her face, amazed that skin could be so fragile and still hold a body together.

"You're not wearing your plastic leg.''

He ceased his nuzzling instantly and followed her eyes to the end of the bed where he had propped the prosthesis. "No,'' he said sharply. "I'm not.''

"Let me see your leg. Please.'' She reached for the sheet to pull it back.

He grabbed it and held it taut over his body. "No.''

His tone was colder, harder, than he had ever used with her. For a moment it frightened her, but only for a moment. She laid her hands over his and tried to work his fingers off the sheet. "Please, Steve. I want to see you."

Angrily he flung her hands off. He raised his hands from the sheet and threw them over his head. She wanted to see? All right, better to let her see. Better to let her get disgusted now before he fell any more in love with her than he already was. Better that she should run from him shrieking in fear and revulsion now than later. He was hideously deformed and the sooner she realized it, the better for them both.

In anguish, he felt the sheet slide away from his body. The cool air from the window air-conditioning unit touched his body. His jaws ached from clenching them. He stared at the ceiling, trying to concentrate on the dancing patterns of light the television cast there. He didn't want to see the look of horror on her face. He wished he could close his ears to any sound of repulsion she might make.

He wouldn't blame her, of course. She had been sheltered from ugliness. Her world had been soft and beautiful, a chrysalis of gentility and graciousness. The world he came from, the jungle war he had lived through, were as foreign to her as life on another planet.

"Oh, Steve."

It wasn't the kind of reaction he had expected. Her voice was breathless, tremulous; her tone emotional, reverent. Tucking in his chin, he looked down the length of his body just in time to see Laura Jane's hands reaching out to touch his pink, puckered thigh. Even though he could feel the shy, light touch, even though he could see her hands gliding over the hair-roughened skin, he didn't believe it. His flesh quivered beneath her sweet tribute, but his heart exploded.

"Steve, you're beautiful." As she looked down at

him her eyes were liquid with tears. He searched them but could find no trace of repugnance, nor even pity, only undiluted love and admiration.

With a strangling sound, he reached for her and pulled her down onto his chest. His hands cradled either side of her face, holding her hair back as she bent toward his mouth.

He kissed her with a new ardency. His tongue pressed into her mouth deeply. It swirled, gathering up all her sweetness. Learning from him, she nibbled at his lips, sucked lightly when he introduced his tongue into her mouth again and went on a darting expedition between his lips with her own tongue.

"God, God, Laura Jane." He held her head tight against his shoulder to stop her ardent kisses and to regain his breath and common sense. His sex was full and surging behind his underwear. Everywhere her skin touched his, he was burning. He thought to ease himself by touching her breasts. But their full soft weight in his palms only made him want her more, not strictly in a carnal sense but for all the healing succor she offered.

"I feel funny on the inside," she confessed. Her hand feathered over his chest and stomach.

Mirthlessly he laughed. His loins were throbbing. "So do I."

"My heart's beating fast." Taking up his hand, she pressed it over her left breast.

His hand closed softly over the delicate mound of flesh. He gritted his teeth. "So is mine."

"Is this how you feel when you make love?" she whispered.

He couldn't vocalize an answer but nodded.

"We can't make love because we're not married, right?"

He moaned and hugged her closer. "No, baby, no. We can't. It wouldn't be fair to you." Nor to him. If he had her once, he knew he would want her every day for the rest of his life.

Sitting up, she smoothed her hand over his cheek. "Then, Steve," she said with simple logic, "let's get married."

It was a subdued group that gathered in the front parlor of The Retreat. The day was equally gloomy. Moisture-laden clouds hung heavily over the landscape. It hadn't rained. Rain would have been a welcome relief from the oppressive humidity.

This day had been both anticipated and dreaded. Twice Granger Hopkins had set a time for the reading of Roscoe's will. Twice it had been postponed. On the first occasion, Rink had been unexpectedly called back to Atlanta to handle some Air Dixie business. Granger himself had asked for the second postponement. Another client had demanded his immediate attention.

Caroline was secretly glad for these delays. She had been promising herself for weeks to start looking for another house, someplace small but with character, someplace away from town but not too remote for a woman living alone. But she felt no ambition to get started on the project. She used the gin as her excuse.

They had ginned more cotton than ever before. She and Rink went early every morning and came home late every evening. The majority of the season's crop had been ginned, baled and was waiting in the warehouse ready for shipment to the various merchants. The Delta Mills order had been flown to Jackson as Rink had promised.

They shared a feeling of supreme satisfaction, but also one of unspoken loss. Without the constant demands of the gin, they had no reason to spend so much time together. Since that night by the swing, there hadn't been a romantic interlude between them, but the desire was there, a living thing, constantly flowing between them.

Granger coughed behind his hand to get their attention. "I guess we're ready." He was seated beside a small table where he had laid a manila envelope.

Laura Jane and Rink were sharing an heirloom love seat. Their hands were clasped affectionately. Caroline sat in a wingback chair at their left. Haney, who had also been invited, sat to their right and slightly behind them in a lyre-back chair.

Granger took a pair of wire-rimmed eyeglasses from his breast pocket and settled them on his beefy nose. Carefully opening the envelope, he took out the multi-paged document and straightened the stiff sheets. He began to read.

Roscoe had never been philanthropic. He had begrudged every cent his wife Marlena had given to charity. What donations he had made in his lifetime had not been made out of a spirit of generosity, but rather for an income tax advantage. In his will, however, he had bequeathed a sum of money to the church he had been an unfaithful member of and to various other community charities.

Granger paused, poured a glass of water from the pitcher Haney had left on the table for him, sipped it and proceeded. He read in an unemotional voice, but with a detectable reluctance. As the terms of the will were methodically read, the reason for that reluctance became appallingly clear. When he was done he folded the papers and stuffed them back into the envelope. He removed his glasses and replaced them in his breast pocket.

The other three in the room remained motionless. Even Laura Jane, who couldn't fully understand the implications of her father's will, comprehended the unfairness of it.

"He didn't leave anything to Rink." Laura Jane addressed Granger, but her eyes made a slow sweep around the room and finally fell on her brother, whose face seemed to be carved of stone . . . or ice.

"That old bastard," Haney said under her breath as she left the room in a huff. She would refuse to accept the money left to her for "years of devoted service to Laura Jane."

Caroline slowly stood and took a hesitant step toward the love seat. "Rink, I'm sor—"

His head snapped up and his golden eyes blazed at her, halting the words before they could leave her mouth. Rink leaped off the love seat with all the sinuous grace of a panther and had the same deadly look of carefully contained violence about him. He left the room without a word. Remorsefully Caroline stared after him. Laura Jane nervously twisted her handkerchief between her fingers.

Granger went after Rink and caught up with him in the foyer. "Rink, I'm sorry." He grabbed for Rink's sleeve and succeeded in stopping him on his way out of the house. "I hated like hell to be the one to read that will. I begged Roscoe to reconsider."

"You should have known better and saved your breath," Rink said bitterly.

"I tried to persuade your mother to keep this house and estate in her name. Long before her death, she signed it over to Roscoe, making it his after she died. At the time I didn't think that was a good idea. Of course, now . . ."

"For the first time in history, there's not a Winston at The Retreat. It belongs to a Dawson now." His tone was scathing as he spoke the name.

"If you think Caroline had anything to do with Roscoe's decision, you're wrong."

"Am I?"

"Yes," the lawyer said emphatically. "She was as ignorant of this as she was of that scholarship."

Rink's head jerked around. "How do you know about that?"

"I know," Granger replied in a low voice. "Just as I know about everything he secretly did for her. I couldn't understand it. I would have thought he was her sugar daddy, except . . . well, he had other girls for that." He eyed Rink keenly. "I finally figured it out. Only lately, though. For years he'd been using her to get to you, hadn't he?"

Rink was admitting nothing. Apparently the lawyer had put together an accurate picture of things, with one vital piece missing. He didn't know about Rink and Caroline those long years ago. "Well, if that was his dying wish, it's been granted. Because he's sure as hell gotten to me this time."

He stalked out, letting the door slam behind him.

In the parlor Caroline watched him go. She had what she had always wanted. The Retreat. But at what price? The man she loved.

"Caroline, what will I do with the cotton gin?" Laura Jane asked in bewilderment as she came up behind her stepmother. "I've only been there a few times in my whole life."

Compassion for the confused young woman acted as a distraction from Caroline's own heartache. She embraced Laura Jane. "You don't have to worry about the gin any more than you ever have. Your father only willed you the profits from it."

"What about you?"

"I'm to be paid a yearly salary for watching over it for you. Granger will advise us both and keep track of everything. So stop worrying. It'll be just as it was before."

"You'll stay here, won't you? You won't leave?"

"You heard Granger. Your daddy gave The Retreat to me." She laid her cheek against Laura Jane's hair and let it absorb the tear that trickled from her eye. She wasn't fooled. Roscoe's motives had been far from benevolent. He had known that by giving her The Retreat, he could ensure that Rink would despise her. She now owned his mother's house. If Rink had ever loved anything, it was The Retreat.

"You'll stay, but Rink won't," Laura Jane said miserably.

"No, Rink won't stay." Then Caroline sent the girl to Haney so she could cry alone.

"What are you doing up?"

"Waiting for you."

"Should I feel honored?"

"I thought we should talk."

"About what?"

"Don't be obtuse, Rink."

"Obtuse?" he asked, his dark brows arching high over his eyes. "Now that you're the lady of the manor you've started using fifty-cent words."

The foyer was dim. It was late. He hadn't returned for dinner and Caroline had no guarantee that he would come back at all. Except for Laura Jane. He wouldn't leave without saying good-bye to her. So she had waited up until she'd heard his pickup in the driveway, then had run downstairs to confront him when he came through the front door. She was standing on the second step. He was on the first. He was looking up at her belligerently.

"I don't blame you for being angry."

"Thanks. I'm glad I have your blessing."

"Rink, please don't."

"Don't what?"

"Don't blame me for Roscoe's will! I had nothing to do with it. I was as flabbergasted as you. Why don't you contest it?"

"Give Roscoe and the town the satisfaction of knowing how much it bothers me? No thank you."

Roscoe's dead! she wanted to scream. When would

the war between father and son end? With forced calm, she said, "No matter what that piece of paper says, The Retreat belongs to you, Rink. It always will. You can live here for the rest of your life if you want to."

He laughed, but it wasn't a happy sound. "The terms of the will only stipulated that Laura Jane could live here for the rest of her life, not me, too. Your hospitality is commendable, Mom," he said, bowing slightly at the waist.

She flinched against his ugly words, but she tilted her chin up. "I can see you're determined to hurt me. All right. If it makes you feel better, go ahead. Call me dirty names."

With lightning reflexes, his hand shot out, caught the tie belt at her waist and hauled her against him. The impact drove the breath out of both of them. He twisted the belt around his fist, grinding his hand against her stomach. His jaw was rigid and hard as he clamped his teeth tight. He closed his eyes.

For only an instant, a heartbeat, he laid his head on her breast and groaned almost soundlessly. Then he released her with a terse expletive.

"I'm sorry, Caroline, I'm sorry." He sighed. "Yes, I'm mad as hell. But not at you. At him. What makes it worse is that there's no getting him back. He's dead and I'm powerless to fight the sonofabitch. There's no way to release the rage inside me."

He banged his fist on the oak banister. Instinctively she reached out to comfort him but withdrew her hand before it could make contact. He would only misconstrue her love as pity and would hate her for it.

"Where did you go tonight?" she asked softly.

He drew in a deep breath that expanded his chest and opened his unbuttoned shirt to reveal a mat of dark curling hair. "Driving. Just driving around town." He looked at her. "This is my home, Caroline. Despite its flaws, I love this town. I could no more turn off my love for it because the people in it aren't perfect than I could love Laura Jane less because she's not perfect. I'll miss it all over again when I have to leave."

"You are leaving, then?"

"In the morning."

Pain knifed through her heart and she clutched her hand to it. Her face crumpled. So soon! He would be gone and this time he might never come back. Now he could send for Laura Jane when he wanted to see her. "Rink, what kind of monster was he? What kind of man leaves no legacy to a son like you?"

He saw her tears and her pain and knew that it was for him, for all that hadn't been. He wanted to hug her to him. He wanted to bury his head between her breasts and breathe the scent of her flesh. He wanted to press his lips into her skin. He wanted her loving comfort. He wanted the temporary forgetfulness making love to her would bring him. At that moment he could almost have begged her for it. But he remembered the words he had been intended to remember.

You'll never have that woman now, Rink. I know you. Your damned stubborn Winston pride won't let you have her. Because I had her first. You remember that. She was my wife and I had her first.

"He left me a legacy, Caroline," he said roughly. "A helluva legacy."

He brushed past her and went upstairs. Slowly she followed and went into her room. Peeling off her robe, she lay down on the bed, thinking that there was no way she would ever rest again.

But when the telephone rang a while later, she was bemused and disoriented with sleep as she picked up the receiver and brought it to her ear.

"Hello."

She listened for no more than an instant before dropping the phone and racing for the door of her room, not even taking time to put on her robe. Her bare feet flew over the hardwood floors in the dark hallway. She barged through the door of Rink's room and raced toward the bed. Her hands landed in the middle of his bare back.

"Rink, Rink, wake up."

He rolled over and stared up at her in disbelief. Her eyes were dilated, her hair was wild, her breasts were heaving, almost spilling out of her nightgown. "What—"

"The gin's on fire!"

Both his feet hit the floor at the same time, almost knocking her over in the process. He grabbed up a pair of jeans that were folded over a chair. "How do you know?"

"Barnes called."

"Is it bad?"

"He couldn't say yet."

"What about the fire department?"

"Already notified."

"What the hell is going on in here?" Haney demanded from the doorway as she knotted the sash of her robe around her waist. "It sounded like y'all were playing basketball and—"

"The gin's on fire."

"Lord o' mercy."

Caroline left Rink's room at a run. He was almost dressed and she intended to go with him. She pulled on the first clothes her hands came into contact with, an old shirt and a pair of denim cutoffs. She crammed her feet into a pair of sandals. Not exactly a firefighting outfit, but she could already hear Rink's boots thudding down the stairs. She bounded after him.

"Rink, wait!"

"You stay here," he shouted over his shoulder as he ran out the front door.

"Like hell." She was right behind him.

"What's going on?" Laura Jane, looking like a doll with her pale pink nightgown and wide eyes, trailed down the stairs.

"The gin is on fire and Rink and Caroline are going to see that it's put out right away," Haney explained.

"The gin is on fire?" she repeated.

Rink's curses would have burned the ears off a sailor as he pumped the motor of his pickup to life. Haney and Laura Jane stood together on the porch, their arms around each other, while Caroline demanded that he unlock the passenger door.

"You're not going!" he roared.

"If you don't open this door, I'll just follow in my car and then you won't know where I am."

Obscenities poured from his mouth, but he pushed open the door and she climbed in.

Steve had heard the ruckus and was crossing the yard with his limping gait. He was pulling on a T-shirt. "What's going on?"

"A fire at the gin," Caroline shouted back.

"I'll help."

"No, Steve!" Laura Jane cried.

"Steve, you stay with Laura Jane and Haney," Caroline told him through the cab window.

"That's right. You stay," Rink said succinctly. The truck was idling now, but Steve was holding onto the door handle and Rink couldn't accelerate.

Meeting Rink's eyes squarely Steve said forcefully, "You'll need my help more than they will. I'm going."

"Steve!" Laura Jane catapulted herself off the porch and flung herself toward him, wrapping her arms around his waist. "Don't go. I'm frightened for you."

"Hey," he said, tilting back her head. "I'm counting on you to keep Haney calm and to have a big breakfast waiting for us when we get back. Okay?"

She beamed up at him. "Okay, Steve. Be careful."

"I will." He kissed her swiftly on the mouth then gently pushed her away before ducking into the cab next to Caroline.

For a moment Rink stared hard at the man, then he jammed the toe of his boot onto the accelerator pedal and the truck screeched out of the drive.

They had much to be grateful for. The fire was a small one and it was contained in only one part of the building. Thanks to Barnes's quick action, the fire engines were already there when Rink arrived.

Heedlessly, Caroline ran into the building to make sure the bookkeeping ledgers were secure in the office. Rink ran after her, caught her around the waist and pulled her out, kicking and protesting. When she was somewhat subdued, he grabbed her by the shoulders and shook her hard.

"Don't ever do anything that stupid again. You scared the hell out of me." After seeing the fierce expression on his face, she wouldn't have thought of disobeying him.

There was plenty to do. Rink supervised the volunteers in moving the bales of cotton still on the loading dock out of harm's way. Steve, despite his leg, worked harder than any of them. Caroline kept spectators out of the way. She reassured them that no one had been in the building. In two hours the flames had been doused.

She and Rink were summoned by the fire chief and sheriff. "It was arson, Rink," the fire chief said. "They made it happen, but your antiquated wiring helped it along."

Rink ran a blackened hand through his hair. "Yeah, I know it was in sad shape. Was there much damage?"

"Nothing compared to what it could have been if we hadn't caught it in time."

"Thank God most of the cotton had already been baled and sent to the warehouse." Now that she had stopped moving, Caroline realized how tired she was.

"Do you know who might have set the fire, Mrs. Lancaster?" the sheriff asked her.

"I do." It was the foreman, Barnes, who answered. "It was one of 'em who set it that called me. I figured he realized what he'd been a part of and chickened out at the last minute. He didn't identify himself, but I'm sure it was one of the guys you fired a few weeks back, Rink."

At the sheriff's request Rink named the men whom he had fired. The peace officer scratched his ear. "Mighty unsavory bunch. What were they doing working for you?"

"They didn't work for me. They worked for my father," Rink said. He glanced down at Caroline and saw the droop of her shoulders. "If that's all for now, I'd like to take Caroline home."

"Sure thing. We'll be in touch when we have something."

Steve opted to ride in the bed of the truck on the way home. He sprawled on his back and didn't move until Rink pulled the pickup to a stop outside the back door. Haney and Laura Jane tumbled out of it as though they'd been waiting for the first sign of them.

Rink went around to open Caroline's door and she all but fell out of the cab and into his arms. Steve eased himself off the tailgate just in time to catch Laura Jane as she ran into his arms, disregarding the soot and grime that covered him.

"Are you all right, Steve?"

"Sure, I'm fine."

"Well, you don't look fine," Haney snapped. "Lordy, Lordy, look at the three of you. I never saw such a motley crew. Y'all go get a bath and I'll have breakfast waiting for you."

They straggled toward the house. Laura Jane released Steve reluctantly and he headed toward his apartment.

"Steve." The veteran halted and turned to face Rink, who had stopped on his way through the back door to address the man. "Thanks," Rink said.

"You're welcome," Steve replied.

Their eyes held for a long time, then they smiled broadly at each other.

Laura Jane's eyes melted with love for her two heroes. Haney sniffed back threatening tears. Caroline squeezed Rink's arm in approval.

Upstairs in her room she peeled off her clothes and let them fall to the tile floor of her bathroom. She would have to throw them away. The smell of smoke would never wash out. She only hoped she could get it out of her hair.

Several doses of shampoo accomplished that. She stood under the shower's pulsing spray and let the warm water wash away the filth and stench of the fire. When at last she turned off the taps, she felt herself again. Stepping over the pile of clothes, too weary to pick them up, she wound her hair in a towel. She had just wrapped herself in a terry-cloth robe when someone knocked on her door.

"Come in."

She had expected Haney or Laura Jane. That it could be Rink never entered her mind. But that was who stepped into her room, holding a tray laden with a steaming carafe of coffee and a glass of orange juice.

"Haney thought you might want to start with this before you come down."

His mind wasn't on what he was saying. The words found their own stumbling way out of his mouth because all his concentration was devoted to the woman with her hair wound in a damp towel and a wrapper barely concealing the curves of her body. Her skin was dewy. She smelled of honeysuckle-scented soap. Her eyes were large and luminous in her face as she stared back at him. There was a slight catch in her voice when she spoke.

"Thank you. The coffee smells good."

She, too, was distracted. Rink's hair was wet and clung in sculpted strands to his head. He was wearing only a pair of tight, faded jeans that rode low beneath his navel and emphasized his sex. His muscled chest was furred with dark, damply curling hair. His eyes glowed warmly as they watched her.

He set the tray on the table, but made no effort to leave. Later it was difficult to say who had moved first. Had he raised his arms a fraction, spread his hands wide as if to receive her? Or had she taken a tentative step first? They didn't remember. All they could recall was that suddenly she was in his arms and he was holding her tight.

Tears streamed from her eyes and she clung to him. All the fear and anxiety of the last few hours rained from her eyes. He whipped the towel from her head and dropped it to the floor. His hands plowed through her wet hair and pressed her face against the hard warmth of his chest. His head bent over her.

"We have unfinished business, you and I, Caroline."

She raised her tear-glossed eyes to his. She smiled softly. "Yes, we do."

"And it's long overdue," he said quietly, letting his thumbs brush the tears from her flushed cheeks.

"Too long overdue."

Reaching behind him, he pushed the door closed.

Chapter 11

THE CATCHING OF THE DOOR LATCH WAS THE ONLY sound in the room. There were no artificial lights on. The sun was just beginning to tint the eastern horizon and only that ethereal light came through the sheer drapes. The lemony perfume of magnolia wafted in from the large tree outside.

She went into his arms, no longer a girl but a woman needing what he had to give, needing to give of herself.

He was warm. So warm. There was a vibrancy in his body that she had recognized the first time she'd seen him. She had always gravitated toward it. She did so now. Wanting that energy to surge through her as it did him, she snuggled close, folding her arms around his lean waist. The hair on his chest tickled her nose. Against the hard curve of his breast, she smiled.

Rink held her tight. His eyes closed with sublime contentment. He explored her through touch. His hands examined the slender curves of her back. They slid below her neat waist to the soft fullness of her derriere.

He cupped her gently in his hands, squeezed lightly, stroked soothingly, pressed arousingly.

His manhood reacted and they both felt it. Their soft gasps of pleasure echoed each other.

"Caroline, Caroline," he breathed into her wet hair before he pushed her away only far enough to duck his head and seal her open lips with his. Their mouths melded together with soft moistness. Their tongues touched. She allowed him the male privilege of dominance and his tongue slid into her mouth. It was a symbolic possession and he made no apology for it. His tongue loved her with lazy thoroughness, darting and flicking, delving and feathering.

All her senses whirred to life. They hummed softly deep inside her. Then, gaining momentum with each thrust of his tongue, they spun faster and faster until her whole body was singing a new song.

She was inundated with sensations. His hair coiled around her fingers as she caressed the back of his head. The soap he had showered with, his brisk, clean cologne, his own special scent, filled her nostrils, her head, intoxicatingly. With gentle plucking motions of her lips against his, she tasted the minty flavor of toothpaste. The soft moans of arousal and the love words he rasped with ragged breaths thrilled her and made her confident.

And she knew that even without intercourse, she was one with this man. Always had been, always would be. Fate had decreed it. From the moment she first saw him twelve years ago, her destiny had been charted.

Lifting his head, he placed his hands on her shoulders and separated himself from her by several inches. Her smoky eyes shimmered as she looked up into his, which were hazy with swirling gold. Slowly, he unzipped his jeans and pushed them down over his hips. Then, his eyes never leaving hers, he peeled them off and tossed them aside. He stood before her naked.

Her eyes drifted over him. Had she been a man, she

would have envied him his physique. He was hard and lean and lithe. His chest was magnificently proportioned. The dark hair that covered it grew in intriguing patterns her fingers longed to explore. The wide fan of body hair tapered to a sleek black ribbon that bisected his flat stomach, whorled around his navel and disappeared into the dense thatch that surrounded his manhood.

It was hard, full, as proud as the man.

Rivers of life coursed through her heart as she studied him. Momentarily she closed her eyes against waves of dizziness. She felt faint. A desire so intense that she thought she might die of it seized her. It was an honest lust, one sanctioned by love because it was only a part of why she loved him.

"Are you all right?"

She opened her eyes and saw him smiling down on her. She laughed in a maidenly, shy way. "Yes. Yes, Rink. I'm all right. It's just that you're so very beautiful and I want you so much."

He kissed her lips with chaste tenderness. "Thank you for the compliment. I'll see what we can do about the other."

He sought the sash of her robe and caught it between his fingers. He tugged on it and it came undone. Moving with deliberate slowness, he inserted his hands beneath the wide lapels and eased the robe aside.

"My God, look at you." His murmur was all but soundless as he gazed at her breasts. As though he couldn't believe all of her could be as perfect, he quickly divested her of the robe and let his eyes roam freely and eagerly over her nakedness. His eyes were wildly excited as they devoured her.

Then his fingertips, lightly, so lightly she could barely feel his touch, took the same path as his eyes. They skimmed the creamy flesh of her breasts, the smooth expanse of stomach, belly and hip. They fanned the dark nest of hair between the slender columns of her thighs. "God, you're beautiful. Beautiful and sweet."

She felt the earnestly whispered words against her flesh as he dipped his knees to lower his face to her breasts. Worshipfully he cupped one in his hand and massaged it. She raised her hands and laid them softly on his hair. She inclined toward him, swaying slightly.

He kissed her. With his thumb he outlined the areola, touched the nipple. It flushed beneath his deft strokes. He looked at it, smiled a quick, fleeting smile, then leaned forward and applied his tongue. Again and again, his tongue circled over the velvety button.

"Rink." His name was a pleading sigh. He heeded it.

He took her nipple between his lips and suckled it. Caroline emitted a sharp, startled cry and arched her back to give him greater access. His cheeks flexed as he drew on her gently. He treated her other breast to the same delicious torment until she was whimpering and clutching at his hair.

"Sweetheart." He buried his face between her breasts as he had longed to do so many times. Splaying his hands wide over her back, he drew her as close as they could get. He hugged her hard for endless moments, then straightened. Adoringly his eyes wandered over her face. He lifted one of her hands to his mouth, kissed the palm and spoke against it. "Touch me. Please."

He carried her hand to that part of him that strained with life, life he wanted to share with her. When he withdrew his hand, hers remained. With her heart in her throat lest she do something displeasing, she closed her fingers around him.

"Ah, God." Whispering her name and endearments like a chant, he covered her hand with his own and instructed her on what gave him pleasure until he couldn't bear any more. His breath was loud in her ear when he groaned, "Caroline, darling . . . better stop."

Trapping her face between his hands, he kissed her fiercely, his tongue plunging deeply. Not ending the kiss, he lowered her to the bed and followed to cover her body with his. She accommodated him and he nestled his hips in the cove of her parted thighs. His belly meshed with hers, his chest settled against the mounds of her breasts.

The kisses he planted on her throat and neck were hot and moist. "If I wait much longer—"

"Don't wait," she said quickly, arching against his hardness.

But it had taken twelve years to get there and Rink wanted to experience all of it without rushing. His hands glided over her breasts. Her nipples were ripe for the tender finessing of his fingertips. He replaced his fingers with his mouth, kissing and licking and nuzzling her breasts until she was almost delirious.

He levered himself above her. His hand smoothed down her stomach, her abdomen, marveling at the fabulous texture of her skin. Then his fingers encountered her fleecy delta and luxuriated in it. He laid his palm over it and let his fingers curve downward between her thighs. They came away dewy with her desire.

He leaned away from her and guided himself to the very threshold of her femininity. They watched each other, watched the play of intense feeling flicker across one another's faces each time the velvety tip of his manhood touched that magic spot. Beyond pride and shame, she touched her hands to his chest and curled her fingers into the mat of hair.

"Now, Rink, please."

His whole body straining, he introduced himself into the warm harbor between her thighs and lowered himself upon her. He pressed deep, deeper, until . . .

His whole body went rigid and his eyes, suddenly clear, speared down into hers. Rapid breathing made a bellows of the chest suspended above her as he braced himself on his arms.

"Caroline." She read her name on his lips. He had spoken it almost inaudibly in his disbelief. "You're a virgin."

"Yes, yes," she cried gladly. Locking her fingers around his neck, she implored him with a sustained pulling motion. "I've always been yours, Rink. Only yours. Claim me."

He paused a moment; then, making a groaning sound of immense gratification, he covered her again and pressed her into the bedding. His thrusts were gentle but imperative. The extended foreplay had made her ready. When her body yielded to him, it caused her but fleeting pain. Her slight gasps were captured by his mouth. They sighed together with supreme emotion as he sank completely into her.

He filled her. She gloved him. And for long moments neither of them moved. They savored the feel of being one, of being as intimate as two separate beings can be, of being grafted together by love and desire and pain.

"I can't believe it. Sweet heaven. Oh, God, Caroline, don't let this be just another of my dreams about you."

"It's no dream, Rink," she whispered into his shoulder. "I can feel you inside me."

Raising his head, he smiled down at her. He kissed her lips lightly. "Can you?" he whispered, and made certain that she could.

Her throat arched as she made a purring sound. "Yes, yes."

He began to move. Out of deference to her, his thrusts were shallow and slow, but no less potent as they drew her closer to a magical sphere.

"Am I hurting you?"

"No, my love, no."

"Caroline . . . Caroline . . ." He could repress his

mounting passion no longer. Reaching the summit, he experienced the highest level of ecstasy he had ever known. It went on and on as his lifeforce pumped into her. And when it was over, he collapsed, spent and sated and loved, into her welcoming arms.

"It sure is taking Caroline and Rink a long time to get down here," Laura Jane complained. She was afraid the breakfast she had helped Haney prepare would get cold and therefore be ruined for Steve.

"Why don't you two go ahead," Haney said.

"I don't mind waiting," Steve offered.

"No. You're starving. I know you are." Laura Jane spooned a heap of fluffy scrambled eggs onto his plate. "How many slices of ham do you want?"

"Two," he said.

"Three," she amended.

Haney set her coffee cup on the countertop. "I'll mosey upstairs and see if I can't hustle them along. I'm sure they'll want to get some sleep, but they really should eat first after being up half the night." She went on her grumbling way, but Steve and Laura Jane barely missed her. They were engrossed with each other.

At the top of the stairs, Haney looked curiously toward Rink's bedroom door. It was open, but when she stuck her head inside he was nowhere to be seen. Nor was he in the adjoining bathroom. At least he didn't answer her when she softly called out to him.

"Humph!" she grunted, planting her hands on her hips. "Now where do you suppose . . . ?" She glanced toward Caroline's room. The door was closed.

The housekeeper's eyes narrowed in contemplation. "I send him up here with a tray for her. Now the tray's disappeared and so has he. Her door is closed and I feel in my bones that it's supposed to stay closed for a while."

She turned toward the stairs again. "Well, it sure isn't any of my business what they're doing in there, but I didn't hear any conversation." At the bottom of the stairs, she glanced back up, nodding her head in approval. "Makes more sense for her to be with Rink than it did for her to marry his daddy, that old buzzard," she muttered as she made her way back to the kitchen.

"Are they coming down?" Laura Jane asked.

"No. Not any time soon, anyway." Haney turned away and began to wash the dishes.

"Why not?"

"They're sleeping, that's why not."

"But they should eat something first. You said so yourself. I'll go wake them and tell them—"

"You sit yourself back down," Haney commanded, turning away from the sink and trailing soapy water onto the floor with an indomitable finger. "They're tuckered out. Now, you mind your own business and see to that hungry young man sitting there."

Hurt by Haney's stern tone, Laura Jane slowly returned to her chair. Steve caught the housekeeper's eye and looked at her inquiringly. He cast a glance toward the ceiling. Haney watched his face as he gradually began to comprehend the situation.

Steve's eyes glinted mischievously. "Laura Jane, after breakfast why don't you come out to the stables with me? You haven't been to see the filly in days."

Laura Jane looked up at him, her lightheartedness returning. "But I thought you would need to sleep this morning."

"Naw," he said expansively. "I'm not tired. If Haney can spare you, I'd like for you to spend the morning with me, help me do some chores."

"Oh, Steve," she said, pressing her hands together. "I'd love that."

Haney exchanged a look with Steve and he winked at her.

"Why didn't you tell me?" Taking up a strand of her hair, Rink whisked it back and forth over his mouth. He was lying on his back. Caroline was on her stomach, leaning over him.

She tweaked clumps of chest hair and traced the swirling patterns with her fingertip. "Because I had to know how much you loved me. If I had told you that your father and I had never been intimate, would you have believed me?"

"I might have. I would have known soon enough."

She shook her head. "I didn't want our first loving to be a test."

His eyes fondly surveyed her face. "I see your point. But what if I had wholeheartedly believed you?"

"Then it would have been easy for you to come to me, Rink." She touched his nipple and watched it bead in response. "But I would never have known the extent of your love. Since you came to me, believing the worst but still loving me, I know that you were willing to sacrifice your pride for your love."

Drawing her down to him, he kissed her long and deeply. When he finally ended the kiss he said, "Not that I particularly want to discuss this right now, but why didn't you ever sleep with Roscoe? Don't tell me any nobility on his part kept you a virgin."

"No, I wouldn't try to convince you of that. I think he intended to consummate the marriage on our wedding night." She closed her eyes and shuddered. "He came into this room. I didn't know how I was going to survive it, loving you as I did." She brought his hand to her cheek and absently rubbed the backs of his fingers over it. "But I had made a bargain and I was willing to live up to it."

She fell silent. Rink stared at the ceiling, not even

wanting to think of her sharing the same space, the same air, with that foul old man. "What happened, Caroline?"

"He kissed me several times. That's all. Then he left me without a word. I was confused. I didn't know what to think. It wasn't too many days later that I began to notice that he was ill. I saw things that I wouldn't ordinarily have seen if I hadn't been living with him. He took huge quantities of stomach remedies, things like that.

"I realized when he didn't come to my room again that he was more than likely impotent and that this stomach ailment was responsible. Of course, I know that for fact now. We never spoke of it. It would have been such a blow to his ego to try and fail that he never tried. We lived platonically."

After a brief silence, he asked, "Would you have ever told me?"

"You mean, to spare us all that antagonism? I don't know, Rink. I asked myself that every day. Why didn't I just tell you and put an end to it?" She ran her finger down the length of his nose. "I have my pride, too. I wanted you to love me in spite of everything."

"It was tough. I wanted you. But every time I thought of you and him, I—"

"Shhh," she said, stopping his words by laying her index finger lengthwise over his lips. "I know. I understand what you were suffering."

"Do you know what he told me after you left the room the night he died?" She shook her head. "I told you he left me a legacy. It was this. He told me that I would never have you because my pride wouldn't let me." His eyes melted into hers and one corner of his lip lifted in a half smile. "He was wrong, wasn't he? He didn't count on my loving you this much." He touched her face. "Then he told me always to remember that you had been his wife, that he had had you first."

She stared at him, astonished. "You mean he deliberately led you to believe that—"

"Yes."

"Oh, my darling." She kissed his cheek softly and brushed strands of hair off his brow. "I thought you just *assumed,* but to think he died wanting you to believe that lie."

Rink laughed scornfully. "He knew me well. It almost worked to keep us apart."

"I'm glad it didn't."

"God," he whispered savagely, "so am I." He wound a handful of her hair around his fist. "When I think of all the hours I tormented myself over it. Every time I thought about you with him, my guts would wrench so hard it hurt. And all that time, you were the same." He touched her lips. "My Caroline of the summer woods. The same. The very same."

He pulled her down and kissed her until they broke away from each other breathlessly. "The same, but different."

She could tell by his softened expression that the discussion about her marriage to his father was over. "Different? How so?" she asked impishly, bending her knees and then raising her feet in the air. She pointed them daintily, like a ballerina. He watched them. They were beautiful feet, slender, high-arched. Her toes were polished a frosty coral shade. He had erotic plans for those toes.

He responded to her flirtatiousness. "For instance . . ." He wedged his hand beneath her. "Your breasts." He took one in his hand and kneaded it.

"What about them?"

"They're larger." He rolled the nipple between his thumb and finger. "This is darker. Not much. But slightly."

"Anything else?"

"You're softer, rounder, much more womanly, but

with the same fawnlike grace of a girl. You're everything
I've dreamed about for years. More."

"You're not disappointed?"

He dragged his tongue along her collarbone and hotly
kissed the top curve of her breast. "No, God no." He
glanced up at her. His eyes were regretful. "But I'm
afraid you were."

"Not I, Rink Lancaster." She kissed his eyebrow.
"Not I."

"But you didn't . . . you know. What all the ladies'
magazines say you're entitled to."

Her three middle fingers played with his lips. "And it
didn't matter a bit. I experienced yours. I watched it, felt
it inside me, knew what it was like for you. I wanted to
witness you loving me."

His arms closed firmly around her. "I do, you know.
Love you. Even though I've acted like a bastard the last
few weeks, said things, insinuated things. The more I
loved you, the more rotten I behaved."

Laughing softly, she laid her head on his chest and
rested her hand low on his stomach. "You don't have to
remind me how rotten you've been at times. But I knew
why. And I forgive you. I love you."

He covered her hand and moved it down. "Mind?"

She cupped her hand over him. "Not at all. I love
touching you."

His hand went to her breast and treasured it. "Let's
sleep for a while."

"You want to sleep?"

"Not really. But I want to wake up with you."

It was shortly after noon when they came downstairs.
Arm in arm, they were smiling at each other, so they
didn't see Laura Jane and Steve until they reached the
wide foyer.

"Steve wants to talk to you, Rink," Laura Jane
announced. She looked like a little girl about to burst for

having to keep a birthday secret. Her eyes were shining.
She couldn't stand still.

Rink looked first at her, then at Steve, who was
nervously rotating the brim of his straw cowboy hat
between his fingers. "Caroline and I are starved. Can it
wait till after lunch?"

"Yes." "No." They answered in unison.

Caroline, sensing what might be on Steve's mind,
diplomatically intervened. "I'm sure we'll all feel better
after lunch." Giving Rink a loving look, she disengaged
her arm from his and went to Laura Jane. "Does Haney
have it ready?" She steered the young woman toward the
dining room. "What does Steve want to talk to Rink
about?" she asked softly.

"Us getting married," Laura Jane whispered back.

"Then I suggest we wait until after he's had something to eat." Caroline squeezed her arm in affectionate
support.

During lunch, Haney brought the cordless telephone
extension into the dining room. "It's the sheriff."

He had called to say that the arsonists had been
arrested. One of them, the one who admitted to calling
Barnes and warning him of the fire, had broken down
and confessed, implicating the others. "It won't do them
much good to plead innocent. I figure we'll have formal
confessions from the other three by suppertime."

"Thanks, sheriff. Be sure that their families are taken
care of, food, rent money, whatever they need for the
next several months and send me the bill."

He hung up and reported the news to the others. As
soon as the sherbet dishes had been cleared away, Laura
Jane excitedly herded everyone into the study. "Go
ahead, Steve," she said, nudging him.

His Adam's apple slid up and down as he swallowed.
"Rink, with your blessing, I want to marry Laura
Jane."

Giving away nothing of what he thought of the

request, Rink sat down in the deep leather chair behind the wide desk. He took a sip of his iced tea, which he had carried with him from the dining room. "And without my blessing?"

Steve's eyes never wavered. "I still want to marry her."

Rink studied the man for a long, tense time. Neither pair of eyes moved from the other. Finally Rink said, "Ladies, will you excuse us please? And, Caroline, please close the door behind you."

"How did you know I'd be here?"

"A hunch." He pushed aside the branches of a pine sapling and came into the clearing. She was sitting beneath a tree, her legs tucked under her, a book resting on her lap. She hadn't been reading it but had been staring into space when he came through the trees. He went to the tree, propped his hand on the trunk and looked down at her upturned face. "Don't you know it's dangerous for you to be out in the woods alone?"

"Why? These are my woods."

"But some sex-crazed man might come along and ravish you."

"That's what I'm counting on."

Laughing, he dropped down beside her and gathered her in his arms. He kissed her lightly several times all over her face, then pressed his mouth with firm possessiveness over hers. She indulged him for only a moment before pushing him away. "Wait. First I want to know what you told Steve."

"I told him if he ever did anything to hurt her, I'd kill him."

"You didn't!"

He shrugged and grinned at her devilishly. "Well, I said it in a nice way."

"But you did consent to their getting married?"

"Yes, I did," he said solemnly.

She hugged him hard. "Rink, I'm so glad."

He eased her away to look at her. "Are you? Do you really think that will be best for Laura Jane?"

"Yes, I do. She loves him. And you don't have to worry about him hurting her. He idolizes her. He's never talked about his past, but I get the feeling that it was dismal. Then the war and losing his leg. I'm sure Laura Jane is like a fairy princess to him. He can't quite get over being allowed to touch her."

"He sounded sincere," Rink said musingly. "I made the condition that Laura Jane would always live at The Retreat. I don't think she'd adjust to another home. He agreed, but insisted that he be given more responsibility. He's touchy about her being an heiress and him a hired hand."

"I would expect that of him. He works harder than anyone to compensate for his handicap."

"He made no bones about the way he feels. He told me, or maybe *warned* is a better word, that their marriage would be a real one." His brow furrowed. "Do you think Laura Jane can tolerate sleeping with a man?"

Caroline laughed and burrowed her nose in his neck. "I get the impression that Laura Jane has been chasing Steve around the stable for months and that he's been the one trying to save her virtue."

"But does she understand the responsibility that goes with sex?"

"Rink." Placing her hands on his cheeks and capturing his full attention, she said, "Laura Jane was born with a deficiency for learning. But she has a woman's emotions and a woman's body. No one should deprive her of what that body needs, any more than it should be deprived of nourishment or air. She'll be happier now than she's ever been. He loves her. He'll cherish her. They'll work the rest out between them."

She could feel his tension ebbing, and the taut lines in

his face began to relax. It thrilled her to know how much he valued her opinion.

"What about you?"

"Me?" she asked.

"What about your needs all these years and the deprivation you imposed on yourself?"

"I survived on memories and dreams. Memories of you in this place. Dreams of what I thought could never be."

He inched down onto the soft grass with her and began to unbutton her blouse. "You thought about me? Every once in a while?"

"Every day. Every hour. And even if I had never seen you again, I would have been thinking of you the moment I died."

His eyes closed briefly with the emotion that swept him. When they opened, they shone down into hers. "I hear thunder. Or is that my heart?"

She smiled. He had said almost those exact words once. "Thunder. It's going to rain."

"Do you mind?"

"I prefer it."

"Sweet, sweet," he whispered across her mouth. "God, I love you."

She helped him take off his shirt. He stood and she was an avid audience as he unbuckled his belt, unzipped his slacks and stepped out of them. Hooking his thumbs in a brief pair of light blue underwear, he peeled it down his hard, sinewy thighs.

His nakedness matched the wilderness setting. In the darkening light, a harbinger of rain, his body stood bold and primeval. Even as she watched, raindrops began to fall on his bronze skin.

Kneeling beside her, he pulled her to a sitting position and took off her blouse. Her brassiere was lacy and sheer, a contrast to those she had worn years ago. Through the silk confection, he touched her breasts. He

teased the nipples until they strained against the tenuous
veil.

"Look at what you've done," she said scoldingly as
she shimmied out of the garment after he had unsnapped
it. "Aren't you ashamed of yourself?"

"Yes," he replied contritely, looking anything but.

He unbuttoned her full peasant skirt and pulled it off,
leaving her only in her panties. Then he bent to work on
the leather thongs of her sandals, which wound seductively around her ankles. When her feet were free of the
sandals, he caressed them, massaging her arches and
wringing the toes between his strong fingers. She
propped herself on her elbows and watched this loving
ritual in wonderment. But when he lowered his head and
his tongue touched the tips of her toes, her breasts
trembled with passion.

"Rink," she cried softly, and fell back onto their bed
of verdant undergrowth.

He braced himself above her. She caught handfuls of
his now damp hair and twisted it around her fingers as his
mouth fused hotly with hers. He enjoyed her mouth as he
would a piece of luscious fruit. Then, as softly as the
falling raindrops, his lips skipped across her face, paused
at her ears. His tongue darted playfully about her
earlobe. He kissed her neck, her chest.

The rain fell on her breasts, making them shine wetly.
He sipped up the gathering moisture. Against her cool
skin, his mouth was hot when it drew a budded nipple
inside. "I never forgot the way you taste. Never."

Restlessly, she shifted beneath him, making a cradle
of her femininity to hold his hard maleness. They fit
together and their sighs spiraled above them. He rubbed
against her suggestively but didn't claim her. She called
his name plaintively.

"Not yet," he whispered against the quivering flesh
of her stomach. "This is for you."

He moved lower, counting each rib with a kiss. His

mouth drifted down to her navel and blessed it with a kiss that made her arch and moan. The tip of his tongue dipped into the shallow dimple repeatedly. Then, employing his teeth and nose and chin, he nudged her panties down over her hips and thighs and legs until she could kick them free.

Caroline felt she would shatter from the pressure building inside her. She didn't think she could stand any more. But he had only begun. His lips drifted over the tuft of dark hair, disturbing it with his light, rapid breath. His tongue discovered the grooves where her thighs joined her abdomen and followed their slanting decline.

"Rink . . ." His name stumbled from her trembling lips as she clutched at his hair.

Gently his hands positioned her, parted her, touched her. But nothing could have prepared her for the sweet kiss he pressed there. His lips were loving, his tongue daring, and together they brought her to a pitch of ecstasy that robbed her of thought. He tantalized and tasted until her whole body began to quake. He had kindled a volcano inside her. When he knew it was about to erupt, he rose above her and drove himself deeply inside.

The hands that gripped his hips, the thighs that enclosed his, the ragged words of love she spoke were his encouragement. His body pulsed inside hers, sparing nothing, driving them higher and higher with each thrust until they exploded together in a shower of dazzling light.

When the crisis passed and they returned to the world, the light had faded. They were in a welcome world of shadow and cloud. They were hidden by a silvery fog that whirled as crazily as had their hearts and minds only moments ago. And their entwined bodies were bathed by the softly falling rain.

Chapter 12

THE BRIDE WORE WHITE. THE SILK DRESS WAS SIMPLY cut but exquisitely fashioned for her slender figure. She didn't look consumed by it as she might have in a traditional wedding dress with yards of fabric and lace. She wore pale stockings and white slippers. The sides of her dark hair were pulled away from her center part and held back by twin white camellias, her favorite flower. She was loveliness personified. Her eyes were glowing, testifying to her happiness. She showed no signs of nervousness.

Her groom did. He fidgeted and constantly cleared his throat and shifted to support himself on his good leg. He tugged at the knot of his necktie, unfamiliar apparel for him. It had been suggested that he not bother dressing up for the occasion, but he had insisted. He wanted this day to be a memorable one for his bride. He wanted everyone to know that this wedding was official and that both of them were well aware of what they were doing and proud of it.

Caroline touched Steve's arm reassuringly as they stood below waiting for the bride. He smiled at her gratefully. But when the minister's wife began to play the wedding march on the grand piano in the back parlor, Steve had eyes only for Laura Jane. And she for him. Her huge brown eyes sought him out in the foyer and stayed on him as she descended the curving stairs on her brother's arm.

Few had been invited to witness the nuptials. Rink and Caroline. The minister, who had so recently officiated at the bride's father's funeral, and his wife. Granger. And Haney, who wept through the entire recitation of vows. Fortunately, the ceremony was brief.

Steve pressed a tender kiss on his new wife's lips and immediately discarded his necktie.

"Steve." He turned and took Rink's outstretched hand. "Welcome to the family."

Steve's face wrinkled into a broad grin as he pumped his brother-in-law's hand. "Thanks, Rink. I'm very glad to be a part of it."

"Congratulations, Steve," Caroline said and kissed him lightly on the cheek. "Laura Jane." Caroline hugged the young woman tight. "Always be happy."

"I will, I will," she said eagerly, bobbing her head. "Let's have refreshments now. I think Steve needs a cold drink."

Everyone was laughing as they filed into the dining room, where Haney had outdone herself with a buffet of ham and turkey, innumerable salads, vegetable casseroles, a traditional three-tiered wedding cake and other desserts. There was coffee and a citrus punch. When Rink was seen spiking Steve's punch glass from a decanter of bourbon, even the minister laughed. It was a festive, lighthearted party, and for Laura Jane's sake, Caroline was glad.

After everyone had eaten, the photographer grouped them for formal pictures. Steve's discarded necktie had disappeared and had to be found and replaced. Caroline brushed Laura Jane's hair and touched up her lip gloss. By the time the photographer was done, no one could see for the spots that danced before their eyes.

The guests departed and the family was left with the ravaged buffet. The bride and groom retired to the upstairs. During the week preceding the wedding, Steve's things had been moved into Roscoe's old room. The couple would share it since it was larger than Laura Jane's bedroom. Caroline planned to redecorate it and make it more appealing and personally theirs.

After they had helped Haney clean up, Rink and Caroline went to a movie in town. When they came in, the house was quiet and dark. They crept up the stairs, hoping not to disturb the newlyweds. They went into Rink's room. After closing the door behind them, he switched on a dim lamp beside the bed.

"I'm getting tired of all this sneaking around," he complained. "I hate one of us having to get out of bed and run across the hall at dawn. Why can't you just move into this room with me, or let me move into yours?"

"Because."

"That's a real good reason." He had already taken off his boots and shirt and was working on his pants. "Maybe I should write it down so I'll remember it."

"Please don't make fun of me. I don't want anyone to know yet."

"They already know," he said. He was down to his underwear. He collapsed into the leather easy chair that was his favorite spot in the house.

Caroline drew her sleeveless cotton sweater over her head and peered at him in astonishment. "Do you think so?"

Speechlessly, he nodded and watched her carefully fold the sweater and drape it over the back of a chair. Her brassiere was flesh-toned. There was a rose woven into the stretchy sheer fabric. Its petals flowered open around her nipple. As though to make up for all the years she had had nothing pretty, she always wore beautiful lingerie.

Finding his voice, Rink said, "Steve and Haney know for sure. They'd be blind not to, Caroline. For twelve years I've had to keep it a secret that I love you. I don't think I've been too discreet the last few days. I'm happier than I've ever been in my life. And it shows, dear heart."

She blushed as she stepped out of her skirt, revealing a pair of tap pants that matched her brassiere, a lacy garter belt and a pair of silk stockings. His manhood responded significantly.

"I don't like the sneakiness either, but for my sake let's not let everyone in on the secret. I'm flouting decency as it is."

She picked up her hairbrush and lifted it through her hair. The lamplight caught the falling strands and burnished them with red highlights. Her back was to him. It curved with supple grace down either side of her spine. The lace border on the tap pants barely concealed the bottom curve of her derriere. Between that lace and the top of her stockings was an expanse of thigh he ached to touch. "How are you flouting decency?" he asked with a thick voice.

Taking a small plastic bottle from her purse, she dropped a dollop of lotion in her palm. She rubbed it into her hands and smoothed it onto her arms. God! She was driving him insane.

"Because legally you're my stepson."

"And illegally?"

She turned toward him, saw him sprawled in the chair, saw his body, hard and male. Her smile was both shy and wanton. "Illegally, you're my lover."

"Come here." Quickly he freed himself of the underwear and threw it to the floor.

She went to him and stood docilely as he rid her of the

tap pants, leaving the garter belt riding low on her hips
and the garters stretching down the columns of her thighs
to the top of the stockings. He squeezed his hand into the
top of one stocking and gently pinched the tender flesh.
Her fingers curved around his ears as he leaned forward
to kiss her thighs, her belly, her stomach.

He guided her down to straddle his lap and his hard
virility was sheathed by her mystery. Her arms went
around his neck and her back arched, bringing her
breasts to his seeking lips. He kissed the rose design,
probed its center with his tongue until it gave birth to
another bud. His lips closed around the hard bead and he
massaged it with his tongue. The brassiere finally fell
away beneath his deft fingers. He buried his face in the
fragrant cleft.

Her thighs tightened around his as she rocked above
him with slow rotations of her hips. His hands stroked up
the backs of her thighs to her hips, where he caressed the
soft flesh and held her fast. Clasping his head tightly to
her breasts, she bent low over it and whispered love
words in tempo to his upward thrusts. He reached higher
and higher, to the very gate of her womb. Then, when
she trembled with her fulfillment, he melted her with his
fire.

Caroline slumped against him and for long minutes
they didn't move. Finally he ran one hand down the back
of her head. He kissed her shoulder. When she still
didn't move, he asked softly, "Is something wrong?"

"In a chair? What have I turned into?"

Smiling, he nuzzled her ear. "A generous, gorgeous,
loving woman with all the sexual passion a young man
dreamed of." He hugged her tightly. "I used to sit in
this chair and dream of you. This is where I did most of
my fantasizing of what it would be like when I made love
to you." He brushed her cheek with his knuckles. "It's
far superior to my fantasies, Caroline."

She raised her head. Her eyes looked like still, moonlit lakes. "Is it?"

"Yes." He touched her hair, her mouth, her breasts. "I still can't believe this is real."

"I can't believe this is *me*, behaving like this. But then you've always been a bad influence on me."

The loving glow in his eyes was replaced by a mischievous gleam. "Aren't'cha glad?"

"Uh-huh." Matching his light mood, she rolled her hips forward.

He groaned theatrically. "Good God, Caroline. Are you trying to kill me? Can't we at least get to the bed first?"

Later, wrapped together under the light covers, Rink found her ear in the darkness and whispered, "You know, if Haney had a bed partner, we could make this into a club." She yanked several chest hairs and he yelped softly. "I only meant that with Steve and Laura Jane in one bedroom and us—"

"I know what you meant." Her smile turned into a yawn. "I can imagine how Steve is feeling right now, but I wonder what Laura Jane thinks of marriage."

They didn't have to wait long to find out. The next morning the newlyweds joined Caroline and Rink at breakfast. They stood in the kitchen doorway with their arms around each other. Steve was wearing a comically sheepish grin. Laura Jane was absolutely radiant. To them all she enthusiastically declared, "I think everybody in the whole world should get married."

Reconstruction had already begun on the gin. Caroline was grateful that Rink was around. She wouldn't have known where to begin the cleanup after the fire. No sooner had that been accomplished than he began to talk about refurbishing. He went over all his plans with her, and she approved them. They included scrapping the old equipment and buying new, replacing the wiring and generally making Lancaster Gin one of the most modern mills in the country.

"We've made a tremendous profit this year. The bank is willing to grant us a long-term loan for the improvements at the lowest interest rate possible. We should take advantage of their generosity."

"I agree."

They worked long hours in the sultry summer heat, but it was invigorating to them both. Too often they had to control their urges to touch each other. They were watched and they knew it and they didn't want to give people any more to talk about than they already had. Gossips were speculating as to why Rink hadn't yet gone back to Atlanta. That worried Caroline, too.

"Rink?" They were taking a short break in the office at the gin.

"Hmmm?" He rubbed a cold soft drink can back and forth over his forehead.

"When are you going back to Atlanta?" She tried to sound casual but knew she had failed when he lowered the can and looked at her sharply.

He took a sip of his drink. "Trying to get rid of me?" he asked teasingly.

Her eyes softened with love. "Of course not," she spoke quietly. "I just wondered why you're doing all this for the gin. I'm being paid a salary, but there's no reason for you to put so much time and energy into it."

He set the can down on a coffee table piled high with outdated trade magazines. Standing, he stretched and went to the window where he could see workers unloading building supplies from a flatbed truck. "This gin means a lot to me whether Roscoe wanted it to or not. I don't profit from it financially, thanks to his will, but it's still of vital interest to me. The gin belonged to my mother's family before Roscoe took it over and put his name on it. Since it's part of my heritage and bears my name, I have to care about it. And if those reasons don't seem valid enough, let's just say that I'm protecting my sister's legacy.''

''I love you.''

He turned swiftly to face her. Her pronouncement was unexpected and seemingly out of context. ''Why? I mean, what made you say so now?''

''Because any other man would have left long ago, bitter and enraged over the circumstances.''

''That's what he wanted me to do. Even now I refuse to buckle under to him.''

''Is that the only reason you're still here, to defy Roscoe?''

He smiled and came to her. Taking her hand, he pulled her to her feet and backed her into a corner between the wall and a file cabinet. The narrow space afforded them a modicum of privacy from anyone who might come in. ''You have a little to do with my hanging around,'' he drawled and began to kiss her.

He tasted salty. He was sweaty. He was thoroughly masculine. She loved the sheer maleness of him. Everything feminine about her responded to it. Inching closer, she pressed her aroused body to his. His lips slid to her neck to nibble and tease. His hand covered her breast and caressed it.

''You can't take that kind of liberty,'' she murmured. ''I'm the boss.''

''Not my boss. I don't officially work here, remember?''

She moaned softly as his fingers idly traced her nipple through her blouse. Bending his head, his teeth pulled free the first button and his mouth savored the warm flesh beneath. ''But I still exercise a certain amount of control,'' she said breathlessly.

''Not over me you don't.'' Her hand went to the fly of

his jeans and pressed the hardness there. "All right. So I lied," he said roughly. "You exercise a helluva lot of control."

"I always thought this place was a honky-tonk." Caroline looked around the dim interior of the tin building.

"It is. But it has the best barbecue east of the Mississippi. An old family recipe imported from Tennessee. What will you have, baby back pork ribs or sliced beef brisket?"

"Can I lick my fingers?"

"Sure."

"Then I want the ribs."

They smiled as the waitress sashayed off with their order. They had to shout over the blaring music coming from the gaudy jukebox in the corner. Couples danced on a sawdust-strewn dance floor, bobbing a two-step or swaying together in a clenching embrace, depending on how romantically involved they were.

A cloud of tobacco smoke hovered just under the ceiling. From the cheaply paneled walls, flashing pink-and-blue neon lights touted various brands of beer. A model with a smile as voluminous as her hairdo and bosom adorned a poster for a radiator shop. Behind the bar, the face of a clock wavered beneath a moving waterfall. That electrically animated marvel made Caroline slightly nauseated if she looked at it too long.

She and Rink were enjoying themselves. They had made a habit of inventing places to go for a few hours every night just to give Steve and Laura Jane time alone in the house. Steve had told them confidentially that he had mentioned a honeymoon to Laura Jane, but the thought of traveling too far afield was frightening to her. She had adjusted to married life beautifully. He didn't want to make an issue of a honeymoon.

"Did you come here often?" Caroline asked, resting her forearms on the table and leaning toward Rink.

"All the time. When I was in high school and too young to buy beer, all of us guys would pile into one car and come out here. They didn't have any qualms about selling it to us. Daddy told me—" He broke off suddenly and Caroline knew it was because he had called Roscoe by the familiar form of address.

"Go on," she prodded gently. "What did he tell you?"

"He told me that during Prohibition this place was a hotbed of bootlegging. More illegal whiskey was run in and out of here than anywhere else in the state."

He became meditative as he absently toyed with the salt shaker. Caroline covered his hand, bringing his eyes up to hers. "It wasn't always bad between the two of you, was it? Weren't there a few good times that you could remember and forget the rest?"

He smiled sadly. "There were a few, yes. Like the time I wanted to smoke one of his cigars. I was about twelve. He let me. I got sicker than a dog and he thought that was hilarious. He teased me about it for years later, but I didn't mind. Then there was the time I got caught painting 'Go Wildcats' on the rival school's team bus. Roscoe defended the whole bunch of us to the school board, reminding them that boys were supposed to raise hell or they wouldn't be normal."

His brow wrinkled. "There's a pattern here, Caroline, that I've never thought of before. If I was involved in some kind of mischief, Roscoe approved. He liked me best when I was in trouble. It was when I stood up for something right that he couldn't stomach me. He wanted me to be like him, a mover and shaker just a little beyond the pale of morality. I don't claim to be a saint, but I've never swindled anybody or hurt anyone just for the hell of it." He met her eyes full on. "I want you to know this. I regret very much that he and I didn't love each other.''

"I know you wanted to love him, Rink.''

"If I ever have sons or daughters, I'll love them for what they are. I'll never try to change them. I swear that.''

They clasped their hands tightly across the table and didn't release them until their food arrived.

By the time they had eaten, the place was getting rowdy. There were more drinkers and dancers than diners. The noise level had risen to a din. As soon as Rink got their check from the waitress, they made their way to the cash register at the end of the bar. Their tab was being tallied up when Caroline heard the first slurred voice.

"Must be nice, huh, Virgil, to move right in where Daddy left off?''

Rink's hands, which had been leafing through a roll of currency, became ominously still. Caroline saw the vein in his temple begin to tick and his jaw bunch in anger.

Virgil giggled. "Reckon you're right, Sam. Ain't nuthin' like havin' your own daddy work out all the kinks for you, so to speak.''

Rink calmly laid his money on the bar. "Rink, let's go.'' Caroline grabbed his arm. He shook her off like a pesky fly. She glanced around self-consciously. Someone had turned down the volume on the jukebox. All the dancers were suddenly still. Others at the bar moved away from Virgil and Sam, who were obviously too drunk or too stupid to know that they had just ignited a very short fuse. As Rink turned to face them, his eyes smoldered with a yellow light that made Caroline shrink in fear.

"What did you say?'' His lips barely moved as he asked his simple question in a deadly quiet voice. One of the men poked the other and they fell against each other laughing.

"Mr. Lancaster, sir," the manager of the tavern ventured, "they're new to town. They don't know nothing about your family. They're just shooting off their mouths. Don't pay them no mind. I'll throw them out."

He could have saved his courage and his breath, for Rink ignored him. "What did you say?" he demanded more loudly. He advanced on the two men, who were teetering on their barstools.

"Well, we was just sayin' how lucky you was to have had your daddy warm up your bed for you before he kicked off."

Caroline raised a trembling hand to cover her mouth and tried to avoid the curious eyes that were aimed at her. She knew they were remembering that for all her finery, she was still Pete Dawson's girl. Trash.

Virgil could barely talk for laughing at Sam's clever way with words. "I'll bet the sheets didn't even cool off none before you moved right in. Did your daddy teach her some good tricks, sonny? Does she do for you what she—"

Virgil never got to finish his question. He never remembered even starting it. Rink's rocketing fist crunched into his chin, lifted him off the stool and sent him flying into the ring of spectators. He was unconscious before he hit the floor.

Sam watched his friend's misfortune with open-mouthed astonishment. He got off his stool waveringly. He smiled sickly at Rink.

"He . . . he . . . we didn't mean nuthin' by it, Mr. . . . uh . . . Lancaster, sir. We was just funnin' with—"

He saw the fist coming, tried to dodge it and took the blow full on his cheekbone. He howled in pain and fell to his knees. Rink stood over him, feet braced wide apart, breathing harshly, his fists balling and releasing at his sides.

"Apologize to the lady," he said in a soft rasp. "Now."

Sam rocked back and forth in agony, both his hands clutching the side of his face as though to hold it together. The only sounds he could utter were guttural whines.

"Apologize to the lady," Rink roared.

Caroline rushed to him and grabbed his arm. "Please, Rink," she pleaded earnestly, "let's go. He can't speak. It doesn't matter. Just get me out of here. I can't stand everyone looking at me. Please, let's go!"

He shook his head as though to clear it. Then he abruptly turned toward the cash register, angrily tossed down a handful of bills and, while stuffing the rest of his money into his jeans pocket, took Caroline's upper arm and dragged her with him as he pushed through the door.

He sped home, but the pickup lacked the responsive engine of his sports car. He cursed it when it sputtered and choked and wouldn't go as fast as he wanted. When they got home, he came around to her side and opened the door but didn't wait for her to get out before he stamped into the house. She followed and found him pacing the library like a caged cat. Judiciously she closed the door behind her as she entered the room and dropped her purse into the nearest chair.

He glared up at her. "Do you see what everybody thinks? They think you slept with my father."

"I was his wife. What are they supposed to think?"

He cursed imaginatively and ran his hands through his hair. "I guess I'm the laughingstock of the whole damn town. What a kick everybody must be getting out of this. Me taking over where my old man left off."

His selfishness overwhelmed her. "Have you given any thought to how *I* feel, to what they think of *me?*" She splayed a hand wide over her chest. "They all thought I had seduced your father into marrying me. Now they think I've seduced my stepson. Whatever they say about you can't compare to the ugly things they say about me. I'm poor trash, remember? To them I always was and always will be. And it has nothing to do with how moral I am or am not. It's a stigma I was born with.''

"But as Roscoe's wife you were about to overcome that stigma, weren't you?''

She tried to avoid answering, but when she saw the smirking knowledge on his face, she had to respond. "Yes.''

"Well, maybe for your sake it's a damn shame he died," he said cruelly. "At least you came out on top financially. I'm sure the contents of his will are common knowledge by now. Everybody knows I was left out of it. The whole town probably thinks I'm mooching off you because you've got The Retreat.''

"Be reasonable, Rink. That's impossible. Everybody knows how successful your airline is.''

"They all know how much I love this place, too. They probably think I'm playing your stud just so you'll keep me around.''

She recoiled as though he had slapped her. "I hate it when you talk like that.''

"Why not talk about it? Let's face facts. Isn't that what I'm doing?" he asked. "What purpose am I serving around here? Laura Jane's got Steve to take care of her. Haney bustles around them like a mother hen. All I'm doing is keeping the mistress of the house happy in bed.''

"Don't you dare sound self-sacrificing. You're happy, too." She cursed the tears of anger and hurt that filled her eyes.

"I was until I realized that everybody thinks I'm taking Roscoe's place in your bed.''

"But you're not! You know that, Rink.''

"The net effect is the same.''

"Because everyone thinks I slept with your father?''

"Yes." The word exploded from his mouth like a missile. The aftershock that followed was a deadly silence. Finally Rink said, "Even dead he's keeping us apart."

Caroline rounded on him, indignation lifting her head to a haughty angle. "Not him. *You*. Your damned pride. Your pride is keeping us apart this time."

"And what about yours?" he flared back.

"Mine?" she asked, aghast.

"Yes, yours."

"What have I ever had to be proud about?"

"That you went off and got yourself a college degree. That you married the richest man in the county. That you live in his mansion. That you're socially above all those who used to look down their noses at you."

"I told you when you first came back that I loved living here."

"But what if everyone knew that the only reason Roscoe married you was to get back at me, that your marriage was a sham? Could you hold your head quite so high then?"

Her guilty silence was as good as a confession. She sank into a chair. Rink's shoulders sagged. In a calmer voice he said, "I can't stand their thinking you were my father's lover and you couldn't stand their knowing otherwise." He threw his head back and laughed. "God, what a wizard of revenge he was. If his first trick didn't work, keeping us apart by assuring me he'd slept with you first, he had this to fall back on."

He went to the door. "Much as I hate to admit it, Caroline, we've played right into his hands. Just as he knew we would."

There was a heart-wrenching finality to the way he pulled the door closed after leaving the room.

Chapter 13

"I'D LIKE TO TURN THAT BOY OVER MY KNEE, THAT'S what I'd like to do," Haney grumbled as she stripped the linens from Caroline's bed. "If any young'un ever needed a whipping . . ."

Caroline sat at her dressing table, trying to massage away a headache. It wasn't working. Her whole body ached as though she had been bludgeoned. And she had been. By her argument with Rink.

The housekeeper heaped the linens in the middle of the floor and unfolded fresh ones. They popped crisply as she flapped them over the bed. With military neatness, she tucked them under the mattress. "Didn't he say anything to you last night, give you any indication that he was going to sneak out of here like a thief in the night?"

"No, he . . . uh . . . We talked for a while. He came upstairs, and a few minutes later I went to bed. I didn't know he was gone until you woke me this morning."

"I taught that boy better manners and his mama did

before me. Imagine just packing up and leaving without so much as a how-dee-doo. Driving that new pickup to the landing strip and taking off in his airplane. I swear to goodness, I don't know what got into him.''

Caroline wished that for once the housekeeper wouldn't be so talkative. The last thing she wanted to talk about was Rink. Her wounds were too new. Every mention of his name opened them up and made her heart bleed. ''I'm sure he had neglected his business in Atlanta for as long as he felt he could.''

Haney threw her a sardonic look. I knew which way the wind was blowing, she wanted to tell the younger woman. She was dying to know what had happened between them to cause Rink to leave so suddenly. For weeks they had been walking around all goo-goo-eyed toward each other. Something had caused Rink to hightail it, and that something had to do with Caroline. She bent down and hoisted up the load of laundry. ''I don't know what I'm going to tell Laura Jane. It'll break her heart that he didn't even say good-bye.''

''You said he left her a letter.''

''That isn't quite the same, is it?''

Caroline's graciousness had worn out. She stood and went to her closet, gathering up clothes to take into the bathroom, silently hinting that she wanted to be left alone. ''She won't mind Rink's leaving so much, now that she has Steve to take care of her.''

''And who's going to take care of you?''

Caroline halted on her way through the bathroom door and spun around to face the intuitive housekeeper. Haney only gave her an arch look before ambling out with an air of superiority, her arms full of bed linens.

Caroline showered and dressed mechanically. She wasn't interested in how she looked. Rink wouldn't be there to see her. She would go on as normal, go to the gin and check on the progress of the reconstruction. It would be more important than ever for her to appear in charge and to stand firm on every decision. Some employees might use Rink's abdication as an excuse to slack off on the work.

When she arrived at the gin, she learned that Rink hadn't been all that impulsive when he'd left for Atlanta during the night. Barnes met her in the office.

He stood when she entered, shuffling his feet uneasily and never letting his eyes meet hers. "Rink—Mr. Lancaster, that is—called me from Atlanta first thing this morning."

She tried to appear unaffected by the news, but her hand was trembling when she pulled open the desk drawer to put her purse inside. "Oh?"

Barnes cleared his throat. "Yes, ma'am. And he said that I was to help you in any way I could to keep things running smooth, and all. He told me to call him if anything irregular-like came up."

"Thank you, Barnes," she said quietly. He hadn't completely deserted her. He still cared enough to see that she wouldn't be left with an inoperative gin. On the other hand, he could merely be protecting Laura Jane's inheritance.

The foreman twisted his hat in his hand. "You know, me and the guys . . . well, we sorta got used to having Rink around again. 'Course he was just a kid when he left here the first time, but we all liked him even then. He was always looking out for us, know what I mean? Not like his daddy, meaning no disrespect. But Rink was always taking up for us workers."

"Yes, I know what you mean, Barnes."

"Well," he said, backing toward the door and mentally cursing himself. Hell, he hadn't meant to make her cry. "If you need anything, you just holler, you hear, Mrs. Lancaster?"

"Yes. Thank you."

When he was gone, Caroline went to the window and surveyed the landscape. Summer's demise was imminent. The flowers and trees were no longer lush. They were drying up, curling and brittle with fatigue, waiting to die. That was how she felt. For those precious weeks she and Rink had been together, her heart had celebrated life. Now it felt as shriveled as the last brave blossoms of summer clinging to life.

"It was never meant to be, Caroline," she whispered to herself. Were they the proverbial star-crossed lovers, doomed before they were even born? Did fate arrange such human catastrophes? Or were they paying for the sins of their fathers, living out a biblical prophesy?

The cause didn't matter because the end was irreversible. Rink had been right. They were both too proud. She had liked what being a Lancaster meant. Rink knew her well enough to know that she wouldn't want to give that up. And for fear that it would look like begging, he would never come to her as long as she owned The Retreat.

Her head came up. Her heart began to pound.

As long as she owned The Retreat.

Could she give it up? What did the house mean to her without Rink in it? That had always been part of its mystique, part of what drew her to it. It was where Rink Lancaster lived. Even when she shared the house with Roscoe, she would walk the halls and imagine Rink there, as a child, as an adolescent, as a young man. Without him it was just a collection of lovely rooms surrounded by four walls.

It had never belonged to her. Always to him. Legal jargon written down on a piece of paper would never change that.

But could she give it up?

A soft knock on the study door brought her head up from the ledgers. "Come in."

Granger stepped into the shadowed room where only the green-shaded lamp on Roscoe's desk shed any light.

"Haney said you were in here. I hope I'm not disturbing you."

Caroline smiled at the attorney. "Come in, Granger. I welcome the interruption."

"You're burning midnight oil. Is that necessary?"

Yes, it was necessary. Because when she didn't bury herself in work she thought of Rink. She thought of him anyway, but at least staying busy helped alleviate the pain. In the month since he had left, the pain had become less sharp, changing into a steady dull ache for which there was no relief. "This bookkeeping has to be done sometime. At the gin I'm constantly interrupted, so I can get more done here after hours. Did Haney offer you something? A drink, coffee?"

"No thank you." He seated himself across the desk from her in the straight-back chair. "How are things at the gin?"

"Busy, chaotic, fine. But you know that. You were out there yesterday. Is there some problem, Granger?" He looked like a man on his way to the gallows. "Why did you come to see me?" Her face paled. Rink. *Something's happened to Rink.*

Granger was sensitive to her rising panic. "No, no. I didn't mean to alarm you. It's nothing tragic." He studied the rug beneath his chair for a moment. "It's just that you've been extended an invitation and I don't know how you're going to take it."

"An invitation to what?"

"An invitation to accept a plaque designating Roscoe as Citizen of the Year at the Fall Festival."

He referred to the citywide celebration sponsored each year by the Winstonville Chamber of Commerce. Caroline couldn't imagine herself having anything to do with the festival, nor Roscoe. "They want to give the award posthumously? Why? Why not honor someone who's living?"

Granger scratched behind his long, droopy ear.

"That's what I asked. Not that I wasn't honored on Roscoe's behalf," he rushed to add, ever loyal. "But it seems that the award committee voted on him last spring. They don't see fit to change their minds and want you to accept the plaque at the opening ceremony of the festival."

She stood and, wrapping her arms around her waist, went to stand at the window. It was raining, a dreary September rain. It fell heavily, despondently. Not at all like a soft summer rain that kissed and caressed naked skin even as hands and mouths did. She pressed her forehead against the cool pane of glass. Would she ever get over missing him?

His picture had been in the newspaper the day before yesterday. Steve had seen it and Laura Jane had come running to show Caroline. Another city had granted Air Dixie access to its airport. In the photograph Rink was shaking the mayor's hand, smiling, his white teeth flashing in his dark face. His hair was falling on his forehead. She had ached to touch it, brush it back.

"You miss him, don't you?" Granger asked quietly.

"Roscoe?"

"Rink."

She turned. "You know?"

His basset-hound face wrinkled into a wistful smile. "I think there was something between you and Rink long before he came home. No"—he held up his hands when he saw she was about to speak—"I wasn't fishing for details. In fact, I'm probably better off not knowing. But that day I was here for Laura Jane's wedding and saw you two together, I was fairly certain you were in love with each other. Am I right?"

"Yes."

She returned to her stance at the window and they were silent for a moment. "Would I be nosing in where I don't belong to ask why he left?"

She shook her head. "You've always been a good

friend to me, Granger. When Roscoe married me, I knew you were surprised, but you never treated me with anything less than the highest respect and courtesy. I don't know if I ever thanked you properly for that.'' She faced him again. "I thank you now. So as a friend I can tell you that there was too much antipathy between Rink and me for him to stay.''

"Namely his father.''

"Precisely his father. And my marriage to him.''

"Rink's proud.''

"Oh, yes, I know." She smiled. Then she looked at the attorney and said levelly, "My marriage to Roscoe was never consummated.''

"I figured that, too.''

She laughed softly. "You're full of surprises tonight. I thought you'd be shocked.''

"I'm relieved. You were too good for him, Caroline.''

She sank back into the chair behind the desk. "He did some terrible things, the worst of which is what he did to Rink.''

"I agree.''

"You knew about all his machinations?''

"Far more than you can count.''

"Then why did you stay his friend for so many years?''

"His *attorney*. Roscoe had no friends. He wouldn't let anyone be his friend. I stayed with him partially to keep him in line. I took a lot of abuse from him, but I hate to think of what he would have tried to pull if I hadn't watched over his business affairs.''

Caroline placed her elbows on the desk and leaned her head on her fingers, rubbing her temples. "He doesn't deserve that award.''

"Do you want my advice?''

"Please.''

"Accept it, smiling graciously.''

"And be a hypocrite?''

"Don't disillusion them, Caroline," he said, speaking of the entire town. "They need their public figures to love and hate and envy and emulate. Give them what they want. For one hour, let Roscoe be what he should have been in reality."

"I guess you're right."

He stood and she joined him on the other side of the desk. Arm in arm, they walked to the door. "I'll tell them tomorrow that you'll accept the award on Roscoe's behalf."

"Granger." She paused at the door. "What would it take, legally, to sign over the deed to The Retreat to someone else?"

This time she had succeeded in shocking him. "You're not thinking of selling it?" he asked, flabbergasted.

"No. I'm thinking of giving it away."

He studied her face and saw the resolution there. It prevented him from prying further. As he pondered her question, he pulled on his earlobe, stretching it even longer. "The Retreat is yours to do with as you wish. I think it might have been an oversight on Roscoe's part, but there was no stipulation that you couldn't give it away, only that Laura Jane be allowed to live here the rest of her life."

"I understand. This wouldn't affect that."

"In that case there would be no problem in your giving it away. If you're sure that's what you want."

Musingly, she nodded her head. "When is the Fall Festival?"

"The third week in October. About a month away." He placed his hand on the doorknob. "They asked for Rink's address. I'm sure they intend to invite him."

Her eyes flickered away from his. "Could you have a new deed drawn up by the third week in October?" When she raised her eyes again, he was smiling down on her fondly.

"You know, if it weren't for these Lancaster men always getting in the way, I think I'd be a little in love with you myself."

"Hey!"

Caroline stopped on the sidewalk and peered over the top of her grocery bag at the young girl who had so rudely addressed her. "Are you talking to me?"

"Aren't you Mrs. Lancaster?"

"Yes." The girl couldn't have been more than twelve, but she had on garish purple eye shadow and blue eyeliner that had been applied with a heavy hand. Her dark hair had been cut to stick up from the top of her head. One earlobe had three holes pierced in it. A colored paper clip dangled from each of the holes. The other ear bore a large, glittering star. Her mouth was a slash of white lipstick.

Her clothes were as outlandish as the makeup, a green miniskirt over a pair of orange mesh hose, a white sweat shirt with a huge pair of red lips and an obscene tongue emblazoned on it. Caroline thought she must be in costume for some bizarre play. What kind of parent would allow a daughter on the streets looking like this? In any event the girl had gained her attention. "How do you know me?"

"I knew Mr. Lancaster. Rink Lancaster. But it was a long time ago. My name's Alyssa."

Caroline's eyes widened in surprise. This was Marilee's daughter, the one Rink had grown so fond of before her mother cruelly separated them. "How are you, Alyssa?"

"Okay, I guess. You were married to Rink's old man, weren't you?"

"To Roscoe. He died a few months ago."

"Sure, I know that. Everybody knows that. A while back I saw you and Rink at the Dairy Mart."

"Why didn't you come over and speak to him?"

She shrugged insolently. "Didn't feel like it. He probably don't even remember me."

"Doesn't."

"Huh?"

"I'm sorry. I was rudely correcting your grammar."

"That's okay. My mama does it all the time, but it don't . . . doesn't seem to do no good."

Caroline laughed in spite of herself. But she sobered when she cast a glance at the group Alyssa had been with. She could well imagine that peer influence was stronger than parental guidance in this case. The girls accompanying Alyssa looked like escapees from a re-form school.

Caroline was immediately ashamed of herself for forming an opinion based on appearance alone. She had put labels on the girls just as people had at one time labeled her. However, when one of the girls, no older than Alyssa, lit a cigarette, she couldn't help but be appalled.

"How is your mother?" Caroline remembered Mar-ilee as petite and buxom, with long blond hair, china-blue eyes and a petulant pout.

"She's got a new husband. He's a jerk. Worse than the last one. I don't hang around there no more than I have to." Then, as if realizing she had revealed too much of herself, she pulled herself erect and said, "Well, I gotta be goin'."

"Wait!" Caroline surprised herself by saying. When the girl stared at her through lashes gummed with black mascara, she was at a loss for what to say. In those overdecorated eyes she saw rebellion, suspicion and a great deal of vulnerability. It was as though a little girl was living behind the lurid mask and wanted desperately to be coaxed out. "Why don't you come to see me at The Retreat sometime? I'd like to get to know you."

Alyssa scoffed with a crude snorting sound. "Like hell."

"No, really, I would." Why Caroline persisted she couldn't say. The girl had touched her heart in some unfathomable way. Rink would hate to see the child he had loved so lonely. If Caroline could help, she wanted to. "I'd like for us to become friends."

The dark blue eyes wavered. "Why?"

"Because I've heard Rink speak of you so often."

"Yeah? What does he say?" Her chin was tilted at a belligerent angle, but Caroline could tell she had been surprised and was interested.

"He talks about what a sweet baby you were, how much he cared for you and hated to give you up."

"He wasn't my daddy."

"I know. But he loved you just the same." The girl began to gnaw at the white painted lips and Caroline thought for a heart-stopping moment that she might cry. "Rink will be here in a few weeks for the Fall Festival. Why don't you come out and see him?"

Her shoulders lifted in a noncommittal shrug. "Maybe. I'm real busy."

"Oh, I understand. It's just that I think Rink would love to see you. Your mother has made that difficult."

Without answering, Alyssa glanced over her shoulder at her friends, who were waiting for her with growing impatience. "Look, I gotta split."

"It was nice to meet you, Alyssa. Please think about coming to see me."

"Yeah, okay."

Caroline watched the girl's slinking retreat down the sidewalk. She was a pathetic sight. Yet Caroline's heart was lighter than it had been in weeks.

"Are you proud of me, Steve?"

"I'm always proud of you."

Laura Jane and her husband of two months were lying together in the king-sized bed in what used to be Roscoe's suite. The rooms were barely recognizable as such now. Caroline had redecorated them for the newly-weds' wedding present. The wallpaper was new but still in keeping with the antebellum architecture of the house. There were new drapes on the windows, new towels and fixtures in the bathroom, new area rugs on the hardwood floors. A chaise and an easy chair with a teatable between them had replaced the rolltop desk in the sitting area.

Laura Jane snuggled closer to her husband. Idly her fingers stroked his stomach. "But I mean especially proud since I bought those things all by myself today. I got the correct change back and everything, didn't I?"

His arm tightened around her. After two months of sleeping with her, he was almost convinced that she wouldn't break in his embraces. "You did everything just right. I knew you could."

He had taken her into the feed store with him. When he'd first suggested that she handle the transaction, he had seen the trepidation in her eyes. But she had studied the bill the clerk had handed her and painstakingly counted out the correct amount of money, then waited until she had been given her change. When they'd left the store, she'd beamed up at him like a child who had done well at her first piano recital.

"I was afraid to try. I remember Rink used to take me to town. He wanted to teach me to do things on my own, but I was always afraid I'd do something wrong and he'd be disappointed in me. I wouldn't even try."

Steve slid his head across the pillow so he could look down at her. "You aren't afraid of disappointing me?" He was teasing and she buried her nose in the hollow of his shoulder.

"Of course not. I want to please you more than I ever wanted to please anybody. That's why I was willing to try my best. I know I'm not as smart as other people. I don't ever want you to be sorry you married me."

He rolled to his side and hugged her against him. "My darling," he whispered into her hair. "How could I ever be sorry about that? I'll always love you no matter what you do, or don't do. You don't have to earn my love, Laura Jane. You have it already. Forever."

"Steve," she murmured, touching his chest lightly. "I love you so much." Sitting up, she pulled her nightgown over her head and tossed it to the foot of the bed.

It was endearing, her lack of modesty. She was childish in her unconcern over nakedness. Because her spirit was so pure, she felt no shame about her body. Like an Eve before the apple, she was free of conscience and restraint. Such spontaneity continued to delight her husband, and he was almost ashamed of the way he enjoyed her lack of inhibition.

She had taught him something about his own body. He had hated to look at it after the loss of his leg. He had despised it. It amazed him that Laura Jane took such pleasure in his body. She continually invented excuses to touch him. Her chinalike hands soothed when he'd thought there was no healing power left on earth. She thrilled him with her curious examinations and aroused him to heights he had never known before. Each caress was a demonstration of the unselfish way she loved him. In his whole life, he had never known such care from another human being.

Now, with a quiet smile on her lips, she lay back down beside him and threw her thin arm around his waist. He threaded his fingers in her long straight hair and brought her face up to receive his kiss. It wasn't long before their hands began to wander. He caressed her back as she rolled atop him. She laid her palms on his cheeks and kissed him repeatedly on the face. Her kittenish tongue teased his ears, something she had learned from him.

She inched down his body and dropped kisses on his

throat and chest. Then her lips opened over one of his nipples and she tested its texture with the tip of her tongue. He almost vaulted off the bed.

"Laura Jane," he gasped.

"Hmmm?" she murmured, not stopping. "When you do this to me, it feels good. Doesn't it feel good to you? If it doesn't, I'll stop."

His hands tunneled through her hair and his fingers closed about her head. "No, don't stop," he gasped. "Not until . . ." He positioned her over him and with a slow, easy movement made them one.

Bracing herself on her arms, she leaned forward and placed one of her breasts against his lips. He kissed the tiny pink nipple until it pearled. His tongue curled around it. She sighed her pleasure.

The tempest inside them continued to build until he clasped her hips between his hands and strained into her. She nestled his head against her small breasts as their bodies shuddered together. Long after it was over they held each other. Then softly she kissed his forehead and lay down beside him.

"I'm glad you taught me how to make love," she said.

He chuckled. "So am I."

"I wish everyone in the whole world were as happy as we are."

"I don't think that's possible. No one could be as happy as I am." He pressed a gentle kiss on her mouth.

"I wish Caroline was happy. Since Rink left, she hasn't been happy." Her perception should have surprised him, but it didn't. He thought that sometimes she was more sensitive to emotions than other people. "Do you think she misses Rink?"

"Yes I do, sweetheart."

"So do I." She fell silent for a moment and he thought she had gone to sleep. Then she said, "I'm afraid she's going to die like Daddy did."

Steve caught her beneath the chin with his fingers and tilted her head up. "What in the world are you talking about?"

"Caroline's sick."

"She's not sick. She's certainly not going to die."

"Daddy used to rub his stomach when he thought no one was looking. Or he'd close his eyes like he was hurting somewhere."

"What does that have to do with Caroline?"

"She's doing the same things. Late yesterday evening when she came home from the gin, I was watching her from the parlor. She hung up her jacket on the coat tree and went up the first two stairs. Then she stopped and leaned over the banister. She rested her head on her hands for a long time. It looked like she couldn't get her breath. I was just about to run and help her when she pulled herself up. It seemed to take all her energy to get to the top." Concern marring her perfect features, Laura Jane bent over him. "Steve, she's not going to die, too, is she?"

"No, no, of course not," he reassured her, smoothing back her hair. "She was probably just tired, that's all."

"I hope so. I don't want anyone else to die until I do. Especially you," she said, hugging him hard. "Don't ever die, Steve."

He held her close and soon he felt her gentle breathing against his skin and knew she was asleep. He pulled the covers over them and continued to hold her. But he didn't sleep. He stared into the darkness, his brow furrowed. He had been worried about Caroline, too. And what Laura Jane had told him only fed that worry.

Chapter 14

FALL FESTIVAL WAS BLESSED WITH A GOOD WEATHER forecast. The morning of the opening ceremony dawned clear and brisk. Caroline decided to wear her new suit. It would be cool enough.

Following a discreet tap on her door, Haney came in carrying a tray. "I hated to disturb you. You should sleep late more often. But I knew you wouldn't appreciate it if I let you sleep through the shindig."

"Thank you, Haney." On the tray was a pot of tea, which she had begun drinking recently instead of coffee, a glass of orange juice and two blueberry muffins. "I wasn't sleeping. Just being lazy."

"That's good for a body now and then. Especially since today is probably going to wear you out. Do you need me to press anything? Want me to run your bathwater?"

"My clothes are ready," Caroline said, sinking down into a chair beside the table where Haney had set the

234

tray. She poured a cup of tea. "A hot bath sounds nice. It's chilly outside."

Haney went into the adjoining bathroom, keeping up a stream of chatter about the coming events of the weekend. Caroline barely listened as she sipped her tea meditatively. "Your bath's ready. Why haven't you eaten those muffins?"

"I'm not hungry." Every time she thought of standing up in front of the whole town to accept that blasted plaque, her stomach lurched in protest. Putting any food into it would be risky.

The housekeeper watched the young woman as she rose and went to her closet to get a terry robe. Through the batiste nightgown she could see that her mistress had lost a significant amount of weight. The figure that had been fashionably slender was now downright skinny to Haney's way of thinking. "Do you think he'll be there?" She bent to straighten the covers on the bed.

"Who?" Haney tossed Caroline such a reproachful look that she lowered her head and answered, "I don't know." She went into the bathroom and closed the door, just as effectively closing the topic of Rink.

When Caroline came down the stairs an hour later, Steve whistled long and low. Laura Jane clapped her hands. Haney's expression was somewhere between concern and pride.

"Man, that's class!" Steve said.

Caroline laughed and the three watching her were grateful for the fluting sound. She wasn't given to laughter lately. "Do you like it?"

"You look beautiful, Caroline," Laura Jane said enthusiastically. "Oh, you're gorgeous."

"She's too skinny," Haney grumbled, but lovingly picked an imaginary piece of lint from Caroline's shoulder.

"I thought as long as they're going to talk—and they

will—I would give them something to talk about. Besides, we're representing the Citizen of the Year. We should dress the part.''

Her two-piece suit was of cream-colored wool crepe. Her blouse was dove gray, almost the exact shade of her eyes. She had tucked all her hair under a soft felt hat the same color as her suit. Its low, dipping brim flirted with her brows. Her makeup was sedate and had been carefully applied to camouflage the violet shadows beneath her eyes. Pearl earrings were in her ears. Her stockings were pale ivory. She wore bone-colored suede pumps and carried a pair of matching kid gloves.

''You all look spiffy, too,'' Caroline commented as she surveyed them proudly. Laura Jane was in pale blue and looked like a collector's prized doll. Steve was in his wedding suit, but Caroline had seen to it that he had a new necktie for the occasion. Haney, too, was in her Sunday best.

''The carriage awaits,'' Steve said, formally offering his arm to Laura Jane. ''Lady Laura Jane, Lady Caroline.'' He turned and she took his other elbow. ''Haney, if you please,'' he said, and they left The Retreat.

The high school auditorium was jam-packed. No one remembered it ever being so crowded, not even when the commencement exercises had been rained out of the football stadium and moved into the auditorium.

Caroline sat up on the stage, flanked on one side by her family and Haney, whose presence she had insisted on, much to the officials' chagrin, and on the other side by those same officials.

To keep her panic at bay, she tried to focus on the American flag standing sentinel in the corner of the stage. The stars seemed to buzz like gnats over the field of blue. The stripes waved. The flag was perfectly still.

Caroline was sick.

She glanced out over the audience and all she saw was

a sea of swimming faces staring at her with avid interest. Diverting her eyes to her lap, she noted that her palms were shiny with perspiration. If she put on her gloves, her hands would be too hot, though now they were icy cold. She swallowed the nausea in her throat and wished that she hadn't tied the bow at her neck so tightly.

Her stomach was growling as it rolled from side to side. Why hadn't she eaten those muffins? If she had, she would have thrown them up. But she was going to throw up anyway. She was going to disgrace herself in front of the whole town.

Why was it so damn hot in here? Her skin was clammy. She looked around. No one else seemed uncomfortable. Steve and Laura Jane were speaking quietly to each other. Haney had found one of her church friends and they were gaily chatting. The mayor, against the rules of the building, was puffing on a cigar as he talked loudly and expansively to the county judge. The odor of the smoke turned her stomach.

As she watched the mayor, he excused himself from the judge and went marching toward the back of the stage. "Well, well, we can get started now. I was afraid you weren't gonna make it, boy. How are you, Rink?"

Caroline swallowed and began breathing through her mouth with shallow pants that were supposed to control nausea. Her whole body went cold, then flushed hot. Her earlobes seemed to be on fire, they burned so.

She heard his voice as he greeted those around her. From the corner of her eye, she saw Haney advancing on him militantly. He stopped the tirade he saw coming with a sound kiss on her cheek. She jerked back, as flustered as a young girl, then squeezed him in a bear hug. Laura Jane vaulted from her chair and ran to embrace him. Steve stood and the two men shook hands.

Then she saw his brown pant legs moving toward her. He stood directly in front of her. She could feel heat and energy radiating from him. And because the whole town was watching, she drew her lips into a stiff smile and raised her head to look at him. "Hello, Rink."

Rink stared down at her and was only partially successful in hiding his shock. Her eye sockets were deeply shadowed. Her cheeks were gaunt. She was pale. She looked like she could stand about seventy-two hours of uninterrupted sleep and about five hearty meals.

But she was beautiful.

It took every ounce of self-control he possessed not to take her in his arms and hug her to him fiercely. The last two months had been hell. He could recount every miserable second of them because he had done nothing but think of her, miss her.

Damn his temper. Damn his pride. He had gotten angry because two drunken jackasses in a tavern had shot off their mouths. He had taken out his angry frustration on her. This time, she had given it back tit for tat. That had both surprised him and angered him more. Mostly because what she had said had been right on target. Roscoe could no longer be blamed for keeping them apart. He was bringing this misery on himself, on her. He had left without a word. What kind of behavior was that for a grown man?

For a man in love?

Ah, but being in love made you mean and crazy. Love made you act like a fool even when you knew you were acting like a fool and couldn't help yourself from acting like a fool. Love made you take a hand so cold it was shocking and say an insipid, "Hello, Caroline. You look lovely," when what you wanted to do was throw your arms around her, beg her forgiveness, claim her as yours and defy heaven and earth to try to come between you again.

Rink sat down beside her. The hem of his trouser brushed her leg and she circumspectly moved it aside. He watched her hands tug self-consciously on the hem of her skirt as she sat with rigid posture on the stage. God, she was precious. She was still the girl in the woods, the Dawson girl, trying so hard to gain approval. His heart ached with love for her. He wanted to shout at her, "What the hell do you care what they think of you? You're head and shoulders above any of them."

Then it struck him that he was as bad as she. He wanted her more than he wanted to live till tomorrow. Yet he had let public opinion keep him from her. She had been his father's wife. So what if everybody thought it had been a normal marriage? He knew better. And even if he didn't . . .

He turned to her so quickly he startled her into looking straight at him. Their eyes collided.

He studied every feature of her face. He cataloged every minute detail. She was as beautiful to him as the first time he'd seen her. He loved her a thousand times more now than he had that summer twelve years ago.

And he knew in a blinding instant that if he had had to go through eternity not knowing her true relationship with his father, he would still want her. He loved her to the exclusion of all else, more than he minded public ridicule, more than he resented his father, more than anything, he loved Caroline Dawson.

"So I'll now ask Mrs. Caroline Lancaster, Roscoe's widow, to come to the podium."

Rink's eyes flew to the speaker's microphone where the mayor had just introduced Caroline. He hadn't been listening to the flowery speech. Apparently neither had she. When the audience burst into loud applause, she jumped.

Rink watched as she visibly collected herself and stood gracefully. She placed her purse and gloves on the seat of her chair, then walked to the podium with more poise than a queen bred to such ceremony. The smile she gave the mayor was tremulous and the audience took her evident emotion to be reaction to his speech. Rink scanned every face in the crowd. She needn't have worried. They approved of her.

She accepted the plaque with one hand and shook the mayor's hand with the other. Moving aside, the mayor offered her the microphone. "Roscoe would have been honored to receive this token of appreciation from you. I and all his family accept it for him and say thank you."

There was nothing hypocritical in her short acceptance speech. Everything she had said was the truth. She hadn't added to the litany of praise the mayor had heaped on Roscoe. She had merely accepted the tribute in Roscoe's stead. She had given these people what they wanted, a hero for the day. To Rink's way of thinking that was well and good.

He watched her turn. Her face was as pale as the bone china in the cabinet at The Retreat. She paused and closed her eyes briefly as she seemed to struggle for breath and equilibrium. She took another step and swayed. The mayor's hand went to her elbow and he spoke her name.

Rink bolted up from his chair. She looked toward him, blinking rapidly as though she were trying to focus on him. Then slowly her eyes drifted closed, her knees folded beneath her and she collapsed to the floor.

A murmur of surprise and alarm rose up from the audience. Laura Jane cried out and clutched Steve's hand. Haney cried, "Lord o' mercy!" and clasped her hands over her enormous bosom. Those closest to Caroline surged around her, dropping to their knees on the stage.

Rink, wild with fear, began plowing through them, shoving men twice his size out of the way. "Get away from her. Get— *Move!* Let me through. Dammit, get out of my way!"

At last he reached her. He fell to his knees and grabbed her hand. It lay lifelessly in his palm. "Caroline, Caroline. For God's sake, would someone call a doctor? Caroline, sweetheart. God, speak to me!''

He clawed at the bow on her blouse and ripped open the first few buttons. He pushed aside her jacket, wreaking havoc on the expensive ensemble. The hat was whipped from her head and sent sailing. Her dark hair tumbled free. With smart, swift pats, Rink slapped her cheeks. Her eyes fluttered open and he gave a soft cry. ''Just rest, darling. What's wrong? What's the matter? No, don't talk. Someone's calling a doctor.''

''Rink,'' she whispered, smiling drowsily and serenely. ''Rink.''

''You fainted, sweetheart.'' Weakly she raised her hand and touched his cheek, his hair.

As though on cue, those ringed around them raised their eyebrows. Someone was heard to mutter, ''Well, I'll be damned.''

''You're going to be fine. I promise. I'll see to it.'' Rink carried her hand to his mouth and pressed the palm against it. He gathered her into his arms so she was lying across his lap rather than on the floor. ''A doctor will be here soon.''

''I don't need a doctor.''

''Don't talk. You fainted. It was the excitement, that's all. You'll—''

''I'm pregnant, Rink.''

Her soft interruption halted his rapid flow of words and he stared down at her speechlessly. She laughed softly at his blank expression. ''That's all that's wrong with me. I'm going to have a baby.''

Her eyes roamed around the curious circle of faces bending over her. The leaders of the community were all listening avidly as the drama that would feed the gossip-mongers for months unfolded before their very eyes. It was people like these who had labeled her and her family trash. It was these people she had tried to impress, whose approval she had made a career of seeking.

Now she wondered why she had devoted so many years to such an empty goal. Her eyes went back to Rink's. Golden eyes that had always stirred in her passion and desire and love. Placing her hand on his cheek, she said, "I'm going to have your baby, Rink."

His eyes shimmered with emotion. Tightening his arms around her, he bent his head and put his lips to her ear. "I love you," he whispered. "I love you, Caroline."

Then, like a whirlwind, he surged to his feet, swooping her up into his arms. "Let us through. You heard the lady, she's pregnant. I'm taking her home. Mayor, put out that damn cigar. It's making me sick and I'm only the father, not the expectant mother. Haney, please get Caroline's things there on her chair. Steve, if you would be so kind as to bring the car around, please. Laura Jane, are you okay? That's my girl."

All the while he was issuing orders, Caroline's head was resting comfortably against his chest. He maneuvered them through the crowd, assuring everyone that she was fine, that she had fainted from the excitement, the heat in the building and the lack of a proper breakfast. "I'm taking her home now to feed her and put her to bed. Everybody go on and have a good time. She'll be fine. I understand pregnant ladies do this a lot."

He smiled down at her, and with the whole town watching as they left the building, she wound her arms around his neck.

"Waking up already?" Rink leaned down and pressed a sweet kiss on her forehead.

"Have you been here all this time?" She had fallen asleep with him holding her hand.

"Every second."

"How long have I been asleep?" She stretched languorously.

"Several hours. Not long enough. I intend to keep you in bed for the next few days."

Her eyes opened wide. "Just to sleep?"

"Among other things." He growled menacingly and hugged her tightly. For a moment he nuzzled his face in the fragrant softness of her neck, then raised his head to kiss her.

His lips met hers with tender pressure. With his tongue he examined the seam of her lips lightly, and when they parted he pressed it deep into the sweet hollow of her mouth. Her arms looped behind his neck and she pulled him down closer.

He surrendered to an urge he had suppressed for hours because it might disturb her. He stretched out beside her on the bed and held her sleepy-warm body against his. Their mouths played with each other. They couldn't stop smiling. But eventually Rink did and looked down at her seriously.

"When were you going to tell me, Caroline?"

He was fully clothed, but his shirt was unbuttoned. She slid her hand inside and laid it flat against his chest. "After this weekend. If you hadn't come home for Fall Festival, I would have called you."

"Would you?"

"If I hadn't, Haney would have."

"She knew?"

"I think she suspected. And Steve. They hadn't said anything, but I could feel them watching me all the time."

"It didn't take me but one look to see that something was wrong. You've lost so much weight." His hand coasted down her ribs to her hipbone.

"The doctor said that was normal. I haven't been eating much. What little I did eat often came up."

"Why didn't you tell me? I don't know whether to beat you or kiss you."

"Kiss me."

He granted her request. With his palm, he massaged her stomach. "My baby's in there. God, what a wonderful miracle," he said, hugging her boisterously. He kissed her again, a hearty kiss that mellowed to one of desire.

His hand slid up to her breast. He had left her in only a silk slip when he had stripped off the rest of her clothes and ordered her into bed as soon as they'd arrived home. The silk was warm with her body heat. He filled his hand with her breast, pushing it up until it stretched the slip's lace cup. He kissed her through the lace, taking teasing love bites of the firm flesh. "Caroline, will you marry me?"

She sighed. His mouth closed hotly around her nipple and sucked. "How could I refuse? You have such a nice way of asking."

He raised himself over her, capturing her face between his hands. "I want you to know something, something I didn't realize until today." His eyes probed deeply into hers. "If you *had* been a wife to my father, I would still love you and want you for myself just as much as I do now."

He actually saw the tears welling up in her eyes. He watched as they overflowed and rolled down her cheeks. "I love you." She caught the back of his head in her hand and urged it down for another kiss. "Yes, I'll marry you."

"Soon?" he prodded. "It's only been four months since Daddy died. People will talk."

She tossed her hair on the pillow and laughed. "After the episode this morning, that's an understatement." She gave her abdomen an affectionate pat. "I'd say the sooner the better."

"This week?"

"Tomorrow," she whispered and he smiled. "What are we going to do after we're married? Where will we live?"

"Here at The Retreat. I'll have to shuttle between here and Atlanta for business."

"I'll shuttle with you."

"Not afraid to fly with me?"

"I've never been afraid to do anything with you."

That earned her another kiss. "While we're here, what are we going to do, switch bedrooms every few nights?" he teased.

"Why don't we use your bedroom and convert this one into a nursery?"

His eyes surveyed the room, then came back to rest lovingly on her. "My mother would have liked that."

Their mouths melted together again. "I can't get enough of you. God, I missed you."

His furred chest moved against her breasts, still damp from his mouth's caresses. His hand covered hers where it lay on her lower abdomen and pressed. The warm sensations of desire spread through her belly and thighs like melting butter. Feathering her lips over his throat, she purred, "Rink, take off your clothes."

"Damn!" he cursed and sat up. His cheeks were flushed and his pulse was pounding in his temple. "I can't. We'll have to postpone our reunion. I promised Haney I'd bring you down for supper as soon as you woke up."

"Oh, golly!" Caroline said, throwing off the covers and thrashing her legs to get off the bed. "I just remembered. We're having company for supper."

"Company? Who?"

"It's a surprise. Find me something to wear." She dashed to the dressing table, picked up a hairbrush and began to drag it through her hair. "Do I look like we've been . . . you know?"

Worriedly she studied herself in the mirror as she patted her kiss-abraded lips with a powder puff.

He tossed down the soft challis dress he had selected from the closet, came up behind her and reached around to take a breast under each hand. His fingers outlined the tight beads of her nipples. "Uh-huh. You look exactly like we've been . . . you know."

He buried his face in her neck, just behind her ear, and nuzzled the erotic spot. Groaning, she breathed, "Rink, I'll never get ready if you don't stop."

"I'm ready." He pressed his swollen masculinity against her bottom. "I've been ready for hours. Do you know how beautiful you are when you're asleep?"

"You know what I mean. Ready for dinner."

"Oh, dinner. Hell." Sighing theatrically, he dropped his hands and stepped away from her.

When they were somewhat composed, they went downstairs to join Steve and Laura Jane in the parlor. Without asking, Steve fixed Rink a bourbon and water and brought it to him where he was seating Caroline on the sofa with comical carefulness.

"Thanks," Rink said, accepting the drink. He looked at his brother-in-law and smiled. If he had had any remaining doubts about Laura Jane's marriage, he had only to look at her and Steve together. Laura Jane glowed with happiness like a beacon. Steve was relaxed, no longer tense and defensive. He had some terrific plans for making the stables more productive. He now spoke to Rink as an equal. The men were getting to know and like each other.

When the doorbell chimed, Caroline, much to Rink's consternation, jumped up and ran toward the foyer. "I'll get it. Enjoy your drink."

"How does she expect me to enjoy anything with her hopping around like a jackrabbit?" Rink complained. "She's supposed to be taking it easy these first few months, isn't she?"

"I can't believe Caroline's going to have a baby," Laura Jane said to her brother.

"What I can't believe is that I'm the last to know."

Rink looked accusingly at Steve. "Why didn't you call and drop me a hint?"

Steve shrugged unrepentantly. "It wasn't my place to."

Rink frowned. He had more to say but was halted by Caroline's appearance in the doorway. "Rink, someone's here to see you."

The young girl's eyes darted nervously around the strange room. She gnawed on her lips, which Caroline was relieved to see were free of freaky lipstick. Gone, too, were the paperclip earrings and the makeup. Her clothes were more traditional, a simple dress with a full skirt. The hair was still spiked, but it had been brushed down in a pixie style around her face.

"She said it was all right for me to come," Alyssa said defensively, jerking her head toward Caroline. "I said you probably wouldn't even remember me, but she said you did, so . . ." She ended on a shrug.

Caroline watched Rink's face go from wonder to shock to delight. He spoke the girl's name under his breath, then repeated it more loudly, gladly. He stretched out his arms as he came toward her. But he didn't rush her. He stopped before he reached her, still with his arms widespread.

Caroline looked down at Alyssa, who had arrived at The Retreat in the town's only taxi. She saw the girl's lips begin to tremble, saw tears in her eyes. Alyssa tried very hard to put up an uncaring front, but she failed. Throwing off the last vestiges of toughness, she plunged headlong into Rink's arms, mashing her face into his chest as her arms went around his waist.

"She's not a half-bad kid."

They were in Caroline's bedroom, undressing for bed.

"Not at all. Only misdirected. Correction. I don't think she's had any direction at all. You should have seen her the first time I met her. She looked like something out of a horror movie."

"How long has this friendship between you two been going on?" He sat down on the bed to take off his shoes and socks.

"A few weeks. We've met twice in town for milk shakes. I invited her here tonight for dinner on the outside chance that you'd be here." She turned from the closet where she'd just hung up her dress. "I'm glad you were," she said with soft significance.

"So am I," he responded. "You've given me another reason to love you. Thank you, Caroline."

"You're welcome." Emotion made her voice as husky as his.

"Did you see the look on her face when we invited her to go to the fair with us tomorrow? That bitch Marilee. I'll bet she's never taken that poor kid anywhere."

"You'll be a good influence on her."

"Not near as good as you'll be. I want us to see her as often as we can."

"So do I. But are you sure you want to go to the fair tomorrow?"

"Why not?" he asked, stepping out of his trousers.

She faced the mirror and with feigned nonchalance fluffed back her hair. "Everyone in town will be there. After today—"

She never got to finish. He came up behind her, turned her around and sealed her lips with his. Finally, he raised his head. "I'm going to parade you all over those fairgrounds. We're going to talk to everybody. And I'm going to tell anybody who wants to know and some who don't just how much I love you and that I can't wait to get our baby here."

She dropped her forehead against his chest. "I love you so much. You're wonderful."

"You're wonderful," he whispered, gently setting her away from him. His eyes wandered over her body with leisurely pleasure. Her Charmeuse slip clung seductively to the curves of her body, detailed her breasts and their pert crowns, formed a shallow cup around her feminine delta, conformed to her thighs. "You're beautiful, Caroline."

He touched her through the satiny fabric, sliding over her form with his gentle, talented hands. Her nipples responded to the provocative fanning of his fingertips. The backs of his knuckles rubbed over the faint triangle and made her thighs tingle.

She knew in a moment she would be lost to all else. "Rink, wait." His hand opened over her and his thumb skated across the satin-covered delta. "I . . . I have something to give you."

"I have something to give you, too," he murmured as he dipped his head. His tongue touched her nipple at the same time his thumb searched and found. "Can yours wait?"

"I . . . I supp . . . suppose so."

"Mine can't," he grated softly as he took her hand and guided it to his sex, which was hard and full and straining against his briefs.

He hooked his fingers under the straps of her slip and pulled it down so she could step out of it. She stood before him naked and quaking with arousal. Lifting her against him, he carried her to the bed. As she lay back, he peeled off his underwear and stretched above her in naked splendor.

He knelt between her thighs. "I love you. I've always loved you, Caroline. I used to dread every dawn because I'd wake up thinking of you, wondering where you were, what you were doing, wanting you, aching for just the sight of you. Now I look forward to every new day because I'll wake up loving you and knowing that you love me."

He touched his lips to her abdomen, knowing his baby slept securely within the body of the woman he loved.

She placed her hands on his beloved head in wonder that life had afforded them such happiness. His lips drifted over the cluster of dark curls. Desire and love spiraled through her like a lazy zephyr.

With his hands on her breasts, he lowered his head farther and kissed the velvety petals of her womanhood. His tongue bade them open. He withheld nothing, gave everything.

"I won't hurt the baby?" He rose above her and settled his manhood snugly against her creamy warmth.

"No."

He possessed her with a fierce passion tempered by love and caring. His taut hips rose and fell rhythmically as he plunged deeply but gently. Ever atuned to her needs, he withdrew, stroked lightly the portal then sleekly delved again. She closed about him tightly, milking him with the walls of her body. They gave and they responded equally in a tempestuous physical exchange of love. When the tumult came, they shared it, hurtling off the edge of the universe in each other's arms.

It was a short while later, as they dried each other after a shower, that she said, "You never did let me give you my present."

"You mean there's more?" Playfully he smacked her bottom as she returned to the bedroom. "It couldn't be any better than what I've already had."

"This is serious." She went to an antique bureau and pulled open a drawer. Out of it she took a folded piece of paper. Handing it to him, she went to the window, giving him her back.

The harvest moon shone a silvery light down on the wide expanse of grass. The river channel could be seen winding through the trees in the distance like a sparkling ribbon. How she loved this place. But she loved the man more.

She heard the paper rustling, knew that he was

reading the deed that transferred The Retreat to him. His footfalls were muffled by the area rug as he came up behind her.

"I can't accept this, Caroline. The Retreat is yours."

She turned to him. "Never mine, Rink. Always yours. That was why I loved it so much. Without you in it, having it meant nothing. You're its heartbeat. Just as you are mine."

She took a step toward him and rested her hand on his chest. "I love you enough to give up the thing I thought I wanted most in the world. Love me enough to put your pride aside and accept it. Please."

He looked at her for a long moment, then at the paper in his hand. He folded it carefully and set it on the bureau. "I accept. With one condition. That you promise to share The Retreat with me for the rest of your life. Promise that we'll love here and have babies here and that we'll never dwell on the tragedies that happened before."

Her smile was radiant. "I promise."

He sealed the covenant with a kiss as binding as the pledge. Then, lifting her into his arms, he carried her back to their bed.

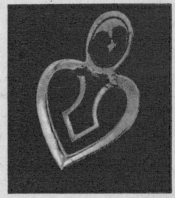

Silhouette
Intimate Moments

more romance, more excitement

───────── **$2.25 each** ─────────

Silhouette

Intimate 💞 Moments

more romance, more excitement

Silhouette Intimate Moments

Coming Next Month

SPINSTER'S SONG
by Parris Afton Bonds

•

THE SWEET RUSH OF APRIL
by Linda Shaw

•

GYPSY WIND
by Lisa Jackson

•

VARIATION ON A THEME
by Billie Douglass